THIS NEW INTERNET THING

THIS NEW INTERNET THING

ROBERT PURVY

CUBBYBEAR PRESS

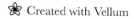

INTRODUCTION

This book is really a continuation of *Inventing the Future* and *The Big Bucks*, although you don't have to read those books to understand it. The characters were all introduced in one of those books, and continue their merry march towards the glorious future here. I hope you enjoy it.

If you find yourself unbearably curious about how the characters got here, and for some inexplicable reason don't want to read those books, there's a plot synopsis at the end.

1

SOUVENIRS

It was spring, 1992. Len was finally ready to get out of the frigid Midwest and move to California. His old friend Stan down the street had sold his house and moved to Miami with his son, leaving his (apparently) estranged wife behind, and that was the last straw for Len. That, plus the fact that the lawn mowing service raised its prices yet again, and there were rumors of another property tax increase in Bloomfield Hills. He was finally sick of it. He figured no one was going to buy a house in the winter, so he might as well dump it while the weather was good and the kids would be out of school soon.

Len was 67. He'd retired from Chrysler almost two years ago, and hadn't really latched onto anything in his retirement that grabbed him. Detroit was going down the toilet and had been for 30 years, and no one was doing anything to stop it. His daughter Janet was making it big in Silicon Valley, he was divorced, and she was his only kid. Her new husband Walt had offered to let him live on his property in the Sierra. He could fish every day, go for hikes and have a dog to hike with him, and best of all, see her and Walt all the time! In fact, he'd already tried living there for a couple weeks and he loved it.

Janet was ecstatic, and also relieved. Now she wouldn't have to worry about him taking care of that gigantic house and going up the stairs in his old age, and he'd be only three hours away. Walt started the process of getting permits for the father-in-law house he, Len, and Janet were going to build for him.

Len had a giant garage sale one Saturday, and everyone in the neighborhood knew that meant yet another long-time Detroiter was leaving. Pretty soon there'd be no one left that they knew anymore. This whole corner of Michigan was a one-industry town, and now that autos were a dying industry, everyone was bailing. No one's kids wanted to live here after they finished college. They moved to Chicago, or New York, or California, and the parents moved to Florida.

Jamie, a 16-year-old kid from the next block, came over and shook hands with him. He called him "Mr. Saunders" and said he was going to be studying World War II in his history class next year, and his father told him Len had some stories he *really* should hear. Len was busy dealing with buyers and told him to come back towards the end of the day when things quieted down.

Around 3:30 Jamie came back with his dad. Len had gotten a couple lawn chairs and invited them to sit down.

Jamie's dad Harry was someone Len had helped out on some project or other many years ago. He didn't even remember what he'd told Harry about his time in the war, but apparently Harry did.

"So Jamie, you wanted to hear about the Big War, huh? Well, I'll tell you what I can. I'm afraid I didn't have a very exciting war, unlike your dad here!"

Harry smiled self-deprecatingly. "He's sick of all my war stories!"

Jamie looked embarrassed. "You always tell the same ones, Dad! I bet there's a lot more you haven't told us yet!"

"You're too young for those!" said Harry.

"Anyway, Jamie, your dad is probably remembering my older brother Jack's experiences more than mine."

" 'Jack', that's the name I couldn't remember. This is important, Jamie. Listen up! I've forgotten most of this myself."

Len grabbed a can of Bud out of his cooler and passed one to Harry. He gave Jamie a Coke. This was going to be a long story.

"So, does the name 'Albert Kahn' ring any bells for you, Jamie?" He shook his head.

"Well, Albert Kahn was the most famous architect in Detroit, or maybe in the whole country or even the world, if you just look at industrial buildings. He built the River Rouge plant for Ford, and almost all the car factories in Detroit, including Chrysler's where I worked."

"OK.." said Jamie, not sure where this was going.

"In the late 20's, the new Communist government in Russia needed to build factories fast, but they didn't know how. Who do you think they turned to?"

"Let me guess: Albert Kahn?"

"You've raised a smart boy here, Harry. Right, Albert Kahn. Now, does the name 'Stalingrad' mean anything to you?"

"I think we get to that second semester. Wasn't there a big battle there or something?"

"A big battle!" laughed Len. "Yeah, I'd say it was a big battle. But we're getting ahead of ourselves here."

"One of the things that Kahn's company built was a big tractor factory in Stalingrad, in about 1930."

Harry interjected, "That's the part that blows my mind. Americans helping the Communists! And you said Henry Ford was behind it, too, right?"

"Yeah, the Commies weren't the bad guys yet. They even sent some of their engineers over to Detroit!"

Harry just shook his head. "Pay attention here, Jamie."

Len continued, "I was only five when the deal first started, but Jack was eighteen, and he got a job with the Kahn company."

"OK."

"They sent him to Russia to work on the Stalingrad tractor factory. He was gone for over a year, and when he came back he didn't want to talk about it much, or even tell us where he went."

"How come?"

"Well, I guess the Russians were pretty secretive even then. You could be shot if you talked too much. Over time that attitude seeps into you."

"Wow. Did he ever tell you any more?"

"Yeah, over time I managed to worm it out of him. He was pretty proud of that gigantic factory! He said he learned more from the Americans than the Russians, though."

"Oh, yeah? Why's that?"

"Well, he said the Russians had studied and memorized and always wanted to do everything *exactly* the way the books said. The Americans were more seat-of-the-pants, practical guys. They always used to argue with the Russians about that. I'm like Jack. He taught me everything I know about mechanics."

Len continued, "So of course we got into the war in December 1941. I was too young to go, and Jack was too old, at least at first. Later on, the draft board got more desperate."

Jamie was looking impatient. "So if Jack was too old, how is this about him?"

Harry said, "Be patient, boy. He's getting there."

"We were both sitting around at home while all the other guys were going off to war. You might not get to study this part, but the war was not going well for us at all in 1942. It was torture for Jack and me not to be part of it. At least I knew I could join up when I turned 18."

"Are we almost to the good part?" Harry elbowed him hard.

"So they had the battle of Stalingrad, the Germans and the Russians, in late 1942, and Jack was obsessed with it. They were actually fighting in *his* factory! He knew every inch of it. It killed him that they were destroying it."

"And so…?" prompted Jamie.

"And so he got it in his head that he wanted to go over there and help out! That was all he talked about."

Harry interrupted. "That's the part that gets me: actually *wanting* to be part of that meat grinder! If they even let him near it."

"That's what everyone told him. My parents, the guys at Kahn, everyone. But he wouldn't listen. One day in October he disappeared."

"So did he get to Stalingrad?"

Len looked like he'd just pulled a shade down over his eyes. His words came more slowly.

"We never saw him again. That was the worst thing for me and my parents."

"Did you ever find out what happened?"

Len took even longer to answer.

"I finally couldn't stand it. I figured I had maybe six months until my 18th birthday when I'd get drafted, and I was going to use the time to find out."

"So what'd you do?"

"Well… I knew he couldn't *fly* to Russia, so he must have taken a ship. I went to New York, and started asking around. Long story short, I ended up at the Merchant Marine hiring office. And they had his records!"

Jamie interrupted him. "Excuse me, Mr. Saunders, back up: you went to New York, *by yourself*?"

"Yep, I sure did."

"How did you get by there?"

"Oh, it wasn't that hard. All the men were off fighting the war, so there was lots of work."

Jamie was seriously impressed. Len was on a roll. He thought maybe he had a reference Jamie would get:

"Hey, have you heard of that new Disney movie, 'Newsies'?"

Jamie had. "Yeah, it's kind of a flop, though, isn't it?"

"I guess so. Anyhow, it's about a newsboys strike in 1899, long before I went there, but selling papers on the streets *was* one of the things I did to make money."

Jamie hadn't seen the movie, so he let that pass.

"Anyhow: what's 'Merchant Marine'?"

"That's the civilians who sail the cargo ships. Jack signed on to one of those ships headed for Russia."

Jamie just waited for the rest of the story.

"Well, maybe you've heard of the U-Boats? Those were German submarines who hunted cargo ships like Jack's."

"Like in the movie *Das Boot?*"

Harry elbowed him again.

"Just like that movie, Jamie. Jack's ship went down. Some survivors were rescued, but not Jack."

Jamie didn't know what to say, but this time he had more restraint and just waited.

"I figured maybe I could find some of his shipmates, so I hung around New York a few more months."

"And did you find any?"

"I did. They all told me Jack was a great guy, did his job well, never fought with anyone. He really wanted to jump ship in Murmansk and get to Stalingrad, and they always told him he was nuts. He thought he could just go to the train station and buy a ticket!"

Len was tearing up, but he wiped his eyes and continued.

"I knew Mom and Dad would want to hear *any* little details about him, so I kept pressing. Finally, one of them, 'Tom,' I think his name was, told me a story that I can still remember word for word. I don't even know if it was all true or not, but I knew my folks would want to hear it that way."

"One night they were playing poker. Jack was losing, but he never complained. Suddenly the ship just exploded when the torpedo hit. It caught fire right away, the sirens sounded, the loudspeaker told them to abandon ship, and they all ran for the lifeboats."

"All of them but Jack got into a boat. Someone noticed he was missing and ran back to look for him. There were flames and oily smoke everywhere."

Harry and Jamie were transfixed.

"He came back dragging Jack. Apparently he'd tried to go down below to look for anyone who was trapped, and the fire and smoke just got him."

"Was he still alive?"

Len just shook his head. "He wasn't sure, but the other guys could tell he was dead. They put him in the lifeboat anyway so he could have a proper burial."

"At that point, Tom put his hand on my arm, and said, 'Your brother was a hero, Len.' We were both crying."

Harry wanted to pause for a few minutes, but Jamie was dying to hear the rest of the story.

"So they all got rescued?"

"Yeah, it was freezing cold, but they survived. Not Jack, of course."

Jamie didn't know what to say. Finally, "Thanks, Mr. Saunders."

Len wiped his eyes again and said, "Well, Jamie, war's not like in the movies. The rescue ship didn't have facilities to keep dead bodies, so they gave him a burial at sea. Tom and all the other guys in the lifeboat stood next to the body as the chaplain read the service and they slid him over the side."

"When I got back home, my own draft notice was waiting for me."

Harry put a hand on Len's arm. "That's enough for today,

Len. Jamie, I guess you've got a good story to tell your history class next year!"

Harry shook Len's hand. "Len, if I don't see you again before you move…"

Len said, "Yeah, good luck to you too, Harry. And especially you, Jamie!"

Jamie shook his hand. "Thanks again, Mr. Saunders! Good luck in California."

The crowds were all gone, and Len figured that was it. He'd have to take the rest of the stuff to the dump. Janet's old Schwinn — he couldn't imagine anyone wanted that heavy old thing, but someone gave him $10 for it. Some of the stuff had belonged to Betty, but if she hadn't asked for it in the twenty or so years since the divorce, well, too late now.

He thought, *"I've gotta tell Janet about that bike!"* and called her. She couldn't believe anyone wanted her old bike. Then he told her about the conversation with Jamie and Harry:

"Hey, you remember the story about your Uncle Jack?"

"Vaguely. Wasn't he killed in the war?"

"More or less. He was on a cargo ship that got sunk by a U-Boat."

"Oh yeah, now I remember. Why, what happened?"

He told her about how Jamie came over to hear his old war stories. She said,

"But *you* didn't even leave the States!"

"Shhh! He didn't get time to ask about that!"

She laughed, "What did you do again? Monitor aircraft production for the Army or something?"

"Hey, logistics won the war as much as the guys firing the guns!"

"And you must have done a great job at it! After all, we won."

Len laughed and updated her on his progress in moving. She told him Walt was submitting his house plans to the county for approval tomorrow.

The rest of the night, he thought about his big move. Did he really want to spend the rest of his life fishing and visiting with Janet and Walt? It might get boring, but it wasn't a bad life, all in all. Detroit was sure as hell no place to retire, and Florida didn't appeal to him. California *was* expensive, but he was going to have a place to live that was almost free, and he'd have all the proceeds from selling his house, too.

Jack didn't get to live this long; he barely reached his thirtieth birthday. What would *he* have done, if he'd survived the war? He might have gone to college and become a full-fledged architect for the Kahn outfit. Maybe eventually the draft would have caught up with him, and he'd have the GI Bill to fall back on, like Len did. *If* he survived.

Len thought about his own college experiences in Ann Arbor. He'd always been good with numbers, and in the war he found he really liked the accounting part of his job! The auto companies were actually *building* the airplanes and tanks and generally knew what they were doing, but the government was paying them. They got a lot of money for it, and someone had to keep them on the up-and-up. Len found that he actually liked doing that!

The civilians made fun of him as a "bean counter," but the Army really appreciated what he did. So in college he got his degree in Accountancy. "You'll always have a job in Accounting," his dad used to say.

After college he got a job with Arthur Andersen, the big accounting firm. They put him on a few "fraud audits," which meant swooping down on a company where they suspected embezzlement, and questioning every single piece of paper and every financial transaction. He absolutely loved it, especially when he found something and the bad guys got caught. They noticed his enthusiasm and the partners started asking for Len Saunders when they had a fraud audit coming up.

He remembered one big case, where a bunch of war profiteers kept up their thievery even after the war was over. Len ferreted out the phony invoices that sunk their case. They paid *themselves*, in a devious way they thought was safe, and Len figured out how their scheme worked. They went to prison. He'd seen some shady stuff during the war, where invoices were padded and non-existent employees drew paychecks, but he'd never quite managed to nab anyone.

It still rankled him that he wasn't made a partner after that. He got an award, but that was it. When he came up for his "make partner or leave" review after eight years or so, he left and went to work at Chrysler. It turned out that no matter how great a job you did, if you didn't bring in a lot of new business, you had no chance of being a partner. Being the guy who sends people to prison was not exactly the best way of selling your services!

Now at least Janet did seem to have that smoothness he lacked. He remembered one epic run-in he had with a VP, Harold Townsend was his name, and Mr. Townsend wanted him to include some revenue in one quarter that really belonged in the next, and Len just refused. He was sure that Townsend held a grudge and kept him from ever getting promoted again. He'd thought of leaving Chrysler, but hey, he had a family to support.

Judging by her steady rise up the corporate ladder, Janet must not be shooting herself in the foot like that. He must have done something right with her! She didn't have kids, though. His brother was dead, so the two of them were the last Saunders left, "*Well, too late to do anything about that,*" he thought. "*Maybe Janet will make it to CEO someday!*"

Janet. He thought back to Retirement Day and all the stuff that happened since then, and how he came to be leaving the state he'd lived in all his life.

2

THAT RETIREMENT GIFT

Two years ago, on June 15, 1990, Len's retirement date came up. He'd have kept working if he could, but old-line industrial companies like Chrysler were pretty strict about retirement, unless you were a bigshot. At age 65, you get the gold watch and out you go.

Len had a lot of people under him, and they organized a farewell lunch. He'd built up his division's finance department singlehandedly, and most of those folks owed their jobs and their careers to him. At lunch, they all took turns telling Len stories, and there were a lot of wet eyes in the restaurant. Mitch, the first person he'd hired and his designated successor, told how, in 1961, Len had taken him to lunch in his Dodge Dart convertible with the top down, and they'd been the envy of everyone on Woodward Ave. Len knew this would happen, of course, which was why he always took his interviewees to lunch that way.

Later on, Judy described her experience going to lunch with him in his 1964 Chrysler 300K convertible, a story that sounded remarkably similar to Mitch's. It turned out almost everyone had a story like that. Mitch yelled out, "Hey, Len, didn't you ever hire anyone during the *winter*?" He said, "A couple of you, but it was a lot harder." Everyone laughed.

Mitch asked him what his plans were now that he'd shaken off his chains at last. He said, "I'm gonna get my golf score down, finally. Get myself in shape. And there's a long list of projects around the house I've been putting off, so I guess now I have no more excuses!" While he had the floor, he took the opportunity to give his goodbye speech, which everyone promptly forgot, including him. He noted that Chrysler was moving to Auburn Hills near his house, and why, oh why, couldn't they have done that ten years earlier? His commute would have gone down to ten minutes!

Everyone laughed, but getting out of Detroit had been on everyone's mind since the 1967 riots. Detroit was rotting away. Just last night, the Pistons had won the NBA championship and riots had erupted, killing 8 people. In 1967 at least there were grievances and riots all over America, but this riot was utterly pointless. What made it worse was that the city officials tried to blame the media for exaggerating it. Some of them made a point of saying that hundreds of thousands were peacefully celebrating the victory and only a few were violent, as if that made any difference.

No one at the lunch wanted to talk about last night, except for the game itself. Mitch gave Len the group present: a 20-year-old bottle of Ardbeg. Everyone knew how much he loved Scotch, and especially about the bottle he kept in his bottom drawer for special occasions, against all company regulations. "Save some for me, for when I come visiting, Len!" yelled out Dan, one of his newer hires. Len couldn't help thinking that he'd probably never see *any* of these people again.

Finally, he shook hands with the men and hugged the women and got into his car, which nowadays was *not* a convertible anymore. Now he had a 1989 Chrysler LeBaron, "the land yacht" as he called it. While they were in the restaurant, someone had tied a bunch of tin cans to the back bumper, as if he was just married. He drove a mile away and then took them off, since he didn't feel like dragging tin cans all the way back to Bloomfield Hills.

Back in the house, he looked at the bottle of Scotch, which he'd been intending to save, and said to himself, "If not *on my retirement day*, when?" He opened it and poured himself a drink and sat down to read the paper. It was too late to get in nine holes of golf today, and he was too tired anyway. Maybe Monday.

He looked at himself in the mirror. He still had some hair, which he was thankful for. A whole lot of guys were bald by his age. His lean, tough body from the Army had melted a long time ago and he had a fair-sized paunch. Next week he'd join the Y and get back in shape before it was too late and he was pushing a walker around.

The weekend felt like any other, with Janet calling at 9:00 am Saturday morning. She'd heard about the rioting and wanted to be sure he was OK. She tried to sound bright and cheery when she said, "So what are you going to do now that you're free?" This was not the first time she'd asked that. *"I'm going to brag about **you** whenever the other old folks talk about their grandkids!"* he wanted to say.

On Sunday night it felt weird that he didn't have that tightening of his stomach that said "back to work tomorrow!" He set his alarm for 7:45 instead of 6:00, although he figured he'd probably wake up at 6:00 anyway. He did, but he lay in bed awake instead of getting up. At some point he went back to sleep again and found himself dreaming when the alarm finally went off at 7:45. *"It's a whole new life!"* he thought. He made waffles for breakfast, something he almost never had time for, unless Janet was visiting.

What to do today? He realized that if he was going to play 18 holes he should have teed off already. *"Can't sleep 'til noon every day,"* he thought. What's on the project list for the house? What about all those books I wanted to read? I should join the

Y, like I've been thinking about forever. It was overwhelming. He ended up puttering around the house all day and taking a nap after lunch. He felt vaguely guilty about that. "*Is this what my retirement's going to be: taking naps?*" He resolved to start doing some of the stuff he wanted to do.

Tuesday morning he went down to the Y and joined up. While he was there, he got on the exercise bike and rode for 15 minutes. Most of the other people exercising looked like retirees, too. At the water fountain he got to chatting with another guy, Ted, who said he came here every morning about this time.

Ted was indeed retired. He'd worked as a production supervisor at an auto supplier in Pontiac. He'd been retired for four years now, and said it seemed like a lifetime ago. Now he was so busy, he said, that he didn't know how he'd ever had time to work! Len was envious and inquired what he was so busy with.

"I don't know; the time just goes!" Ted said. His kids were always calling him and his wife to come over and watch the grandkids or take them to Little League or whatnot. He had some charities that he worked with, and sometimes it seemed like he was the only one who ever did any work! The other people were retirees like him, and they were always going off on cruises or down to Florida in the winter, or else taking care of their grandkids like he was. So yeah, staying busy was no problem at all. He'd thought he was really going to work on his golf game, but now he was lucky to get in one game a week.

Len was both encouraged and appalled. Was this what retirement was like — just being busy with *nothing*? He didn't have grandkids to take care of, and he didn't want to go to Florida in the winter, either. But still, maybe volunteering *would* be a good thing. He asked Ted what sort of volunteer work he did. Ted worked at an animal shelter taking care of the dogs, which he loved doing, and he gleaned food for a local food bank. Len didn't know what "gleaning" meant, but Ted explained that he picked up food that the supermarkets couldn't sell, and took it down to a food bank.

Ted looked at his watch and said he had to hurry home and take his wife to her doctor appointment. He asked if he'd see Len tomorrow, and Len said it was his first time here, so he didn't know.

On the way home, Len thought about Ted's volunteer work. At Chrysler he made decisions that involved a fair amount of money, or arbitrated difficult disputes between people. Now he'd be doing... what, exactly? He thought about the job before Chrysler, too, and how much he looked forward to being a detective on the fraud cases. Maybe there was some way to do that again! Detective work wasn't about solving murders or having a shoot-out with the bad guys, after all.

The rest of the week was similar to Tuesday: he'd go to the Y in the morning, have lunch, take a nap, and work on little projects around the house. It was summer so he had a lot of yard work. He thought maybe he and Ted could become friends, but it seemed like Ted was always busy doing something with his family or his charities.

He'd always been interested in the stock market, but in Finance at Chrysler, he had a lot of restrictions on what he could invest in, plus it just seemed too much like work, so he'd never done much with it. Thursday afternoon he went to the library and looked at Value Line and some of the other financial publications, and he signed up to get the Wall Street Journal delivered. He looked into Janet's company, 3Com, but that didn't seem to be doing much, and neither did her previous company, Apple.

When he was looking at Value Line, he saw some "technology" stocks. None of them seemed to be doing much. *"Why the hell is that?"* he wondered. *"That's gotta be the future. Janet used to be at Apple, but now what happened to them?"* He remembered back when he was a kid, there were all these shady car-related companies in Detroit. Everybody and his brother was starting a company in their garage. They'd get a story in the paper, collect some money from gullible investors, and then you'd never hear of them again. Some of those guys belonged in prison.

He wondered if this same thing was going on with computers now. It had to be; where there's money, there are fraudsters. But how would you find out about it? And who was going to pay you to do it?

Anyway, that reminded him: he should get a better computer! And a modem. He picked up one of those computer magazines while he was at the library and leafed through it. Most of it went completely over his head, but he definitely got the idea that he should get one of those 80486 PC's at least. His old PC was almost a joke. He wasn't exactly sure what he would do with a modem, but he picked up a brochure at Sears on something called "Prodigy." He asked Janet about it, but she didn't know much.

He thought about her a lot. Knowing that a great guy like Walt was there for her really made a difference. He'd never had that feeling about her first husband, Kevin or whatever his stupid name was. What a loser.

Now he didn't need to worry about her all alone in that house any more. Of course, they didn't have as much crime in Silicon Valley as Detroit did. Thank God she'd gotten herself out of here after college. Jeez, Detroit has been declining for 30 years now. Maybe he should sell the house and get out, too. But where?

His old neighbors Harry and Helen had moved down to Florida last year, and they invited him to come visit during the winter. He got sick of the cold and snow, so he went. It was definitely nicer weather, he had to give them that. They had a condo in Fort Lauderdale. Their neighbors Harry and Judy down the hall seemed to drop in constantly, or else they were dropping in on Harry and Judy. They were from New Yawk, but Harry and Helen always told them to give it time; they'd recover eventually. Bridge games seemed to take up their days, if Harry wasn't playing golf that day.

The complex had regular bingo games at night, and Helen bragged that she was running eight cards at a time now, but some of the old-timers could do sixteen. Their other obsession seemed to be fighting with the homeowners association. The current controversy among the owners was about the pool service and what a lousy job they were doing, and when the monthly maintenance fees would go up. To Harry, maintenance fees were a *good* thing: They meant that he didn't have to mow the lawn in the summer, rake leaves in the fall, and shovel snow in the winter. Len admitted that he was sick of that stuff, too, but he was noncommittal when Helen said he really should move down and start enjoying life. "*You call this enjoying life?*" thought Len.

"But it never snows here," Helen said. "What about the hurricanes?" he asked. That was only a problem if you owned a house, they said. And anyway, the hurricanes were never really *that* bad. The TV always exaggerated how terrible it was going to be, and then it was nothing but a heavy rain.

Some of the older people Len knew moved to be near their grandkids. He thought that was dumb, too. In ten years the kids would be too old to need you anymore. Maybe their parents would drag them to visit you once a month in the nursing home. In any case, Janet didn't have any kids, so that was out..

He found himself looking forward to their weekly phone calls more and more now. She was climbing the corporate ladder like nobody's business! He wondered where she got it from. Not from him, for sure. He'd made it as high as Department Manager at Chrysler after a lifetime of work, but hell... she'd be a CEO real soon at this rate. She got tired of hearing him say how proud he was of her. Every time she told him how many people she had under her he wanted to tell her again, but he'd learned to stop himself. She didn't need any more encouragement.

Now she and Walt seemed to be worried about *him*. He'd made the mistake of mentioning the nice bottle of Scotch they'd bought him for his retirement gift, and even though she never mentioned it, he just *knew* she was thinking about it. He'd never be a drinker. His father had had a weakness for that, and his mother had made him vow to never touch the stuff. Now it wasn't quite *never*, but still, just once in a while. He planned to keep it that way.

On Sept 23rd, she said that she and Walt wanted to come visit for a week! What could he say? He knew they must be worried about him, so at least he could show them he was doing fine. He didn't know how they'd amuse themselves here, but at least Janet could show Walt all the places she'd hung out growing up. It had to be a lot different than Walt's childhood in northern California. They thought October would be a good time.

He thought about going fishing in a couple weeks, if he could find a place to rent. Janet had begged him not to sell the cabin up north, but for some stupid reason he'd gone ahead and done it. He wondered if the new owners were actually using it, or maybe they'd let him rent it! That would be fun. The time he got to stay in Walt's cabin while they were on their honeymoon was pretty fun, too, even though he had no idea how to catch those kinds of fish. California lakes didn't seem to have walleyes or Northern Pike, and in fact they all seemed to think Northerns were trash fish to be exterminated. Snobs.

3

JANET AND WALT COME TO VISIT

In October, 1990, Janet and Walt came to visit Len at the ancestral home in Bloomfield Hills, Michigan. Len met them at the airport. Walt had never been there. He said if he hadn't married someone from Detroit, he'd probably *never* have come.

Len hated Detroit's decaying Metro airport. Janet said it reminded her of all her trips home when she was at MIT. Nothing had changed since then, she said, except it was older and shabbier.

They got on I-94 and then north on M-39. Walt asked if they were going to go through Detroit, and Len reassured him that he probably didn't need to worry about flying projectiles. Later this week they could go in there if he really wanted. Len hadn't been to Detroit since he retired, and he couldn't think of any reason he *would* go, except maybe to see a Tigers game.

He'd been retired for four months, and still hadn't settled into any real activities yet. Whenever Janet called him, she always seemed worried about that. He always laughed it off, with "Hey, I worked my whole life, and before that I was in the Army! Can't a guy just enjoy some relaxation finally?"

They wound through the streets and ended up at Len's house in Bloomfield Hills. Walt was seriously impressed. The streets and trees were beautiful, and the house was *way* better than Walt's and, actually, most houses in Silicon Valley. Four bedrooms, three baths, two stories, on a third of an acre. And this wasn't even the best house on his street.

Len showed them to their room on the second floor. Walt complimented Len on what a nice house he had. Len was self-deprecating.

"It's a pain in the ass keeping it up these days. And how am I going to get up these stairs when I get old?" He smiled.

Janet had been worrying about that very thing, but this wasn't the time to mention it. They put their suitcases in the room, got settled, and came back downstairs. Len was sitting in front of the TV, and held up his bottle of Ardbeg.

"Hey, what do you say we open my retirement gift? I think this qualifies as a special occasion!"

Walt said, "Well, that's right gentlemanly of you, sir. Don't mind if I do," and Len poured him a glass. He offered one to Janet, who declined. Walt noticed that the bottle was nearly full, and glanced meaningfully at her. She was always worrying that he was drinking.

"Well, what do you two want to do this week? I have plenty of time to show you around now that I'm retired."

Walt said, "Thanks, Dad. Janet's been wanting to show me her old haunts around here, and we're going to take you out to dinner tomorrow!"

"Oh, boy. I usually get the early-bird special these days, if I go out at all."

They both laughed. Janet said, "Too early for dinner for me! We'll take you at a civilized hour."

"OK, I guess I can have a snack at 4:30 to tide me over."

On Monday, Walt and Janet walked around the neighborhood and drove to her old high school, and Janet reminisced about her childhood here. Walt had never been to Detroit, and after a lifetime of hearing about Motown, he really wanted to, so they planned that for Tuesday. He thought it couldn't really be *that* bad, could it? Len nervously advised them to go during daylight hours and be home before dark.

Tuesday morning after rush hour, Janet drove Walt downtown. They parked at Renaissance Center, a group of skyscrapers that was one of the crown jewels of the Detroit Renaissance, originally started twenty or so years ago by a group led by Henry Ford.

Janet looked around and said, "Wow, most of this wasn't here when I was growing up!" Walt agreed that it was impressive. It seemed to be a gigantic hotel, so they walked around the lobby and then bought tickets on the Detroit People Mover, an elevated monorail that went all around the downtown district. That hadn't been there before, either. They got off at Cadillac Center, because Walt liked the name.

Walking around, Walt marveled at how it *looked* like a big city, and yet it was missing all the people. The streets were almost empty. Janet remarked on this, too. There would be a parking lot or an empty building right down the street from an impressive skyscraper. She remembered coming here as a child when it was a real downtown.

They got back on the train. It was getting towards noon, and Janet said, "So are you up for Greek food? I always used to love going to Greektown."

Walt was agreeable, so they got off the train at the Greektown stop and walked down Monroe Street. She said, "There's a place that I used to go to when I came home from college. I think it's called Golden Fleece. I hope it's still there!" It was. They both had gyros, which were as good as she remembered them. Neither was still hungry, but she insisted they had to try the baklava.

Walt asked, "So you liked to come down here? I hope you don't mind my saying so, but Detroit does look like it's seen its better days."

She admitted, "Yeah, most people in the 'burbs never come here anymore. Do you want to walk down to the River? I remember doing that a lot." He agreed. While they were walking, she asked,

"So, is it everything you imagined?"

"I don't know," said Walt. "I was picturing car factories and Motown bands."

She laughed. "That's a different part of town. We can go to a car factory if you want. I think some of them have visitor tours."

Walt pondered that. He'd seen factories before. How exciting could it be?

"There's the Henry Ford Museum and Greenfield Village, but those are way out in Dearborn. Maybe we should go there on a different day."

Walt said, "Now *those* I've read about. Maybe later this week?"

They got to Riverfront Park, which seemed to be mostly a concrete walkway along the river, with a railing to keep people from falling in. It was pretty deserted.

"So that's Canada over there?"

Janet said, "Yep, Windsor. We could go there today if you want."

"What's there?"

Janet hesitated. "I think they have a casino now. And way less crime."

Walt was silent. They walked a while, then turned back and got on the People Mover again. They got off at Renaissance Center again and drove home. Walt said,

"Well, that was fun. Now I can say I've seen Detroit. Thanks, Janet!'

"Yeah, we can get home well before dark. It's still too early for dinner, or else we could go to Buddy's Pizza. That's about the only good thing in Detroit anymore."

"Add that to our list." They drove home, with traffic

noticeably worse than in the morning. Len was watching TV.

"Well, you're back in one piece! How was it?"

Walt answered, "It was, uh, interesting. I can see Detroit *used to* have a real downtown."

Len agreed, "Back in the day. What did you see?"

Janet filled him in on their itinerary. Len got the bottle of Scotch out.

"How about a drink before dinner?" Walt agreed and Janet demurred. While they were sipping, she said, carefully,

"Hey, I was thinking. Mom didn't come to our wedding, so she's never met Walt. We should probably go visit her while we're here."

Len looked pained. "Without me, you mean." It had not been an amicable divorce, and Janet had upset Betty by telling the judge she wanted to live with him, not her. This was very unusual, but Janet had held her ground. Relations with Betty had been chilly since then, at best.

Walt picked up the signs but ignored them, and said, "Where does she live?"

"In Mount Clemens. About 40 minutes away."

Walt said, "Sure, if you want" with the same expression as he'd have used if they were going to a funeral.

"It'll be a short visit," she said, while patting his hand. She went to the phone and called her mom, and when she returned she said,

"OK, it's all set. We're going there for a quick visit tomorrow night." Walt nodded.

The next evening they drove over there. She knew Walt wasn't the type to bring up emotional stuff, so she started,

"I guess you figured out that Len and Betty don't exactly get along?"

Walt said, "Yeah, I kinda got that. Messy divorce, was it?"

"You could say that."

"And they didn't have any kids besides you?"

"Nope. I'm really not looking forward to this. But she did

tell Dad's sister that she wanted to meet you, so she knows we're here."

Walt was silent. She continued,

"When I told the judge I wanted to live with Dad, Betty completely lost it. I didn't think she'd ever speak to me again."

"How old were you then?"

"I was 15."

He didn't think she wanted any comments, so he stayed silent.

"God, I can remember it like it was yesterday. I was living with her temporarily in an apartment in Bloomfield Hills while the divorce went through. I'd started high school at Kingswood, where we went on Monday, and I just *loved* it."

"That *was* a pretty nice campus," Walt agreed.

"Kingswood was the first time in my life I was ever treated like I mattered. Like I could do things on my own."

"And?"

"And she wanted me to move with her to Mount Clemens."

"You didn't want to go?"

"Hell, no. I wanted to stay in Bloomfield Hills with Dad. And definitely not change schools."

"Makes sense. I haven't met Betty yet, but your dad's a great guy."

Janet had tears in her eyes.

"Dad *always* encouraged me. He used to take me to the library every week, when Mom just wanted to take me shopping."

Walt put his hand on her arm. "Well, you turned out pretty good, as far as I can see."

"Oh, Walt…" she trailed off. They got to Betty's house and rang the bell.

Janet hadn't seen her since her own wedding in the early 70's. In her mind, Betty was still the attractive, fortyish woman in smart, tailored clothes she was then. She'd tried to prepare herself to imagine her mom twenty years older, but still, it was a shock. She'd gained at least thirty pounds and had that sort of short, poofy hairdo that older women tended to have, very large glasses, a white blouse with a black sweater over it, and way more makeup than she ever used to use.

"Janet! And this must be Walt! I'm so glad to finally meet you!" They shook hands. "Come on in!"

Janet hugged her longer than she expected to.

"Mom, how *are* you? You look great."

Betty stepped back to take a better look at Janet.

"Oh, I'm old, but thanks for saying so. But *you* look fantastic, dear. I can tell you're taking good care of yourself." She took their jackets and hung them up. "Let's go sit down. Can I get you anything?"

Betty said, "So you two have been married now for how long? I've lost track."

Walt said, "Let's see: we got married in March 1989, so it's a little over a year and a half now."

"Wow. And you both already owned houses, right? Which one did you pick?"

Janet took this one. "Walt's house was much better than mine, so that was a no-brainer."

Betty said, "And I think you're in construction, aren't you, Walt?"

"I'm a general contractor, yes. I've had my own business for almost ten years now. Two full-time employees and a lot of contractors."

Janet thought she detected some condescension in Betty's voice. Walt ignored it, if he even noticed.

"And that's how we met!" said Janet, putting her hand on his arm. "Walt started working on my house, way back when."

"Isn't that sweet!" said Betty. "No kids, though?" They both shook their heads.

"So you're still working, Janet?"

"Like a married woman doesn't have to work? Is that what you think?" thought Janet. Instead, she said,

"Yeah, I've been at 3Com for over five years now."

"Three Com, is that what you said?" asked Betty, pronouncing it slowly. "What do they do?"

"3Com does computer networking, Mom," said Janet.

"Oh, you always wanted to do that computer stuff, didn't you? I remember when you were in high school and the boys had it and the girls didn't. You were so upset!"

Janet just smiled. "What are *you* doing now, Mom?"

"Oh, I'm just a secretary at GM Labs in Warren. I know your father would call that being a traitor to Chrysler! But the money's good."

Walt said, looking around, "This is a very nice house you have here, Betty!"

"Oh, thanks. I inherited it when my parents passed away. It's getting pretty old now."

Janet remembered going to their funerals, and realizing that this was the house that Betty wanted her to live in. *"Yuck!"* was her reaction then.

Betty made them some herb tea, and they chatted a little more about her side of the family, most of whom Janet remembered. Betty suggested, half-heartedly, that they could go visit them while they were here, but Janet didn't respond one way or the other. She asked what her first husband, Ken, was doing now, and Janet told him what she knew, and that he had two kids with his second wife. Somehow, she just knew Betty was thinking, *"That should have been you, sweetie!"*

Finally, Walt glanced at his watch and said, "We should probably get going, hon. Dad's going to wonder what happened to us!"

Janet looked relieved, "Well, it was great seeing you, Mom! You'll have to come and visit us next time you're in California!"

Betty had no plans to go to California any time soon.

"For sure! It was great seeing you, too, and especially meeting you, Walt!"

In the car, Janet imitated her nasal voice. *"I think you're in construction, aren't you, Walt?* Like you're out there swinging a hammer or something. Snooty bitch!"

Walt was placid. "Oh, I'm used to it. Hey, at least that's over!"

Len was only mildly curious about Betty's new life after the divorce. He finally said to Janet, "Can I tell you what the proudest moment of my life is, so far?"

"Sure, Dad!"

"It was when you told the judge you wanted to live with me instead of her!"

There were tears on both their faces as they hugged. Eventually, Walt said, "Hey, can I get in on that?" They made it a three-way hug.

Later on that evening, Janet had a flurry of phone calls and stayed in the kitchen for a long time. Finally she came back and said, "OK, I'm seeing my friends from high school tomorrow night! Can you boys entertain each other?"

Walt didn't particularly want to be the one guy in a group of women where he didn't know anyone, so skipping that was fine with him.

4

THE IDEA

The next night on that visit back in 1990, Len and Walt went to Len's favorite steakhouse for their Boys' Night Out. It was a traditional men's restaurant, beloved by generations of car guys. There were still a few of these places in Silicon Valley, but Walt rarely got a chance to go to one. The maître'd recognized Len and said, "Mr. Saunders! It's been a while since we've seen you here. Welcome back!"

Len said, "Thank you, and let me introduce my new son-in-law, Walt Campbell!" They shook hands and he showed them to their table.

They both ordered a martini and took their time on the menu, although it was a foregone conclusion that they were both having filet mignon. They ordered from a mature gentleman who came to their table and did *not* say anything like, "My name is Jason and I'll be your server tonight." It was so refreshing. They settled into their martinis. Walt let Len speak first, since he was the host and the oldest.

"So, Walt, how are you enjoying Detroit so far?"

Walt thought and then said, "It's everything I expected, Dad!"

Len laughed. "That's good. Wouldn't want to disappoint you, would we?"

"No, sir!"

"It's too bad you came after baseball season. We could have gone to a Tigers game."

Walt vaguely remembered when he and Len had first met in the hardware store, and they'd talked about the Tigers being in the World Series.

"Oh yeah, you *were* a baseball fan, weren't you? I guess the Tigers aren't quite as good as the first time we met."

"Hell, they're not even a .500 team anymore."

Walt commiserated. "We had Oakland this year, not that I care about the A's much."

"Yeah, they kinda got slaughtered in the World Series, didn't they?"

Walt agreed. Their salads came, so they tucked into them. When they were done, Walt said,

"So you've been retired for, what, six months now?"

"A little less than five."

"How are you finding it so far?"

"Well… it's an adjustment. I was afraid I'd be bored, but so far I'm keeping pretty busy."

Walt didn't want to just say, "Doing what?" so he waited.

"I go to the Y almost every morning. I've been visiting a lot of the relatives I'd sorta lost touch with, and some of them live a long way away. And I've done some volunteering."

"Oh, yeah? What sort of volunteering?"

"I go to some grocery stores and pick up the food they can't sell, and take it down to the food bank. Helping feed hungry people — that's pretty satisfying."

"Very good."

Len was silent for a while.

"Oh, one more thing: I managed to get the modem connected to my computer and get signed up on Prodigy! It took me two days, and five phone calls to their support line, but I did it!"

"Wow, that's more than I can say! What's 'Prodigy'?" asked Walt.

"It's this electronic bulletin board-type thing, where you can get news, sports, stock prices, and stuff like that. Janet doesn't know much about it."

"Nor me. Do you have to pay for it, or what?"

"You pay a monthly fee," said Len. "Of course, it ties up your phone while you're on. And they have ads. I've been getting pretty absorbed in the investing stuff. There are a bunch of forums where people discuss stocks and what-have-you."

"So that's why your line was busy last week! We thought maybe you had a girlfriend!"

Len laughed. "No such luck. Anyway, it's fun. Maybe someday I can send Janet an email!"

Now it was Walt's turn to chuckle. "Or you can just call. We do have a phone, last I checked."

Len smiled and thought for a while.

"I've been wishing I didn't sell that fishing cabin I had up in the northern part of the state. Being able to just spend a few weeks there, or even longer — now that would be something!"

"You could just rent a place, though, right?"

Len agreed that he could.

"How did you like staying in my cabin while we were on honeymoon?"

Len snorted. "You call *that* a cabin? Up where I used to go, that would be called a mansion!"

"You liked it, is that what I'm hearing?"

"Hell, I think I could live there for good!"

That was what Walt was thinking, but he didn't want to come out with it just yet.

"It gets kind of tough in the winter. I know you have

winter here, too, but up there you can be without power for days when it rains or snows. And no snow plows, either."

"Hmm. Hadn't thought of that. Anyway, I had a good time up there. Thank you again!"

"Anytime, Dad! We'll have to have you out again next spring."

They chatted about this and that for the rest of the meal, then Len asked for the check. Walt didn't complain.

While they were back home and watching TV, Walt said, "So, Dad, do you really think you'd want to live in our cabin? 'Mansion', I mean!"

Len remembered vividly his reaction when Walt said that. His immediate response was to make a joke of it.

"What, and give up all this?" asked Len, spreading his arms out expansively.

Walt laughed. "I see your point."

"Wow!" said Len, thoughtfully. "That *is* sort of appealing. But then where would you and Janet stay?"

"It does have two bedrooms, you remember."

"That's true." Len admitted. After another ten minutes, he said, "You're not really serious about this, are you?"

"I don't know. I just worry about you trying to manage this gigantic house all by yourself."

"*When you're getting old,*" he didn't have to add, because Len thought that, too. "*And going up and down the stairs.*"

"Well, it's an interesting idea. It's a pretty big step."

Walt agreed. They didn't discuss the subject any more that night. Around 10:00 Janet came home and kissed Walt.

"Well, how are my boys? Did you have a good time?"

Walt said, "Dad took me to his favorite steakhouse, and it was fabulous!"

"Oh, boy, what did you have? As if I didn't know."

Len said, "I steered him to the filet, of course!"

"And I bet you talked about me all night!"

Walt tried to look alarmed and said, "Darn! I knew there

was something we forgot to discuss!"

Len said, "So how are your friends?"

"Oh, you know. Married with kids. Some divorced. There are a couple with really good jobs."

She sat down. Walt said, "I thought I'd help Dad winterize his house tomorrow!"

Len looked surprised. "What does a guy from California know about winterizing houses? How cold does it get out there, 50?"

Janet said, "Hey! I think I put on my winter coat twice last year." They all laughed.

Walt said, "I did some reading before we came. Do you put up storm windows, or is that a thing of the past?"

"Storm windows! God, that takes me back. No, I got double-pane windows years ago."

"Good, that didn't look fun. Well, you and I can walk around tomorrow and see what we need to do."

The next day, Walt and Len went to the hardware store to get a new furnace filter. On the way, Len asked, "So, Walt, how hard is it to build a small house?"

"What do you mean by 'small' ?"

"Say, like a typical mother-in-law house."

Walt pondered that one. "I don't know, I've done a few projects like that. Say, six months or so, depending on how many people help, and *after* you get the permits. Why?"

"Oh, just wondering. You got me thinking about moving out there."

"I did? Oh, yeah, I guess we did mention that. How handy are you?"

"I can swing a hammer, sometimes. Use duct tape when it's called for."

Walt laughed. "Which is always!"

Len said, "I don't know. I've been here my whole life. It'd be pretty hard to pick up and move."

Walt didn't say anything.

5

THE NEXT BIG THING

Matt Finegold was a friend of Janet, in his mid thirties. He and his wife Miriam had hired Walt Campbell, her husband now (but not then), to fix up their house, and it turned into the Remodeling Job from Hell. Miriam had wanted to go Full Lawyer over it, but Matt had smoothed things over and paid Walt what they owed. She still hated Walt and harbored a grudge against Matt over that, too. So when Janet and Walt got married in March, 1989, he'd gone to the wedding and she'd invented an excuse to stay home.

Miriam was constantly around rich people at her psychologists' clinic in Palo Alto. Her patients all seemed to be either rich ladies or their teen-aged kids. The husbands, or ex-husbands, almost never came in. In almost every case, the men were executives in some tech startup that had gone public, or else they were venture capitalists or lawyers.

The director of her clinic, Abigail, was married to one of those rich guys, and they led a life that Miriam would kill for. They hosted fundraisers for the local arts groups; their kids attended Stanford and Yale, they went to Ashland for the theater festival every year, and their house was so tastefully decorated it had been in Architectural Digest. Her kitchen had a Subzero refrigerator, a Viking professional range, and an island in the middle with a granite countertop and a wine cooler built in.

Abigail and Bernard, her husband, were fixtures in the Palo Alto social scene. When their kids were in high school, they were leaders of the parents' groups, running silent auctions for stuff the local artists produced, or having a charity ball that was an imitation of San Francisco's Black and White Ball. Palo Alto public schools were some of the best in the nation and they were a big reason why up-and-coming Silicon Valley executives wanted to live there, but the parents were always being asked to give even more.

Bernard sat on the board of TheatreWorks, where his main job was raising money, and he was very good at that. Abigail trailed along behind him, sweeping up the wives as new clients forf her clinic, and it seemed like at least half of them wanted her services.

Abigail talked to everyone and Bernard, as a venture capitalist, even knew the people who were *not* in the news yet, so she was current on all the gossip. Miriam checked in with her regularly about Valley stocks, and Abigail's verdict on 3Com was not good. Their stock was going nowhere, they were dependent on selling Ethernet adapters which would eventually be built into the computer, and Matt really ought to jump to some startup if they wanted to get rich. Miriam wanted that very much.

Matt listened to her telling him this, patiently at first. Lately, she'd been getting more insistent. Matt's problem was, he just didn't *know* what the next big thing was, as he kept explaining. The big boom in PC's of the early 80's was over. Steve Jobs had left Apple and it was floundering without him. The really smart guys (or at least they saw themselves that way), were telling the press that handheld computers, where you used a pen instead of a keyboard and mouse, were the wave of the future. Some of the original Macintosh team had formed a company pretentiously called General Magic, which was supposedly going to own this market. Matt didn't even bother applying, since he knew they wouldn't hire him.

But in late 1989 Abigail heard of a new entrant in this Next Big Thing sweepstakes, and told Miriam about it! One night she said to Matt,

"Have you ever heard of GO Corp? Some of my colleagues were talking about it."

Matt had, of course.

"Sure. Some kind of pen thing, isn't it?"

"Yeah, it sounds pretty interesting! You can carry the thing around in your hand, and it recognizes your handwriting."

"Supposedly. That's a pretty hard problem. Why, what did you hear?"

"Well, just that they have a lot of venture capital. One of the other psychologists knows a guy who works there. Could be the next big thing!"

Matt looked weary. "Right. Next big thing," and ostentatiously picked up the Mercury-News.

Miriam decided to wait until later to pursue this further. As they were watching the ten o'clock news, she said,

"So this GO thing: would it be worth getting an interview there and checking them out?"

"I don't actually know anyone there. They haven't been around that long."

"You can't just send in your resume?"

Matt looked alarmed at that idea. "Send in a resume, cold? That's what losers do."

She looked puzzled. "Why? How else do you get an interview? That's what I did at the clinic."

"Different world here, Miriam. In high tech your headhunter calls them for you. Or you call someone there you know. Or if you're really hot shit, they call *you*."

"And you don't have a headhunter? Aren't those the people who call you all the time?"

"More losers. Bottom feeders. Deal with one of those and everyone thinks *you're* a loser."

Miriam felt like there was some kind of status hierarchy here, and while she'd *thought* she understood it, maybe she was wrong. She didn't want to irritate Matt any further right now. A little more research was clearly called for.

Abigail told her on Monday that GO was a hot startup, and Matt definitely should get in early. Mitch Kapor, who had been largely responsible for Lotus 1-2-3, was a buddy of Jerry Kaplan, the founder. Most importantly, John Doerr, of Kleiner, Perkins, the Valley's most prestigious venture capital firm, was behind it! How could you go wrong? This was the VC firm that had backed Lotus, Tandem, Compaq, and Sun. Having them behind you was like having God on your side.

GO was a leader in something that was certain to be as big as personal computers: "pen computing." Abigail told her about Grid, a startup from the early 80s that made a laptop long before anyone else, and *that* thing used a pen. It was so cool because you didn't have to learn to type! GO was going to go further than Grid and let you write in cursive, just like you'd write a note to someone, and the computer would recognize your handwriting. There were even rumors that Microsoft was interested in pen computing, and once Bill Gates got into something, all the smart money got out. So you had to be quick about exploiting it. Time was of the essence.

Miriam had never heard of Kleiner Perkins, but she was soon name-dropping it with almost everyone she talked to. She was gratified to find they all recognized the name immediately. She just had to get Matt into GO while there was still some founder's stock left (another Valley term she'd picked up).

But how? Matt had already poured cold water on the idea. Miriam told Abigail what he'd said, and she just laughed. Kim

Burdette was the leading headhunter in the Valley, and she was connected to *all* the startups. Surely Kim could get Matt an interview.

Miriam was excited. Might she, for once, know more than Matt about how high tech really worked? She'd find out tonight.

At dinner, she said, "So, have you ever talked to Kim Burdette?"

Matt looked surprised. "The headhunter? No. How do *you* know about her?"

She pointed to her temple.

"Oh, I know a lot of things. The Valley's a small place, you know."

He chuckled, and waited for her to say more.

"Abigail was telling me Kim's the top headhunter in the Valley. She knows all the startups!"

"Does she now?"

She caught the mocking tone in his voice. Now it was her turn to let *him* speak.

Matt finally asked, "So was there a reason you brought this up?"

"Well, remember last week you said you didn't know anyone at GO Corp?" He nodded.

"But the proper Silicon Valley thing was to have your headhunter call the company for you?"

Now it was clear. "Ah. So you want me to have Kim get me into GO? I'm slow here, sorry."

She just pointed to her temple again.

"Sorry, honey. I'm just not interested in leaving 3Com, right when I'm on the brink of a major promotion." His tone was final.

Miriam went in the kitchen for some imaginary chore to hide her mood.

∾

At work the next day, Matt asked his friend Dan, "So have you ever used Kim Burdette for anything?"

Dan laughed. "Amazingly, no. She's sent me on a zillion interviews, but both my jobs since Xerox, I got without her! Someday, maybe… why? Did you talk to her?"

"No, not yet. Miriam is pushing me to call her."

"Really? Why?"

"She's got this idea that I have to join a startup and make us rich. So we can move to Portola Valley, I guess."

Dan pondered that. He knew so many people from Xerox who had already made it, and here he was still struggling. Personal computers had exploded, networking was exploding, so where was his pile of money? He sighed.

"So, you're going to call Kim? I really like her, actually. Not a slimebag headhunter at all. You can see why everyone in the Valley loves her."

Matt felt encouraged. He called and left Kim a message. He wouldn't tell Miriam about it.

Kim already knew all about Matt, of course. Kim knew everything. She had a hand-drawn org chart for 3Com, like she did for all the high-tech companies.

He met with Kim for lunch, and she was every bit as engaging as Dan had said. They had a long getting-acquainted session, where she seemed to be finding out about him indirectly, by asking about *other* people and companies, rather than direct questions. She was not the "I know more than you and I'm not telling" sort of power person, either. Lots of little gossip items seemed to come out randomly, and Kim seemed as amused by retelling them as Matt was.

Finally, they got around to GO Corp. She hadn't actually placed anyone there yet, but she said she'd call for him. She didn't know much about them; just that they seemed to be well-connected with the venture capital world. She mentioned a few other startups she was working with but didn't think any of those were right for him.

Matt came back and told Dan he was on the money about Kim. She might not find him a job, but you didn't get the feeling you had to wash your hands after meeting her, at least.

They had another chat about GO. Pen-based computers: it did have a superficial appeal to it. You can't use a keyboard or mouse on a handheld device, obviously. But really — was this a revolution or just another input device to add onto Windows or Mac?

It seemed like all these people who had missed the PC revolution were just *desperate* to jump on something and *call it* a revolution. Every week, PC Week had a story like that. At the same time, there were people who really *had* built a big new thing back in the day, and now they were bored with just selling and improving it. They wanted to relive their youths and do it again! It was kinda sad, actually, like Jake and Elwood in The Blues Brothers movie getting the band back together again.

The Macintosh people were especially that way. Their names were worshiped like they were Mick Jagger or Paul McCartney or something. Any day now, those guys (they were mainly guys, but there were a few women as well) would issue a press release that *they* were going to create the next big thing, and everybody better just *stand back*! After all, they did it once. How could they miss?

Dan was cynical about all this. Matt was too, but he seemed more willing to believe the hype. Dan thought it was because of his wife.

∿

MIRIAM HAD BEEN BUSY. Every night it seemed like she had some new bit of wisdom on GO to impart.

GO was the new, hot thing, and this was Matt and Miriam's chance for big money. It seemed like everyone else had already cashed in on the PC revolution, and 3Com was not going to do it for them. They'd be lucky if their stock bought them a new car; forget about the house in Portola Valley. Time was wasting.

GO had a deal with IBM; GO was working with Microsoft; pen computing was going to be as big as personal computers were. It went on and on. She lectured him about how, if you carried the computer in your hands, you couldn't use a mouse or a keyboard, and your fingers were too big anyway. The pen *had* to be the key.

This didn't particularly impress Matt, since he was always hearing stuff like this. Styluses had been around forever. Everybody thought they had the next big thing. He had his interview in another week, so he figured there was nothing more to say until that happened.

Miriam was undeterred. She told him about all the top-drawer talent GO had managed to attract. Abigail had told her that Robert Carr, the brains behind dBase; Mitch Kapor, from Lotus; and of course, John Doerr from Kleiner Perkins were all behind it. Miriam had never heard of any of those people before, but the way Abigail said their names, she felt like she was hearing about an upcoming blockbuster with Meryl Streep, Sylvester Stallone, and Robert De Niro; a guaranteed hit!

6

LET'S GO ALREADY

I t was September 1990, GO and IBM had announced a few months ago that they were working together, and the news was all over the tech press *and* the general press. Miriam was insisting, more and more frantically, that Matt *had* to get a job there, before they went public and all that founder's stock was gone. Finally, he caved in and asked Kim to get him an interview.

He drove up to Foster City, which was *way* farther north than almost any Valley company he'd ever heard of. Foster City was this soulless strip of landfill, containing the 92 freeway, office buildings, shopping centers, and strip malls with absolutely zero character, not that the Valley had much character anyway. You could buy a townhouse along one of the many waterways connected to the Bay, if you craved that *faux* Florida vibe.

The interviews were surprisingly unstructured for such a hot shit company. He'd have thought they'd have some supersophisticated interview process, with coding tests, teams of interviewers who cooperated with each other, and all that, but it was pretty much like any other tech interview. They asked him about his work at 3Com and at the University, why he wanted to work at GO (*"To make a lot of money, like all of you!"* he wanted to say), and generally explained how pen computing was going to take over the world.

All of them had ready answers for why Microsoft and Apple wouldn't just add pen support to their own operating systems. According to them, really supporting a pen required such a different *Weltanschauung* that it would be "a bag on the side" if you added it to Windows or MacOS. "A bag on the side" was the standard tech insult for any addition that didn't really fit. *"These guys have really all drunk the Kool-Aid"* he thought.

Matt got the feeling that they were all pretty burned out and just wanted to get back to work, but at the same time they knew they needed a lot more help to do what they were attempting. GO had gained a reputation for "vaporware," the industry's term for products that existed only in presentations and press releases, and they resented it. He knew better than to ask in the first interview when the product was actually going to be delivered, but he had the distinct feeling it was "soon."

That night, Miriam grilled him about the interview. He told her he thought it went well and they'd probably call him back in, but you just never knew. This was unsatisfying for her, but she'd just have to live with it. Only a loser would pester a company he'd interviewed about its intentions. Maybe if he had another offer with a deadline on it, he could let them know, but he didn't.

Naturally, he told Dan about it.

"Hey, I interviewed with GO up in Foster City yesterday!"

"So how'd it go?" Dan and he were always sharing their job search news. Dan had been through a bunch of Valley prospects before settling on a transfer within 3Com, but Matt didn't know if he'd been to GO or not.

"Pretty good, I think. It's hard to tell. Did you ever interview there?"

Dan looked irritated. "Fraid so. Thankfully, they didn't make me an offer."

Matt laughed. "Well, it could be *you're* the lucky one. We'll see."

"So what do they want you to do for them?"

"Not clear. I don't think it's Directory services, anyway. Maybe it's really managing of some sort."

Dan thought about this, but there wasn't anywhere to go with it. He looked at his watch and stood up.

"Well, good luck. I have to go to a meeting!"

Time passed slowly for Matt. He thought that Miriam regarded this whole process as similar to taking the SAT and having her Mom bug her about how well she thought she did. She would sit by the phone if she could. Conversation at home was strained.

Finally, the call came! They wanted to have him back. This time he was talking to Kevin Doren, the VP of Engineering. *It's gotta be serious now*, he thought. Miriam was ecstatic. She wanted to go out and celebrate, but with a lot of effort he calmed her down and got her to wait for the offer.

He met with Kevin and a couple of other guys, one of whom was clearly assigned to get more technical with him. Finally, in walked Jerry Kaplan, the CEO! "This is either their best effort to sell me, or the last chance to veto me," he thought. "Hopefully the former."

Jerry was wearing a blazer and an Oxford shirt with no tie, like practically every executive he ever met. He tried to look bright and chipper, but the strain on him was impossible to miss. It seemed clear to Matt that he could *lose* the offer if he really tried, but basically it was his. Kaplan mostly gave his spiel about pen computing and what a great opportunity it was.

The next day, his offer letter came by courier. This time there was no stopping Miriam. She'd bought a bottle of Veuve Clicquot and had it chilling in the fridge just to be ready for this. "What would she have done if I *didn't* get the offer?" he thought. Anyway, they each had several glasses and then decided they were too drunk to go anywhere, so they continued celebrating at home.

The next day he went into work and turned in his notice. Eric Benhamou immediately called him and tried to talk him out of it, hinting that a big promotion could be in his future. He thanked Eric profusely, said he'd enjoyed working at 3Com *so much* and learned all about networking, but now it was time to grab an exciting new opportunity. They both knew all the lines to this play. "Don't burn your bridges & leave 'em smiling" on Matt's part; "thank him for all he's done and wish him the best" on Eric's part, etc. etc. His two weeks passed uneventfully, and Janet organized a little celebration for him on his last day.

On his way out the door for the last time, she caught up to him and walked with him to his car. She said,

"Well, we're going to miss you, Matt."

She'd already said that at the celebration, so he figured there must be more. She continued,

"Let's keep in touch. You never know!"

Now that they weren't rivals in *any* sense, real or potential, they could be allies. He said,

"Yeah, you never know. What are *you* going to do? You seem to be doing pretty well here."

She smiled. "Yeah, I don't really feel like I'm actually *doing* anything anymore. Eventually someone will figure that out!"

He laughed, "Oh, come on. You could be VP of Engineering anywhere you want nowadays."

"But what *do* I want? That's the question. Right now, Walt and I are both worried about my dad."

"I remember your dad. God, please tell me nothing's wrong!"

She suddenly realized she'd made him think Len had cancer or something, and quickly said,

"No, no, sorry, nothing like that. It's just that he retired a few months ago, and I don't think he's adapting well at all. A couple times lately I've talked to him and it really worries me. He's never been much of a drinker, but… I'm not sure *what* I heard."

Matt didn't really know what to say, so he asked,

"Why? You think he's depressed, or what?"

She hesitated a little. "Walt's had some friends who retired and started drinking, or just sat in front of the TV all day, and I can tell *he's* worried. He's always called Len 'Dad' since he didn't really know his own father very well. My first husband would never do that."

Matt smiled a little, thinking of Miriam's father Marv. He'd never in a million years call *Marv* "Dad." He always thought old Marv looked down on him for being from the poorer part of Queens. Marv was a VP in his company, while Matt's father was "just" a salesman.

But there was nothing much more he could say about it.

"Well, hang in there. Let's have lunch after I get situated up there."

"For sure." They hugged, and Matt drove home.

Miriam was at work, but Mookie was thrilled to see him, wagging his tail furiously. They went in the back yard and played ball for an hour or so. Then they went inside, Matt grabbed a beer from the fridge and headed for the couch, and Mookie curled up next to him.

7

CASSIE MOVES UP

It was January 1991. Cassie Decker had been working for Janet for over five years now. She'd been promoted to manager and had three people under her.

Matt had left months ago, and now Cassie was *really* depressed. Everyone she knew was either gone, transferred, or moved up the management chain so far that you couldn't really talk to them anymore. She was at that stage of a job where all your old friends are gone, a whole bunch of new people have joined, and you feel like a stranger there. It was definitely time to move on.

But move on to what? Had she really gotten all she could get from 3Com? Now she could interview as, basically, "a manager of Support." That seemed kinda blah. Even if she couldn't become an Engineer overnight, maybe she could transfer to something at least a *little* more technical and build up her resume.

Finally she hit on it: Quality Assurance! You don't have to be a great engineer to get that job, and in fact, if you were, you wouldn't want it. She resolved to have a chat with Hope Stinson, the manager of software QA. Hope had always seemed a little too political for Cassie's tastes, but maybe that would be OK for a short-term job. She was the sort of person whom nothing stuck to, a Teflon manager. Cassie had to admire that, in a perverse way. A product goes out that's embarrassing for its bugginess, and Hope always manages to shift the blame to the schedule not giving them enough time. Or she didn't have the proper resources to put on that product. It's never *her* group's fault for not finding the bugs or raising a flag.

She had lunch with Hope, who was ecstatic to find someone she already knew and who knew 3Com's products. So they agreed Cassie was going to be the QA manager for some of the higher-level products, like the new network management product that Dan was working on.

Hope and Janet were always carefully and elaborately formal with each other, like all the managers at 3Com, so this was sweet for Hope: she was stealing one of Janet's best people. She made sure to be extra-nice to Janet to rub it in, in fact Janet thought she was almost sickeningly nice.

When Cassie talked it over with Janet, who had already heard, Janet was genuinely happy for her. She had always thought Cassie was someone to nurture, so if this was what she wanted to do, hey, nothing lasts forever. They agreed that Cassie would recommend someone to replace her from her own group, if she thought one of them was ready to lead the group.

When the announcement came out officially, Cassie thought, "OK, one problem down. Farzad, you're next." She went looking for a new apartment, since kicking her boyfriend out of the one they shared would be too awkward.

DAN'S GROUP HAD LAYOFFS, but Dan escaped. Apparently his transplant from email had worked and he was blooming in the new location. Cassie knew in advance that this bloodletting was happening, but there was nothing she could do about it. Life goes on.

Shortly after that, in March 1991, he quit anyway. He was going to work at Oracle, of all places, not on the database but in their networking group. It sounded like a desperation move to Cassie, but she wished him well. He told her that Patrick, the Marketing VP said to him, "Oracle? Are you *nuts*?" The previous year, Oracle had had "irregularities" in their accounting, the stock had crashed, and some financial analysts were ready to count them out permanently. But apparently Dan knew the VP he'd be working for and wasn't worried about their future, or so he said.

She consoled herself with, "*Well, at least I have a different job now, even if everyone I used to know is leaving!*"

She moved out on Farzad. He took it pretty hard. She thought, "*Yeah, but I bet your parents were, like, 'Finally! You'll find a nice Muslim girl now.'* " She hadn't really dated much since that. Her church had a Singles group, but none of those guys interested her much.

Her mom was relieved, too. She never thought Cassie should marry an Iranian guy, and *especially* not have Muslim children. But now that she was single again and past thirty, she was getting anxious about the grandchildren thing. Cassie's sister and brother were both married already, but neither had kids yet. When she went to church, she'd see the toddler care room outside the church, and get twinges of "*I want one of those!*"

Her new job seemed to involve a lot of going to Engineering meetings as the QA representative, and saying, "We don't have the resources for that." Or being silent. It was rare that she had anything much to say, unless a product had actually been completed and turned over to QA.

Normally, the engineers and product managers plus top management initiated and defined products. Sometimes it came entirely from top management, like the Microsoft deal on LAN Manager. Other times it was more bottom-up, like Dan's new email system. In either case, the "chartering" of a product team was what made it a real product. The product team had to include a tech writer, someone from QA, and of course engineering and marketing representatives. Usually the writer & QA person are afterthoughts, and of course they viewed that as a snub.

Hope, as the overall QA manager, compensated for this lack of *technical* status by wielding *political* power. When products were being discussed, she was always there, tuning into the interpersonal dynamics and figuring out who held the real power, regardless of what the org chart said. Being on Hope's bad side was a very bad career move.

Nonetheless, she would always say at big meetings, ritualistically, "We need to be involved from the very beginning of the project!" Cassie would nod her head dutifully, although she wondered what she could possibly contribute at that stage. She didn't realize, yet, that what Hope really meant was, "We should be able to prevent the product before it even gets started."

Cassie's direct reports were all assigned to various projects and charged with writing Test Plans, which she reviewed. She found that to be an excellent opportunity to learn more networking. She could read their design specifications, compare them to the test plans, talk to the engineers, and generally pick up the lingo. She wished she could actually run the tests, but that wasn't her job, damn it. Still, the bug reports were educational.

Hope had one favorite underling, Jeffrey, whom she often went to lunch with. Jeffrey had figured out that succeeding at QA was not about product *quality*; it was about product *prevention*. Hope was teaching him.

One day in the summer, Mike, a guy she and Janet both knew slightly, called her. He had left to join a startup called Momenta, and apparently it wasn't going too well. They'd both be happy to hire him again if that was what he was angling for, so they agreed to meet him for lunch. They met in the 3Com cafe, since he certainly knew the way to Headquarters and Janet and Cassie didn't have to drive anywhere.

There really weren't too many startups right now. Microsoft was devouring everything, and everyone knew that if you had any kind of interesting company, their minions would approach you with an offer to "work together." That meant, "give us all your technology, and *maybe* we'll issue a press release about how great you are. Or maybe we'll just buy you out. Or build it ourselves." It was like Don Corleone's men making you an offer. Politely.

Momenta had attracted a lot of attention and a lot of venture capital for a "handheld computer" and they were very snooty about which people they would hire. Cassie had called their number and apparently she didn't make the cut. Janet and Cassie were dying to hear whatever Mike was willing to tell them. It didn't seem to them like computer technology was far enough advanced that you could build anything useful, but hey, you never know.

Mike looked vaguely disoriented, like he was on a weekend pass from prison and he dreaded having to go back inside on Monday. He talked about the Company Culture at Momenta, and it really did sound like those C's were capitalized. All the founders had worked at other Valley companies and hated the bureaucratic, secretive, competitive culture that many of them had. So they had jointly resolved, in weekend meetings, to be different and better. The "weekend" part was intentionally inconvenient, and the people who'd been to one would talk about it like a religious cult's retreat.

They used the word "teamwork" so often that Mike thought they must have a keyboard macro on everyone's computer so you could get it with one keystroke. There was a set of precepts called the Momenta Maxims, which all began with 'P': People, Process, Productivity, Performance, and

Perspective. When you joined, you had to sign a plaque with the Maxims, in front of the whole company. People joked that you used to have to kneel to do this, but that was just an urban legend.

Furthermore, there were precepts for how to have a good meeting: start on time, listen to and respect all points of view, reach a consensus, and end on time. These were encased in a plastic icon that was present in every meeting room. If you thought someone was disobeying one of the precepts, you could pick up the icon and wave it at him or her.

Janet had heard enough, and finally asked,

"So, with all this happy-happy, what are you actually building? Or can you talk about it?"

Mike talked about his work like it was already in the past, even though he was still doing it.

"I'm working on one aspect of the handwriting recognition software, with the stylus. That's actually one of the reasons I want to get out: that stuff will never work!"

He hadn't actually *said* he wanted to get out, but that was pretty obvious by now.

Cassie said,

"Really? I've heard of those systems, but I've never tried one."

"Yeah, don't. It's never going to work, and in fact, we now have a keyboard only because one guy managed to beat that into everyone's head. They hate him for it, too."

Janet laughed. "Sounds about right. That's got to be a hard problem!"

"You think?" he said, sardonically.

Cassie said, "I don't know if you knew Matt Finegold or not?"

"Vaguely."

"Anyhow, he's at GO Corp., which I guess is one of your competitors. I haven't talked to him lately."

"Oh, yeah, we know about them. Also General Magic,

and Apple with their handheld thingie. Everyone's trying to do this."

Janet said, "Are any of them succeeding at it?"

"That's the big secret. I don't see how, myself."

They talked about what Mike would do if he came back to 3Com. It was finally settled that he could work in Cassie's group.

8

THE COMPUTER BIZ

Miriam had the hardest time understanding the computer industry. Matt had to explain, over and over, that just because he was in a hot company (GO Corp.) that didn't mean they were rich, *yet*. They couldn't move to Atherton yet. And might never be able to, the way things were going. "If everyone thinks you're great, why isn't that enough?" was her attitude.

"Well, first you have to ship a product and make a profit," he would explain. She'd interrupt him:

"OK, so when does that happen? Why does it take so long?"

She'd visited their offices and seen the prototypes, and he'd shown her the trade press articles about GO. They were all glowing. GO had a big partnership with IBM. So what was the hangup?

"Miriam, bringing out a PC product is like running with a bag of steaks through a pack of hungry hyenas, with a few lions watching from the bushes. And Marlin Perkins and David Attenborough narrating from a sound truck. The people you're carrying the steaks for don't even have a role to play yet."

"What does that even mean?" she said, angrily.

"The lions are the giant companies, like Microsoft, Apple, IBM, and AT&T. The hyenas are the software developers and peripheral makers. And the Perkins and Attenborough team are the trade press,"

Miriam tried to take all that in. It was pretty overwhelming.

It was spring, 1991, and the top brass were all at Esther Dyson's conference in Tucson, Arizona. The thing that Matt had worried about when he interviewed there was actually coming to pass: Microsoft was stabbing them in the back. He was hearing back from the conference that Microsoft was announcing their own "PenWindows," a pen-based extension to Windows. Apparently they'd faked their "alliance" with GO, and now they were ripping them off.

Gates did this to everyone in the industry, so why was GO expecting anything else? Matt had seen up close how they'd taken advantage of 3Com to get their start in networking with "LAN Manager." Whenever any company, anywhere, had any interesting technology for the PC, Microsoft acted like the street mobsters in Queens where Matt grew up: "Hey, that appliance business you have? That's ours now. We'll call when we need your signature on anything."

When Matt made the mistake of trying to tell her this, she became enraged:

"How can they do that? Those are *your* ideas! Don't you have a patent on them? Can't you sue them or something? And anyway, IBM is on *your* side!"

He got tired of walking her through the process of a lawsuit. Microsoft could drown them in legal motions, subpoenas, discovery requests, and on and on, before they ever got in front of a judge. No one could afford those legal fees and no one could wait all that time for a verdict, which Microsoft would appeal even if they lost, meanwhile stealing the market from you.

Matt tried another tack. Way back at the University when he'd had a summer internship at DataPoint, he'd explained to her what "fear, uncertainty, and doubt" meant when IBM did it. Microsoft was doing the same thing now, when they told the industry that *they* were going to support pen input, and everyone should wait rather than deal with GO. They had the power to freeze everyone in the industry.

Miriam had forgotten all that. She couldn't or didn't want to understand that it was just business. This was her chance to move to Portola Valley or buy a vintage house in Old Palo Alto, after all, and it was slipping away. The discussion subsided, but she was still seething.

WITH THE CREW AT GO, Matt didn't notice any changes. The execs were back from Tucson, and everyone knew the conference hadn't gone well and Microsoft was stealing their ideas. The execs spent hours closeted away in meetings, looking earnest, and it was impossible to hide the fact that something was up. They would tell everyone the official story on Friday at the beer blast / comms meeting, but surely the *real* story would leak out before then.

Still, for now it was business as usual. It would have been career-limiting to utter a discouraging word about GO's prospects. Everyone had faith in Jerry Kaplan and Robert Carr, and the Friday meeting would put it all into perspective.

There were rumors that they were getting off the Intel processor family entirely, which would be a radical shift for everyone in engineering. The Intel 8086, 80286, and 80386 chips were what people in the Valley lived and died with. Whenever you met someone from another company with *any* sort of computing device, "What's the processor?" was always the first question.

The IBM PC and all its clones ran on Intel, of course,

Microsoft owned DOS and now Windows, and it was basically a shared monopoly. Matt had always wondered why GO was ever on Intel in the first place. Surely Microsoft would squeeze them out, he'd always thought, and now it was coming to pass.

It was impossible to keep something like this a secret in a small company like GO. Pretty soon the word was out: the processor was going to be the Hobbit, from AT&T. Engineers feverishly gathered information about the Hobbit all week long, and analyzed its design vs. the ARM chip. It was like Computer Science grad school again for Matt. Arguing about chips and how well they ran particular languages and operating systems was raw meat for engineers. Nothing else could make a bunch of programmers geek out like that. The actual business reason for the switch was something they didn't give as much thought to.

"ARM" meant Advanced RISC Machine, or Acorn RISC Machine, "RISC" meaning "reduced instruction set computer," which was the new hotness in the computer industry. The Intel chips were "CISC" or "complex instruction set computer" meaning they had complicated instructions designed to make computer languages run fast, while RISC designers had a philosophy of "just make a few simple instructions blazing fast, and let the compiler guys deal with it." ARM's big selling point was that it used less power, so you could put it in a battery-operated device, i.e. something you carried around.

For Matt, there was a much more serious issue than "which chip is better?": they were partnering with AT&T. He had a sick foreboding about this from his time at 3Com: AT&T was big, bureaucratic, and stupid. They would take forever to decide anything, and then make the wrong decision anyway. It was a former telephone monopoly and nothing would ever change those guys' mindset. No one ever made money dealing with AT&T.

His conversations with Miriam kept getting worse. She'd

start out interrogating him about how it was going, and recount what her boss Abigail at her clinic said about the PC business. This was starting to annoy him. "*What the hell does that stupid shrink know?*" he said to himself. Abigail had been hearing for years about how Bill Gates and the Beast From Redmond were stomping through the Valley and stealing everyone's technology, and she really wanted someone to stand up to them for a change. GO had been Miriam's big hope for getting rich, and now it was slipping away. Matt's instinct was just to lay low for a while and see what happened. Maybe he'd bail out later. This left Miriam unsatisfied. How could he even consider walking away from all that effort?

It seemed like she was picking fights about other stuff more often, too. The remodeling job years ago that they'd fired Walt for, and finally hired someone else to finish was a continual source of complaint. The kitchen island that had triggered so much trouble for Walt was never quite good enough for her. She'd seen Abigail's and it was *so* much better: bigger, with a better granite top. Even though Matt and Miriam's house was nicer now, it was still in a just so-so neighborhood, and nothing would change that except moving.

He called up Dan Markunas, his old buddy from 3Com, who was now working at Oracle, just two exits down 101 from his exit. They met for lunch at Tokie's, a sushi place roughly halfway between them, in Foster City.

Dan and Matt hadn't seen each other in months, since they'd both left 3Com. They sat right near the sushi chef, who took their orders and started handing them the wonderful sushi Tokie's was known for.

Matt said, "So how's Oracle? Is it as bad as everyone says?"

"Hah! It just depends on what part of it you're in. Our part is run by Porter Berwick, an old hippie from Xerox. I guess *some* parts of Oracle *are* sweatshops, but I really like it so far."

"So what does your division do?"

"We're called the Network Products Division. SQL*Net is the main product, which makes tons of money because all the customers buy it. Maybe that's why Larry leaves us alone."

Matt took all that in. They talked about what a network products division at Oracle would do. Apparently Porter had a vision that was about much more than SQL*Net, and they had a lot of networking talent. Deep knowledge of database technology was not a requirement for getting hired there, although at one time every secretary at Oracle knew how to do an outer join. Matt wasn't sure what an "outer join" even was, but apparently it was some SQL thing. They laughed about Larry Ellison's outsized reputation around the Valley, including the time he'd quoted Genghis Khan's "It is not enough that I succeed. All others must fail." That one had provoked a letter to the editor in the San Jose Mercury News about the example he was setting for children.

"Anyway, enough about me. What about you? How's GO?" Dan asked, knowing that there was probably a good reason for this lunch.

"Well, not great," said Matt. "You know what we're doing there, right?"

"Some kind of handheld device with a stylus, and that's about all I know," said Dan. "Doesn't it recognize your handwriting?"

"*Sometimes* it does. Anyhow, they showed it all to Microsoft some years ago before I got there…"

"Uh-oh," interrupted Dan. "I know where this is going."

Matt laughed. "Yeah. You and I saw it with LAN Manager. Now it's happening here."

"So, let me guess: Microsoft is announcing their own version of it, and everyone should wait until it's ready?"

"Wow, you're really good at this, Dan!"

Dan nodded his head, and continued, "So what's GO going to do now? I know: claim this validates our vision for the future, and welcome Microsoft into this market that we pioneered?"

"Well, maybe that's what we say in public."

"But in private…?"

"In private, we're getting off Intel and partnering with AT&T."

Dan buried his face in his hands.

"Matt, Matt, Matt. No one makes money dealing with AT&T. No one. Didn't you tell them that?"

"It's above my pay grade, Dan. They don't listen to *me*."

Dan knew Matt was going to be looking around for another job soon. But he was still curious about one thing.

"So you said you're 'getting off Intel.' What does that mean? Onto what?"

"Have you ever heard of the Hobbit processor?"

"No. Who makes that?"

"Who do you think?"

"Oh, God, no," said Dan. "The plot sickens."

"I mean, yeah. Getting off Intel makes a ton of sense. But everyone's moving to the ARM instead."

"Now *that* I've heard of, at least. What's the deal with ARM?"

Matt said, "ARM is a low-power device that the Apple Newton is using, supposedly."

"OK, yeah, right, I guess I did read that. So what's wrong with using ARM?"

Matt shrugged. "Not AT&T's choice, I guess."

"Wow. Just wow." Dan shook his head.

"Yep. Yep."

"So what are *you* going to do?"

Matt said, "Well, just see how it shakes out, for a while anyway."

"It only gets worse from here, Matt."

"Miriam is pretty invested in us getting rich from GO. She

keeps hassling me about it. I think it's really her mother who's doing the talking, but she goes ballistic if I say that."

"What, she wants you to stay with it, or go somewhere else, or what?"

"She thinks GO should sue Microsoft and make a big stink about it."

"Yeah, that always works well."

"She's been watching too many lawyer shows, I think."

Dan was silent. He said, finally,

"Well, we're hiring, so if you ever want…"

"I might take you up on that," said Matt. "I don't feel like going down with the ship here. But what would I be doing there?"

"I'm not sure, but you can come down and have lunch with Porter, so it's not really an 'interview' " he said, making the air quotes with his fingers.

Matt looked agreeable. Dan said he'd set it up.

9

THE INTERNET, IN PERSON

It was November, 1991. Janet was attending her first Internet Engineering Task Force (IETF) meeting in Santa Fe, New Mexico. The IETF was the group that actually defined how the Internet would work. It wasn't a big corporate or government bureaucracy, and almost no one wore a tie, except for Vint Cerf, the spiritual father of the Internet, who was in a three-piece suit. Janet shook his hand and he was as gracious to her as if she were a visiting President.

It was freezing in Santa Fe, and she had to stop at an outdoors store and buy a stocking cap. The IETF had a practice of meeting in cities outside tourist season to save on costs, and they were certainly adhering to it now.

Why was she at an Internet conference at all? 3Com wanted to *appear* hip and with-it without actually doing much, and sending one of their top managers to a meeting like this was an easy way to accomplish that. That was the first reason.

The second reason was that Janet had been making herself a pest about the Internet in top management meetings for the last couple of years. The rest of the management team pooh-pooh'ed "this Internet thing" as just something for the academic types, with their big Unix machines. 3Com was happy to sell them Ethernet adapters and let them play all they wanted.

Normal business people didn't use that stuff; they used Novell, or IBM, or DEC, or Apple protocols. Someday, they all believed, everyone would move to the global "standard", OSI. OSI, or "Open Systems Interconnect," whatever you wanted to call it, was a standard produced by the ponderous CCITT (the French initials. It was "International Telegraph and Telephone Consultative Committee" in English). That was at least run by the telephone companies and by extension, the United Nations, so it was a *real* standard. Those organizations would rule the networking world, and the Internet would always just be for the pointy heads.

They made fun of "the world-wide web", which had been announced in August of that year. Janet didn't even try to get their approval to buy a NeXT machine to host a "web server," since none of them even knew what that was. She knew they'd never approve it.

But this conference had 350 people in attendance! It was going on all week. There were subgroups meeting on ATM (the new network system that supposedly would be used by the telephone companies and handle voice, video, and everything); AppleTalk; X.25 (the old public data network); routing; SNMP (the management protocol); and many more things she knew nothing about. They certainly seemed to be serious, busy people. Conspicuously missing was Microsoft! As far as anyone could tell, they'd never heard of the Internet.

She walked around the reception looking for people she knew. There was Peter Deutsch, whom she *sort of* knew from Xerox, although she mostly knew *of* him. Chandy, from 3Com. But hello! It was Dan Markunas, her old buddy from Xerox *and* 3Com. He saw her at almost the same time, and they hugged.

"Dan! How's Oracle?" Dan had left 3Com earlier this year

and gone to work at Oracle in their Network Products Division. They hadn't seen each other since then. Many people at 3Com thought it was a stupid move, since Oracle had had a big stock drop the year before. She wasn't one of them, since the people saying that were mostly the same ones who thought the Internet was going nowhere. These were people who spoke about the Microsoft LAN Manager deal as "strategic," and thought Bridge's router business was never going to go anywhere, so they let Cisco take over that market. She sat in these big management meetings where they all debated what business 3Com should be in. It didn't seem to hurt your management career if you were always wrong.

"Oh, it's great! I'm busy learning Unix. I have a private office again! How are you? Is 3Com getting into the Internet?"

The bit about the private office was rubbing it in. They had both had one at Xerox, but nobody at 3Com did. That had been a big bone of contention when 3Com acquired Bridge back in 1987, since Bridge had them and 3Com had insisted on abolishing them, so they could have a uniform company culture.

She didn't want to say too much about her struggles at 3Com, so she just said, "I'm trying. It's hard. How about Oracle — what are you working on?"

"I'm doing this database to help people manage all the text files you need with Unix and the Internet. Learning all about /etc/passwd (he pronounced it "etsy-password"), DNS files, and all that."

She thought she'd get him back now for that private office jab:

"A database! Naturally, that *would* be Oracle's answer to everything."

He smiled. "Yeah, well, that *is* what brings in the money. Anyhow, I guess I'll see you around. Which working groups are you going to?"

She looked through her program, and said, "Oh, I'm not sure. There's so much here I don't know. How about you?"

"I'm going to the Internet Message Extensions working group this morning. This afternoon is a talk by Dave Perkins! You remember him!"

She tried to recall who that was. "Oh, yeah. Didn't he leave?"

"Yeah. He's at Synoptics now."

"Well, I'm sure I'll run into you again." She continued circulating. She wasn't the *only* woman there, but it was mostly men, like most tech gatherings. Everyone looked at her name badge to decide if she was worth talking to. The "3Com" part attracted a lot of attention. They either wanted to ask if 3Com was getting into the Internet, or tell her that they were using 3Com Ethernet adapters. She tried to look polite at the latter group. Some of the guys had other intentions, but she figured her wedding ring ought to handle those.

She ended up going to the Router Requirements meeting, feeling vaguely that routers were something that 3Com sold and her group was responsible for managing them in the corporate network, so they must be important. No one else from 3Com was there, although walking around chatting, it seemed like almost all of their competitors were. She took careful notes for the folks back home.

At lunch, she went to a restaurant with Dan, a bunch of people she didn't know, and Mitch Kapor, the creator of Lotus 1-2-3. Kapor was very down-to-earth and she couldn't wait to tell the people back home about the famous guy she met!

As they got back to the conference, Dan asked, "Do you want to meet for breakfast tomorrow and catch up? I'm dying to hear what's up at 3Com?"

Janet said, "Sure. You can tell me what Porter is like as a VP, too!" Porter Berwick was a guy they both knew from Xerox, and he was the VP of Dan's new division.

Everyone wanted to know what 3Com was doing with the Internet these days, and she was embarrassed to have to say "Not all that much!" They talked about Gopher, which was a new Internet protocol some people were really excited about, and they threw around the names of Usenet groups as if *everyone* read those things. Once in a while she looked at one of those groups, and she'd even made them available to the company, since there *were* a few newsgroups that were directly relevant to some of the engineers. It seemed to generate a staggering amount of traffic, and everyone sympathized with her when she told them that.

Someone mentioned a British guy, Tim Berners-Lee, who was pushing something called "the world-wide web." Now she had heard of *that*. No one was quite sure where that was going, but they all seemed to think it was worth paying attention to. She made a note to herself to stay on top of that one.

It seemed like everyone wanted to hire her! She was that rare "woman in tech," and they all figured that 3Com was going nowhere and she *must* be looking for a job. She was polite to them but didn't let it go beyond that.

ON MONDAY AFTERNOON AFTER LUNCH, as Dan waited for the elevator at his hotel, he saw another guy with a badge for the conference. There was just *something* about him that said "I'm not a techie!" and Dan was intrigued. If he didn't have the badge, Dan would have thought he was an entertainer at a local lounge, except he wasn't quite good-looking enough for that.

The guy stuck out his hand and introduced himself, "Hi, I'm Stan." Stan had a two-day beard stubble, sunglasses up on his head, and long wavy hair greased back. He was wearing a sport coat over a flowered shirt open at the throat, and several gold chains around his neck. No one in tech dressed like that.

They chatted. Stan had heard of Oracle but didn't know anything about it, and seemingly didn't have much interest. Dan said, "So what brings you to the IETF?"

Stan said, "It's exciting, man. It's the future!"

"Yeah, maybe so." Dan agreed.

"Oh, it definitely is. Can you imagine if everyone had this at home?"

Their elevator came and they got in. Dan said as the doors closed,

"Maybe someday. What would they all do with it, though?"

Stan's face lit up. "I know what the *guys* will be doing, at least!"

Dan started to get some idea why Stan was here. "Watch porn, you mean?"

"We like to call it 'adult entertainment'."

Dan smiled. He was about to ask if that was what Stan did for a living, but they got to their floor and Stan got off.

"It was nice to meet you, Dan." he said. "Maybe I'll see you around."

Dan had seen the little room at his local video rental shop with the X-rated videos, not that he ever went in there. He thought of Paul Reubens, or "Pee-Wee Herman," who'd been arrested for masturbating at a local porn theater and always wondered why Reubens didn't just rent a video. But he'd never even considered that you could send porn over the Internet! It was barely fast enough for text, for God's sake. Maybe a photo if you had plenty of time to wait. Almost since the dawn of computing, guys had created adult images and sent them around for their own amusement. Sometimes they did it on a normal line printer, with parentheses placed at strategic points.

But ordinary people watching a video? Forget it. Stan was a real visionary, but he was just a *little* ahead of his time.

Dan saw a couple other 3Com'ers at the conference and

wondered if 3Com was finally, *finally* getting with it. He'd been in a division at 3Com that was working on part of "the Internet," namely SNMP, or Simple Network Management Protocol. They were doing a "management station," which at least two other large companies were doing (Sun and HP), and it had almost zero chance of succeeding in the market, but at least it gave him some credibility in a technology with actual market appeal. Email, he'd discovered, had almost none in the wider market.

The next morning he met Janet at one of those cool little Southwestern cafes that were all over Santa Fe. Dan had always wanted to try *huevos rancheros*, so he ordered those. Janet just had a bagel.

She wondered how life outside of 3Com was. He knew she was open to other opportunities, since that dinner at her house shortly after the wedding, but he figured all the headhunters must know about her by now. Then she surprised him:

"Hey, do you like fishing?"

"Fishing? I love it. Why, what brought that on?"

"Well, we're moving my dad out from Detroit to live in Walt's cabin in the mountains! He's going to fish every day."

Dan was amazed. "Your dad? I met him at the wedding, right? What, is he retired now?"

"Yeah, he retired last year, and we were worried he was going to be bored and start drinking or something. Walt, especially, since he's lost a few friends that way."

"Wow. So is he going to like living by himself out in the middle of nowhere? I mean, I'm assuming here."

Janet laughed. "No, you're not wrong. Walt's cabin *is* pretty isolated. Dad stayed in it while we were on our honeymoon, and he's been raving about it ever since. Dan and Walt are going to build a new house on the property for Dad to live in. We call it "father-in-law quarters!"

"Like mother-in-law quarters. I like it! And Walt's a contractor so he knows how to do stuff like that."

"Yep. I'm going to help, too. It'll be a nice break from work."

"Janet's joining Walt's business! Don't hurt your hands, though. You need those to type!"

"Not really. Mostly I just go to meetings and talk on the phone these days. Anyhow, thanks, I'll be sure to wear gloves."

Dan took all this in. "Wow, my dad used to go fishing all the time before he got married. We always went on vacations in northern Wisconsin to fish."

"Same with us, but it was northern Michigan. I bet my dad and yours would get along great!"

"Yeah. Len will have to have me up there to visit and fish with him some time!"

"It's a deal."

They talked about their friends at 3Com. She said that Matt had left to join this startup in Foster City, called "GO Corp." which Dan already knew all about. He'd just had lunch with Matt a month or so ago.

The funniest news was from a guy, Mike, whom Janet knew but Dan didn't, who'd gone to a startup called Momenta, which was trying to build a handheld computer. They were a bunch of pretentious Apple wannabes, whose motto was "1,000 days to greatness" to appeal to those people who'd missed the original Macintosh effort. She regaled him with stories about their "culture," like this one:

Mike had just joined the company, and Kamran Eliahan, the president, was asking him to affirm his faith in the Momenta Maxims in front of the rest of the company.

"He asked him, 'Do you believe in the Maxims? Are you willing to live your life by them?' Can you believe that?"

Dan snorted. "What are 'the Momenta Maxims'? Do they carry them around on a little wallet card?"

"I forget, but I remember they all begin with a 'P'. People, Process... I forget the rest."

"Is 'Pretentiousness' one of them?"

Now it was Janet's turn to laugh. "That's what I said, too. Patronizing?"

"Piety!"

"Or 'Pointless' "

Dan said, "How about 'Psychedelic'?"

She thought about how that was spelled. He had her there! She wiped the tears from her eyes with her napkin, put it on the table, and motioned for the check. They were both leaving tonight, although the conference was going on all week.

As for Santa Fe: it was freezing, but there were lots of great restaurants and tons of art galleries. He spent part of that afternoon just gallery-hopping, observing that, as always, any piece of art in a gallery cost at least three times what he'd be willing to pay. But hey, they have to pay their rent, too. He thought he'd stick to going to the "artists' open studios" tours, where you could deal directly with the artist, see *all* their work, and maybe bargain with them.

10

WHAT'S A BBS?

I t was February, 1992, that part of winter when the weather in the Midwest has been crappy for months with no end in sight. Len had been living with it all his life, but somehow, now that he knew he *could* give it up and move to California, it became intolerable. Day after day after day it was the same shit: gray skies, temperature in the 40's, and piles of dirty slush on the side of every street. The snow was definitely not a magic carpet of white on tree branches like on postcards.

He was having a good time on America Online, though. He'd started out on Prodigy, but that pretty quickly became too nanny-ish for him. They depended on advertising by big companies, and those people did not like paying for people to criticize them in mean ways. Once he made the mistake of saying something unfavorable about his modem, and he got a nastygram from Prodigy warning him that his account could be suspended if he kept that up. So he'd moved over to AOL, after getting a floppy from them in the mail almost every day.

Those dark, cold, early nights were much more bearable when he could dial up AOL and explore things. He got absorbed in the chat rooms about investments, and now he spent hours in Lotus 1-2-3 typing formulas into his spread-sheets and computing the 90-day and 30-day moving averages of his favorite stocks and mutual funds. He knew one other financial analyst down in Florida (whom he'd never met in person, of course) whom he emailed with almost every day.

Then it was baseball. There were *so* many statistics you could compute, and they were stats you'd never see in the papers. He bought the Bill James baseball books and found a community of people who were also into the stuff, and he spent hours arguing with them.

Janet had been living in the online world for almost 15 years now at Xerox and 3Com, and she didn't see any reason to do it at home, too. The first time he'd asked her a question about Prodigy, he was dumbfounded that she knew absolutely nothing about it!

"Isn't this what you do for a living, honey?"

"It's totally different at work, Dad. We don't use modems at all. It's all Ethernet."

"I don't even know what that is, Is that better than a modem? Mine says it's 1,200 baud. How many bauds is yours?"

Janet laughed. "Ethernet is ten million bits per second."

Len did some math in his head. "Ten million versus twelve hundred. I guess I'm in the wrong business, huh?"

"Yeah, that's why I don't do it at home, I guess. That, plus the fact that it's work!"

"Well, it's a hobby for me, honey. At least it is when it works!"

She thought she should at least try to help him out, though, so she asked him some questions about what was going wrong. It turned out that Dad figured it out for himself as he was explaining it to her, which was what she hoped would happen.

"So I should know more about all this, I guess. Have you gotten into Usenet yet?"

"Usenet?" he said. "Never heard of it. Is that something I should try?"

"Hmm. That's what everyone seems to be doing at work. It seems like everyday, someone comes and complains about it to me. And it sucks up almost all our bandwidth, too!"

"Now that you mention it, people do mention stuff like that sometimes. It sure sounds like a big deal. How do I get on that?"

"Oh, jeez. I'll have to ask Cassie about that. You remember her from the wedding, right?"

"Was she the cute little gal?"

"Dad gets a pass for language like that," she thought. "Yeah, Cassie does lots of online stuff at home. She probably knows."

After they hung up, Len asked some of his AOL buddies about this "Usenet" thing. They all said you couldn't get to it through AOL, but *maybe* he could get on a BBS and do it that way.

"A 'BBS' ," he thought. *"One more rabbit hole to go down. It never ends!"*

He shut the computer off for the night. *"Who's on Carson tonight?"* he wondered. Johnny Carson was rumored to be retiring soon. He'd better enjoy it while he still could.

The next day he didn't go online at all. *"Screw that stuff,"* he thought. No matter what you did, there was always some new mystery you had to solve by asking around. Whatever happened to the old days, when you went to the library and *looked stuff up?* Or maybe you bought a magazine about it. Or went to a bookstore and bought a book. This computer stuff — it wasn't written down *anywhere.* And the worst thing was, as soon as you figured out how to do something, they changed it! There was no professionalism, none at all.

And that was if you could even find what you wanted in the first place! This game was rigged for teenagers or hippies with nothing better to do. Janet was going to find out the answer for him; how long should he wait before calling her and asking? He didn't want to be a pest.

The next afternoon he went down to the Best Buy where he'd bought his PC, and asked Jerry, the salesman who sold it to him, if he knew anything about this "Usenet" thing. Jerry looked puzzled and asked him to repeat the word. Then he disappeared into the back of the store. Len walked around and checked out the computers on display. Finally, Jerry came back with a document with the words, "Horst Mann's List" and a date at the top. It was nothing but a bunch of weird names and telephone numbers.

"What the hell's this? Who is Horst Mann?"

Jerry looked embarrassed. "Horst Mann is this guy who keeps track of all the bulletin board systems in the Detroit area. I've never used any of these, but someone there might know."

"What am I supposed to do with these numbers?"

Jerry explained to him what a BBS was. He found a magazine on the rack that had an article about BBS's, gave it to Len, thanked him for coming in, then went to help another customer.

When Len got home, he poured himself a glass of Scotch and sat down to read. This was going to be a chore.

"*This is for high school kids, not for someone like me,*" he kept thinking, and put the magazine down several times. "*Where are the grownups in all this?*" he wondered. At least Prodigy and AOL were run by actual companies, not a bunch of kids.

He didn't touch the computer for the rest of the week. On Saturday morning he talked to Janet as usual, and she had some news for him. Cassie found the names and phone numbers of some bulletin boards that offered Usenet! It had taken her a lot of digging to find one in the Detroit area, but she even said Len could call her up if he needed help. How could he give up on it now, after she went to all that trouble for him?

On Saturday night, instead of going to bed he dialed up one of Cassie's bulletin boards. The menu didn't say anything about Usenet; it just said something about Internet. He thought that must be it, so he selected it. Now there were various menu choices he didn't understand, like "ftp" and "telnet" but one of them said "newsgroups." That looked promising.

But now what? There were a bunch of subheadings, like alt.* and rec.* and comp.* with numbers after them. What the hell did all that mean? He typed 'h' for Help, which seemed to be a common thing you could do online, and that was no help at all. This stuff was obviously written for people who already knew it. He shut the computer off. Tomorrow he'd call Cassie and plead for some assistance.

After Janet had told Len that Cassie might be able to help him, he dialed her and she picked up.

"Hello, Cassie? This is Len Saunders, Janet's father. I hope I'm not bothering you?"

"Hi, Mr. Saunders! No, it's fine, I'm just sitting around. We met at Janet and Walt's wedding, right?"

"That's right, I remember you. I hope you're doing well!"

"Just great, Mr. Saunders. And you/"

"Great. Len, you can call me Len. Anyhow, I'm hoping you can get me straightened out on this Usenet thing. I got on that phone number you gave Janet, and I just got all confused."

Cassie laughed. "You and everyone else, so don't feel bad, Mr. Saunders. Anyhow, I tried it myself after I gave her the number, and I made some screenshots of it. Can I send you those and a document that explains it all a little better?"

"Oh, you're an angel, Cassie." He gave her his address.

She was still curious. "So Janet didn't tell me much about what you wanted to do on Usenet. Did you have a particular group you wanted to follow?"

"Well, I don't know if she told you I'm on America Online

or not, but I follow the forums on investing pretty closely, since I used to be in Finance at Chrysler. People talk about something called misc.invest sometimes, so I thought I'd start with that."

"OK, that's not one I follow, but I guess I'll start now! Maybe I'll see you on there."

He laughed. "It'll probably be a while before I get up the nerve to say something! First I have to figure out how the thing works."

"Oh, you'll get it! Call me if I can help you out any more."

"Thank you, Cassie dear, and I'll be watching the mail for it!"

Cassie called Janet and told her about the call. Janet was amused. She dialed up Cassie's bulletin board and tried getting on misc.invest herself, so she could help Dad directly.

11

THE OUTING

I t was summer 1992. Len's garage sale was history, anything left over went to the dump, and he sold the house. The real estate market in Detroit was even worse than he thought, and he had to cut the price several times to move the thing. He said goodbye to Jamie and Harry, thankful he wasn't going to have to go to Jamie's US History class and tell the story of his brother Jack yet again.

The movers came and he got in his LeBaron and drove it to California in five days. That big boat of a car used a lot of gas, but it was built to be *comfortable* and it really was, even in blazing heat. He had some books on tape to listen to, and it really wasn't bad at all.

He moved into Walt's cabin up in the Sierras, and he and Walt were planning to build a separate house for him, with Janet's help. When they weren't there, which would be most of the time, he'd take care of the main house.

"Fishing every day" — that was Len's retirement dream, along with "get out of Detroit." Now it was real. He was also spending a lot of time online, so his evenings didn't all revolve around sitting in front of the TV. He got a Labrador, whom he named Mickey, after the great Tigers pitcher Mickey

Lolich. Everyone assumed he *must* be named for Mickey Mouse, but at least occasionally, someone knew who Mickey Lolich was. Mickey took to riding in the boat immediately, so the two of them became inseparable. Sometimes when they were coming in, Mickey would jump off the boat and swim to shore. Everyone told him Labs liked to swim, so now he was seeing it.

Len wasn't in Silicon Valley, but he was nearby, and his daughter *was* there. Whenever he got online and talked about investing, he realized he didn't understand this computer business, and he wanted to. It was so different from the car business he'd spent his life in, where even the tiniest change in a taillight takes two years, and a 20-year veteran was still The New Guy.

He didn't have any technical training, and he was too old to start doing what Janet did. All he had was a lifetime in finance and accounting. But at the very least, he could learn how it worked so he could invest better. There had to be some major fortunes still to be made there. Maybe he could become richer than Janet! The threat of that would make her work a little harder, at least.

Janet must have been reading his mind. She got the idea to take Dad and all her friends out fishing on the ocean. She and Walt had initiated their romance on his fishing boat, so this had sentimental value for them, too. Len jumped at the chance to actually talk to some of these Valley people.

Len & Mickey, Cassie, Dan, Matt, and Bernie the Bernese Mountain Dog all met at 6:00 am at Pillar Point near Half Moon Bay one Sunday, just like that fateful trip three years ago.. Despite the early hour there were eight boats ahead of them for the launch ramp. While they waited, Matt said to Cassie,

"So I hear you're a big mucky-muck now! Congratulations. How is it?"

She made the "tiny" gesture with her fingers. "A *small*

mucky-muck. Maybe just a 'muck'. And it's only in Testing. How's GO?"

"It's going," he said, pointing down.

"Well, we'd love to have you back at 3Com!"

Finally it was their turn to launch. Janet knew the first mate's duties by now. She ran through her checklist, hopped into the boat, and then signaled to Walt, who backed the boat into the water. Janet got the engine running in reverse, Walt backed a few feet farther and then when the boat was floating, he drove away and parked. He came back, she threw him the ropes, he pulled the boat over to the dock, and they all jumped in. Walt turned the boat around and they headed out to sea. Bernie and Mickey barked at the other boaters, then they retired to the cabin to lie down.

They all stood in the bow. Cassie said to Len, "So, Mr. Saunders, how are you doing on the Internet? I haven't heard from you in a while."

"Len, Len. I'm starting to get the hang of it, finally. Thanks again for all your help, Cassie."

They talked some more about what he'd discovered on his own, and Cassie threw a whole bunch of new terms and buzz-words at him, and he felt like he should write them all down, but he didn't have a notebook.

Walt steered them out to where the pelicans were gathered, figuring that they always know where the fish are. He cut the engine, and everyone threw their lines out. Len and Matt stood next to each other at the rail. Len knew Matt had *some* kind of issue with Walt, and that was why his wife wasn't here, but that old stuff didn't interest him. He waited for Matt to speak. Finally,

"Mr. Saunders, how are you liking California so far?"

"Oh, it's a pretty big change from Detroit, but I'm adjusting. Tell me about you! I don't think we talked much at the wedding. So you used to work with Janet?"

"Yeah, but not anymore. Now I'm at this struggling startup, GO Corp."

"Struggling, huh? What does GO do?"

Matt explained how they were building a handheld computer that you operated with a pen, and Microsoft and the big guys were stepping on them. Len had spent his career with the Number Three carmaker, Chrysler, so he could sympathize with that.

"So how did GO get started? Was it one of those VC funds? Did a rich guy stake them?"

"A bunch of rich pricks!" laughed Matt. "Yeah."

This rang a bell with Len. "Oh, yeah, I've heard about them."

"'Vulture capitalist' is another term!"

"And what does Microsoft have to do with it? They don't make those little tiny computers, do they?"

Matt looked tired. "They think no one should do *anything* with software, unless they control it."

Len thought about that. "Doesn't the government have a say in that? I mean, at Chrysler we couldn't even get technical information from GM without official permission!"

Dan overheard. "Maybe the government could. If they were paying attention."

"Well, those vulture capitalists didn't get where they are by being nice guys. Anyway, will this gadget read your handwriting? That sounds impressive."

Matt was sheepish. "I guess it would be if it really worked."

"That's tough. So what is GO doing about those big companies?"

Matt gestured at Dan, who was on his other side. "Well, we're partnering with AT&T, for one thing. Dan here is trying to get me to jump ship and join him at Oracle!"

Dan called out, "No one makes money working with AT&T. Matt should know that by now!"

Len's first instinct was to be shocked at this casual disrespect for Ma Bell.

"Really? Aren't they going to own everything, eventually?"

"That's what they *want* you to believe."

"But you don't?"

Dan said, "Let me ask you this: Cassie told me you're on the Internet! What do you think about that?"

Len looked puzzled. "You mean those newsgroups? They're kinda chaotic, but you can find some useful stuff once in a while. What's that got to do with AT&T?"

"Exactly," said Dan. "They think it's just a toy for the pointy-headed guys. Janet and I both went to the IETF…"

Len raised an eyebrow quizzically.

"Sorry, the Internet Engineering Task Force. We both happened to go to their meeting last November, and AT&T was barely even there."

"So?"

"So, their attitude is, this 'Internet' is all toy stuff, and everyone's going to come around to their way of thinking, sooner or later."

"But they're not?"

Matt jumped in. "We've been hearing that forever, and it's always five years away. Meanwhile, the world is going Internet."

Len tried to absorb that.

"Well… I guess it does seem like that, doesn't it? I gotta tell ya, I only ever hear 'Internet, Internet.' If the phone companies are going to do anything, they better get going."

Dan said, "I wouldn't hold my breath."

Just then Matt's rod tip started bobbing up and down. He had a fish on, and everyone reeled in to give him space. He fought the fish for five minutes or so, Len put the net down in the water, and Matt led the fish to it.

"Nice fish!" said Walt. He weighed it, and shook his head. "Too small, though," unhooked it and eased it back into the water. Len was dumbfounded.

"I've never caught anything that large in my life, and it's too *small?*"

"Well, Dad, this is the Pacific Ocean. We have bigger fish here than back in Michigan!" Janet smiled. Len just shook his head and threw his line back in. Matt and Dan wandered over to the other side of the boat. Janet came over and put her arm around Len's waist.

"How's it going, Dad? How do you like this kind of fishing?"

He chuckled again. "It's different, that's for sure. I'm used to casting a lure out and reeling it back in!"

"Yeah, here you just wait for the fish to bite."

"Hey, before you wander off, I wanted to ask you something."

"OK."

"Matt and Dan made me think this Internet thing might be big. What do you think?"

Janet smiled. "Sometimes it seems that way. Did Dan tell you we both went to the same conference about it last year?"

"Yeah, he did. How was that?"

"You mean how did we like it, or how did we both end up going?"

"Both, I guess."

"Well, Dan went because Oracle is supporting *all* kinds of networking. I went because I wanted to see what was going on, and I needed the break. Dealing with stupid people all day long makes me tired."

Len took that in for a minute or so. He thought back to the big execs at Chrysler and how he didn't get along with them. But that wasn't what he wanted to talk about right now.

"So you were impressed?"

"With the Internet? Well, they certainly seem serious. There were a lot of groups meeting on serious topics. They're not all hippies in tie-dyes, if that's what you were thinking."

Len laughed. "I'm glad you said that. It does kinda seem

that way sometimes from the outside."

"Yeah, that's what the top execs at 3Com think about it. Like it'll all blow over."

"A passing fad!"

"Or so they think. I'm going to go see how my hubby's doing." She wandered over to Walt.

Len thought about all this. On the misc.invest newsgroup that Cassie had helped him get on, no one ever talked about *investing* in the Internet, even though they were all using it. Same with the AOL investing forums. Or if someone did mention it, it was only asking if they could get to their broker or reach CompuServe over it. They were nearly all people who had Internet access through their work or school and just took it for granted. There were "technology stocks" or "computer stocks" but no "Internet stocks." *How do you invest in this?* he wondered.

Dan overheard the conversation and came back.

"Yeah, Janet and I had a good time in Santa Fe. Did she tell you we met Mitch Kapor?"

"Who's Mitch Kapor?"

"Oh, sorry. He's the guy responsible for Lotus 1-2-3."

Len knew what that was, since he used it every day.

"So who's going to make money if Internet is the next big thing? Not those little doodads Matt is working on, I don't think."

"Hah! I think he's figured that out for himself. Microsoft wants to own *everything* and they don't care if they have to steal it from someone."

"Is that right? Maybe I should just buy Microsoft stock."

"Not a bad idea."

"But you're at Oracle, right?"

Dan nodded.

"Their stock's done pretty well lately, too."

"You've noticed, huh?"

"Oh, yeah, I'm retired, so I have lots of time to follow

these things."

Dan felt like he *should* follow the stock market more than he did, since he understood it all pretty well. They talked about the online forums Len was on, the mathematical analyses he did on the data, and what stocks and mutual funds he liked right now. Both of them watched *Wall Street Week* religiously.

They also talked for a long time about fishing in the Midwest. Dan had grown up fishing in northern Wisconsin, which was pretty similar to Len's experiences in Michigan. Then they moved on to baseball, Dan being a Cubs fan and Len a Tigers fan. They both noted that the last time the Cubs were in a World Series, they played the Tigers.

Len thought, "This is what my son would be like, if I had a son." He invited Dan to come up and visit and go fishing with him. Dan accepted at once.

Len got a bite. He knew enough to keep his rod tip up while he fought the fish, and Dan netted it for him. Janet and Walt congratulated him, Walt weighed it, and said, "Looks like a keeper! Good work, Dad!"

Dan got out his camera and aimed it. "OK, let's get the three of you together, with the fish." They put their arms around Len, who held up the fish, and Dan took the classic fishing picture.

"I'll mail this to you when I get it developed, Janet." said Dan. "Along with whatever other photos we take today!"

Walt put the fish in the bucket. It was a good day already.

This was a hot spot. They all started catching fish, and Dan's camera stayed busy, including in Len's hands when Dan himself caught one.

As they were heading back to shore, Cassie joined Len at the rail.

"So, Mr. Saunders, good day?"

"A very good day, young lady! And for you?"

'I caught one, so yeah. Hey, can I ask you something?"

"Shoot!"

"I'm thinking of adopting a child!"

Len was speechless. Almost.

"You? But you're not married!"

"Well, duh. I know several single women who've adopted kids on their own. We can do it now."

Len really didn't know what to say.

"I guess times are changing, huh?" She nodded. "Well, good luck to you, because you'll need it."

"Thanks. By the way, don't tell Janet."

"My lips are sealed. But you said you had a question. Now I'm dying to hear it."

"Would you be the godfather?"

This was way too much for a 67-year-old man. He pictured himself as Marlon Brando in a tux with a cat on his lap.

"Are you going to ask me to have someone beaten up someday if I say yes?"

Cassie doubled over laughing.

"No, no. Good idea, though. Let me think of someone."

Len laughed, too. "In that case, I'd be honored. Do you have it all lined up yet?"

"No, but I've been getting certified as a potential parent, which takes a long time. Lots of one on one meetings with a social worker, a visit to your home, etc. Then when that finishes, I can do what they call a 'fost-adopt.' You foster the child for a while with the intention that you'll adopt her if she works out."

"Wow. I had no idea about all this stuff."

They were approaching shore, so they had to cut the discussion short. Len just said, "Well, I'm eager to hear how this turns out. Let me know when you need me!"

Janet overheard the tail end of this, but she didn't want to ask Dad what it was about.

On their way home in the car, Len asked Walt,

"So I gather you and Matt have some history?"

Walt looked uncomfortable for a second, but overcame it. "You could say that. Just business. We resolved it." He clearly didn't want to elaborate.

"Well, anyway, he's in this startup that he and Dan don't think is going anywhere. What do you think, Janet?"

"About GO? Well, you don't mess with Microsoft if you want to survive."

"I guess that's what they did, huh?"

"Bill Gates thought they were inventing a replacement for Windows. Uh-oh!"

Len laughed. "Yeah, they seem to be the big bullies, right?"

"For sure." They didn't talk about Matt anymore.

Len had one more question. "So this Internet thing: is Microsoft going to end up owning that, too?"

"Well, so far they're ignoring it."

"But…?" Len prodded.

Janet took a deep break. This was going to be a long explanation.

"Usually with something new, they wait for someone else to prove the concept first. Then they swoop in and announce they're supporting it, but now it's going to be *much better!* Meaning, they have their own additions, which of course they control."

Len had never heard this before. This was the kind of thing he came to California to figure out.

"So, how does that work? Why does anyone care what additions they make?"

"They include it all in Windows, and suddenly the customers are all using it, and no one else can sell it anymore."

"That sounds pretty shady to me. Doesn't the government get on them for that?"

She looked annoyed. "You would think. So far they

haven't."

Len thought about all that. Finally, he said,

"Well, I guess it's no different than car add-ons that become standard equipment after a while, huh?"

"Except there are several car companies." she said. "Microsoft kinda has a stranglehold."

"But there's Apple!"

"Yeah, there's Apple. They're not real competition, though. More of a niche."

"An *expensive* niche!" he said. "Have you looked at the prices for a Macintosh?"

"Dad, I sign purchase orders for those all the time. So, yeah. I know what they cost."

"*My daughter!*" thought Len. "*Always thinks she's way ahead of me. I still know a few things she doesn't, though.*"

Len drove back up to the cabin that night, let Mickey out in the yard to do his business, and got on the computer again. He looked on his various forums on AOL to see if anyone had anything to say about GO Corp. There were a few postings, mostly about how Microsoft was eating their lunch, which was what Janet had told him.

12

THE PRICE OF SUCCESS

After the fishing trip and Dad's visit, Janet had a horrible Monday. Her weekly meeting with her peers on the management team started out bad and went downhill fast. Patrick, the VP of Marketing spoke confidently, like every other VP of Marketing she'd ever known.

Then came the moment she dreaded; Patrick complimented her on 3Com's excellent internal network. She smiled, expecting there would be more. There was. He said he had some questions and suggestions for her, and could she meet with him after the meeting and go over them? Of course she could.

It got worse, though. They went around the room, and Jerry, the VP of Sales, reported on their results so far this quarter. Hardware adapters were selling like hotcakes, as usual, but he knew that management wanted him to sell "systems." He was supposed to sell large packages of servers, 3Stations (those diskless workstations that no one wanted), Bridge routers, and LAN Manager software, not just the "onesie/twosie" sales that actually paid the bills.

Those were large, complicated sales that took a year or more to complete. A single mid-level manager didn't have the budgetary authority to buy that. So Jerry had to organize a whole sales team and come back over and over again to present his story, all the while his competition was doing the same thing. He might invest a year in some prospect and then lose the deal. He hated it and so did his salespeople, who only wanted easy deals.

Janet had heard this over and over again, and she got almost physically ill when a VP of Sales said they were "transitioning the salesforce." When the Xerox Star was coming out, "transitioning the salesforce" to sell the Star was the big story. Then she was young and naïve enough to believe it.

Now Jerry said that at every management meeting. Except now that everyone was tired of hearing it, he was looking for someone else to blame. Naturally, Janet's department was convenient. So she had to meet with Jerry after the meeting, too, so they could "brainstorm" on things to help his sales teams when they were at a customer site. She wondered if there was a special school where executives learned to use management jargon like "transitioning" and "brainstorm." But Janet had gotten very good at hiding her feelings in public.

Even though Kristen the HR lady had left after the great email debacle (Janet had fallen into the habit of calling her Miss Smarmy, after hearing it from Dan and Matt for years), the new HR people were just as bad. They seemed to have insinuated themselves into everything at the company. An HR representative sat in on almost every meeting, even if it had no obvious HR subject matter. Their function, as far as she could tell, was to assess who was Up and who was Down in the popularity charts this week.

She didn't even bother mentioning "the Internet" at these meetings any more, because she didn't want to get a reputation as a kook. These people all thought it was just some academic thing, and no serious business person was ever going to use it. She was going to have to find some way of getting into it other than her regular job, and if that meant leaving 3Com, so be it.

That night, Walt was already home when she got there. Bernie the Bernese Mountain Dog nearly knocked her down in his excitement.

"Hey, how was your day?" he called out from the couch.

She made a face, said "Yuck!" and went to change clothes. When she came out, she sat next to him and he put his arm around her.

"Tell me about it."

She was silent for a long time. It was so nice just snuggling with Walt. Bernie curled up on the couch next to them. Finally,

"I'm so sick of that place. It gets more and more bureaucratic every time I turn around. You don't really notice it at first."

"Hmm. So you're thinking about leaving?"

She thought for a minute. "Maybe. I don't know where I'd go, though."

Walt didn't try to suggest anything. This wasn't his area. In contracting, you'd just ask "Who else is hiring?" but this was a different world, and she didn't expect an answer from him.

"What would you do if you could do *anything*?"

"*Anything?*" she said. "I'm not even sure it would involve computers at all!"

Walt laughed. "Whoa there! You're making pretty good money doing whatever it is you do."

She laughed, too. "Yeah, just kidding. I don't know. It would be nice to make so much money we really *could* do anything."

"Is that realistic, though? I mean, you hear about people like that, but I don't know any."

She thought back to that conversation about startups at the 1981 National Computer Conference, where they introduced the Xerox Star.

"There *are* startups where you get a lot of stock. Dan was at one. But it's kinda hit-and-miss whether you get rich or not. Mostly not."

Walt had heard all this before, but not in any detail, so he was curious.

"But you still get your regular salary, right? Or do you have to take a cut?"

"Nowadays, they get venture capital funding, so they can pay everyone's regular salary."

"OK. So it sounds like a win. You still get paid, I mean… even if you don't get rich."

She remembered what Dan told her about his startup, and what she'd heard about the early days of Apple and 3Com.

"Yeah. It's different, though. You know you could go bankrupt at any time."

Walt laughed. "Hell, I have that every day! Half of my clients, you don't know if you're *ever* gonna get paid!"

"I don't know how you do it, honey," she said, squeezing his thigh

They sat for a few minutes. Janet closed her eyes and mused on how nice it was to have a husband who didn't think he knew better than she did.

Finally, Walt said, "So do you really want to work at one of those startups?"

"I don't know. It's pretty intense. You wouldn't see me very much!"

Walt considered that.

"Hmm. I don't know… how long does that go on? Until you make it?"

She snorted. "Or fail. Or worse, become one of those zombie companies."

He looked puzzled, and she continued, "Those are the ones that haven't failed *or* succeeded. On life support until they finally pull the plug."

Walt felt like he'd said all he could at this point. Janet

didn't feel like there was anything more to say, either. But she'd already made her decision, although she hadn't realized it until now:

She had had it with managing. Everyone thought she was good at it, and she probably was. She knew how to keep her feelings to herself in big meetings, to never put the big executive on the spot in front of other people, and to always use management buzzwords like "teamwork" and "align" without being too blatant about it. This must have been the part that her Dad couldn't pull off in his career. When she was a kid, he tried to hide that he was still pissed off when he got home from work, but she could tell.

Her favorite part was helping her underlings develop in their careers and get promoted. Like Cassie. Most of all, she always seemed to be calm and in control without being bossy, and that was why people looked up to her.

But that was old hat now, and she was sick to death of being constantly interrupted no matter what she was doing. Being the big boss, or even the medium boss, meant that everyone felt they had a claim on your time and you *always* had to be available to them.

Even worse, your inbox and your voicemail box was constantly full of messages from people who *wanted* something. It might not be your job to do it — in fact, it almost never was, but you were still expected to find the right person and make sure it got done. And today's management meeting really drove it home: all these incredibly stupid people whom you had to pretend to take seriously. And most of them would stab you in the back if they saw even the slightest advantage for themselves.

She thought of what Matt Feingold had said to her when he left 3Com, "You could be VP of Engineering anywhere you want nowadays." At the time that statement left her vaguely uncomfortable, and now she knew why: she didn't want that job.

What would she have to do as VP Engineering in a startup? Speak to countless hordes of investors, interviewees, customers, and press and give the same spiel over and over. Convince them to join the company, give money, write about you, or God knows what else. Sit in endless meetings, all day and every day.

In return, you got invited to do it even more, in even bigger venues, for more and more money. What was the point? Walt didn't want that rich-person life, *at all*.

He'd made that very clear the time she'd dragged him to a "mandatory fun" event as her husband. It was a "pool party" in someone's backyard, and you didn't *have* to swim but it was strongly encouraged. The other attendees were other VPs and Directors from all over the company, and it was catered by the chefs from Osteria in Palo Alto. There were attractive young people circulating with trays of Margaritas and white wine.

Naturally, everyone wanted to meet Janet's husband. While they were checking out the water temperature in the pool, Patrick, the VP of Marketing introduced himself:

"Hi, I'm Patrick Logan." Walt stood up and shook Patrick's hand.

Janet said, "Walt, Patrick is my colleague in Marketing."

Walt said, "Nice to meet you, Patrick. Are you new to the Valley?"

"No, this is my third job out of Stanford. How about you? Did you go to school around here?"

Walt knew that "school" meant "college" to someone like Patrick, and he was trying to find out what college Walt had gone to. He decided to leave him guessing.

"Yeah, I did. Long time ago, though. So are you going in the water?"

Patrick looked nonplussed. "No, I never really liked to swim. Hey, it was nice meeting you, Walt." and he drifted off.

All Walt's conversations seemed to start out like this. It was always "where did you go to college?" or "what do you do for a living?" Some of the more persistent ones bored in until they figured out that he didn't finish college. Then when they found out he was in construction, they wanted his business card. He had to admit that was sorta nice for his business, but still, he found the whole thing tedious, like he didn't belong in this crowd and didn't even like them.

"Management" was always painted as a one-way street for young programmers: you graduated to being a manager, and eventually you didn't write code anymore, and pretty soon you couldn't even if you wanted to. If you were very lucky, you became the CEO of something, which was like being the Duke of whatever in a 19th Century European country.

If you were *not* one of those Dukes, you became one of those migrant VPs or Directors, who wait until a startup goes public and then sell themselves as the "professional management the company needs now," with "a proven track record of success." There were always lots of them around.

Yuck. So could she return to being a regular engineer and write code again? That was going to take some doing.

13

THE FUTURE: WHEN, AGAIN?

A ll the rest of 1992, Len continued exploring the online world from his cabin up in the Sierras. His visit to Janet and Walt and the fishing trip with her friends had given him a lot to think about.

He kept busy doing bookkeeping and financial work for various businesses up here. They all needed it, and they were more than happy to have someone who actually knew what he was doing. He did the books for his church *gratis*.

So Cassie wanted him to be a godfather! A single girl wants to adopt a baby and not get married. He couldn't get over that. The only single mothers he'd ever heard of had either lost their husbands in the war or gotten divorced. Cassie hadn't written to him since the fishing trip, so maybe she'd dropped that crazy idea.

He kept looking on the online forums for anything at all about investing in the Internet. There was almost nothing. Some people said, "Well, Novell is the leader in PC networking, so if there are going to be a lot of PC's connected, Novell will benefit! Or Microsoft."

But he looked into that, and Novell as an investment made no sense at all. They had the world's most bitter feud with

Microsoft, and Janet had already told him that that was a *very* unwise move for any company. Furthermore, their chairman Ray Noorda was pushing 70 and retiring soon, and there was no very clear succession plan. They were also making a lot of wild acquisitions without any obvious strategy.

He hashed it out with his investing friends online and they all seemed to agree on this as a philosophy:

"If this Internet is going to be as huge as we think it is, then the small players will either get acquired by the big players or driven out of business. The big players may find some way to profit from it, but only if they're smart. And some startup companies may come along, but there's no way to bet on that."

So they set about trying to figure out two types of investments:

1. Large companies that would benefit from the Internet, rather than being rendered obsolete.

2. Small companies that would get snapped up by the big ones.

Len spent hours and hours, all through the fall and winter nights, looking at the big companies in computers and networking and trying to figure out which ones had the smarts to adapt to a new world. Or maybe there were some who were *already* doing the right thing, even if they didn't know it yet!

He picked up on Oracle, not least because Janet's friends Dan and Matt were working there. Their stock had been steadily rising. It wasn't meteoric, but still, the direction was clear. Was this anticipating the Internet, somehow, or was it just that everyone needed databases? Whatever, he bought some of their stock.

Then, in the middle of March, Cassie phoned him. It was *not* about her adopting a child, as he'd expected. She had two pieces of news: first, she'd left 3Com and joined a little company making a handheld device, called Palm Computing. Len thought back to his conversation on the boat with Matt about GO Corp.

"Uh-oh. Haven't those things already flopped?" But he was too polite to say that. It turned out that Palm already had a product out with Tandy, called the Zoomer, and it was not exactly setting the world on fire. But Cassie explained that it had a female CEO, Donna Dubinsky, and Donna had really impressed her as someone who knew how to run a business, and particularly, *this* business Their chief architect, Jeff Hawkins, had impressed her as well. Besides being brilliant, he seemed to be practical, and those two qualities didn't often go together. So she saw it as a bet on *people*, not on a business plan. Len had no reason to be *proud* of Cassie since she wasn't his daughter, but still! She should have been. She was a girl after his own heart.

Cassie was going to be their head of Quality Assurance, which sounded impressive to Len. A guy with that title at Chrysler would be a VP and have his own parking spot at the Headquarters building, and a private bathroom! But this company was a little bit smaller, in a tiny office on El Camino near Chef Chu's . She said they walked over there for lunch, so he knew they were too small to have their own cafeteria, at least.

Her second piece of news was about some new program for the Internet she'd seen, called Mosaic! Len had heard some rumblings about this on AOL, but he didn't know what to make of them. Cassie explained that it was a program for looking at the World Wide Web. He asked if he could get it on his computer, and she said, "No, it's just for Unix so far."

"So why are you telling me this?" he wondered, but didn't say. He wrote down the name and figured he'd ask Janet about it the next time he talked to her.

"Mosaic!" he thought after they hung up. *"Why would Cassie think this was important enough to tell a Nobody like me?"* He called Janet.

"Hi, honey!"

"Hi, Dad. How are you?"

"Good, thanks. Hey, have you ever heard of something called 'Mosaic'?"

"Mosaic? No. Should I have?"

"*Once more, I'm way ahead of her!*" he said to himself. "Oh, Cassie just called and told me about it. She said it was some new thing for the Internet, but I can't get it yet. I figured maybe you could."

She spelled it out and he confirmed it. "Mosaic. OK, I'll ask around. Did she tell you she left 3Com?"

They talked about Cassie's new job and exchanged miscellaneous news. The next day, Janet asked three of her people if they'd ever heard of this 'Mosaic' and one of them, Bill, sent her a copy of a newsgroup posting by a guy named Marc Andreesen at the University of Illinois. She read over the list of features:

• Friendly Motif user interface.

• Color and monochrome default X resource settings.

• Multiple independent toplevel windows.

• History list per window (both 'where you've been' and 'where you can go').

• Global history with previously visited locations visually distinct; global history is persistent across sessions.

• Hotlist/bookmark capability -- keep list of interesting documents, add/remove items, list is persistent across sessions.

and now she understood why Cassie was excited about it. "*Wow. This does look impressive.*" It reminded her of when she'd first seen the Xerox Alto and the graphical user interface: it was something the world was waiting for, even if they didn't know it yet.

"*We have to bring this up and show people!*" she thought, and asked Bill if he knew how to use a Sun machine, so he could build it. Bill's face lit up and he said he'd get right on it. She thought of offering to help, but then realized she'd probably just get in his way. "*Gotta fix that.*" she said to herself.

Shortly after lunch, Bill came to her cube looking pleased with himself.

"OK, do you want to see it?"

She got up and he remembered something:

"Oh, we need you to open up port 80 on the firewall!"

Janet did remember how to do that much, at least. She followed him back to his cube. Margo and Tony gathered around the Sun and brought up the program. Margo said,

"Do you remember the URL for the Bluegrass website?"

Tony said, "I think it's at Xerox PARC. parcvax.xerox.com maybe?"

Janet perked up at the word Xerox. Margo typed it in, and one window on the screen filled with an index of bluegrass musicians. If you selected one, it opened into a page about that musician. Then you could go back to the index again. Tony motioned her to get up and he sat down at the keyboard and opened another window. He typed in a URL that led back to Andreesen's website at the University of Illinois. It had images mixed in with the text! Janet said, "Oh my God! After Xerox I didn't know when I'd ever see this again!" Of course the Xerox Star had that feature over ten years ago, but she didn't want to bore everyone again with her Good Old Days stories.

People in nearby cubes overheard the excitement and started gathering around. There were all sorts of questions about it: does it have sound? Can you email from it? How do you code one of those pages? They spent a good hour talking about it, and everyone wanted to sit down and try it themselves.

Janet thought, "*OK, I'm the senior manager here. I bet they're wondering what I'm going to do about this!*" She decided *not* to pour cold water on it. These people were excited about something! That was worthwhile all by itself. What 3Com would actually *do* about it, she had no idea yet.

"OK, Tony, can you put this up on the server so everyone doesn't have to build it themselves?"

"Way ahead of you," he said. "It's already up there!"

Several people went back to their cubes to try it out themselves. Patrick, the same marketing Director who'd asked Dan if he was nuts when he left for Oracle, walked by and looked in, curious.

"Hey, what's this?"

Janet said, "It's called Mosaic, for viewing the World Wide Web."

"Ah, I've heard about that. What's special about it?"

She sat down and gave him a brief demo, with Tony and Margo excitedly interjecting features that she forgot to mention. Patrick smiled but didn't say much. After ten minutes or so, he looked at his watch, and then said,

"So does this let you do anything on the Internet that you couldn't do before?"

Janet hesitated. He continued,

"I mean, it's a GUI for the Internet, and that's great, we need that, but is there more?"

Tony and Margo figured Janet was the one to handle that. She said,

"Well, possibly it opens up the Internet for the non-computer user, just like the Mac and Windows did for computing in general."

Patrick said, "We're not really in the business of selling Internet to average people, though."

She didn't know what to say to that. He went on,

"Anyhow, if you think the Executive Committee should see a demo of this, why don't you put it on the calendar for next week?"

Janet said she would, although she thought she'd need to do some strategizing so she didn't ruin her credibility with more of this Internet stuff.

Everyone looked a little deflated by all that. She wanted to give them back some of that energy.

"So, do we have a website internally, at least?"

They looked at each other. Margo said,

"I can look into that."

"Great, Margo. Then maybe we can create a demo to show to the executives!"

Then she had another thought: I'll do it myself! That'll show everyone."

"Actually, Margo, I think I'll work together with you on this, if you don't mind. It'll be good for me!"

Margo looked surprised. Janet doing actual programming? *Really?* But she hid it well and said she'd send Janet the site she was thinking of using.

Now they were excited again. They spent the next fifteen minutes talking about what they'd put in the demo, and Janet gave them some ideas on how to display the projects the execs really cared about.

She left them as they were dividing up the work for the demo. She chuckled to herself,

"Well, if someone asks why we're doing this and not our actual jobs, I'll just say the Executive Committee asked for it! It's even true, more or less."

Back at her desk, Margo had already sent her the FTP address of the server at Illinois, and said it was the same place that Mosaic came from. She panicked for a second, "Uh-oh. Now what do I do?"

Of course as a senior manager, she could just "ask" one of her people to teach her, and maybe that's what she'd end up doing. Still, wouldn't *they* all be surprised if she just knew how to build a web server! That would be so cool.

"I'll call Dan! He'll know." she thought. Dan was at Oracle now, but hell, they used to work together on actual Mesa code at Xerox. He wouldn't judge her. She found his number and dialed it.

"Hello, this is Dan Markunas."

"Hi, Dan, it's Janet Saunders. Is this a good time?"

"Janet! Nice to hear from you. To what do I owe the pleasure?"

"Well, I'm hoping you can give me some technical help. I want to build a web server!"

Dan was flabbergasted and asked her if she couldn't just direct one of her people to do it for her. She politely gave him to understand that she wanted to do this one herself, and he walked her through the process of ftp'ing the zip file with the source, unzipping it, typing "./configure" and "make," and so forth. He didn't mind waiting while she did each of those steps, and once the 'make' process seemed to be taking a long time, he said it was looking good and to call him back when it was done.

They had several more calls that afternoon. Dan had seen all the little glitches in the make process and gave her the fixes. This was so fun! On the way home, she stopped at Computer Literacy to get some books. Dan told her to get the Stevens book, *UNIX Network Programming*, so she got that.

Walt noticed the books under her arm when she came home.

"Hey, gonna do some reading?"

She beamed at him.

"Yeah, I'm going to do some real work for a change!"

"Whoa! They're sure paying you well for the *other* kind of work. Are you sure you want to do this?"

This was going to be a long conversation, so she sat down,

"What part of *your* job do you like the best? Managing the people and dealing with the clients? Or actually seeing the thing come together?"

Walt didn't have to think very long on that one.

"Well, you can either earn workingman's wages, or you can earn like a boss. That's the way I look at it. The boss' work kinda sucks, but that's why it pays."

She thought about that a while. Without much enthusiasm,

"Yeah, I suppose."

Walt put his arm around her but didn't say anything.

"I can see myself turning into one of those bullet-headed old guys at TRW. The ones who are lifers."

He ruffled her hair. "Nope. Still got hair up there."

Walt thought she needed a pep talk.

"Hey, you're bringing in big bucks for us! Everyone I work with asks why I don't just retire and let you support me."

She laughed. "I don't see you as a househusband, somehow." He agreed.

Walt was such a good guy, such a better husband than Ken. He wasn't always telling her, not in so many words, that he was a better engineer than she was. He had his own world, which was completely alien to her. His subcontractors were people he'd learned to trust, usually because he'd gotten rid of the ones he couldn't. Sometimes the customers were flaming assholes, like Matt's wife Miriam, and he just had to be polite and keep his cool. At the same time, he had lots of workers who were undependable and who'd desert him in a second if someone offered them more money. She admired him so much for that.

What would Walt do if she *stopped* bringing in so much money? She could see her future as an executive where the promotions get harder and harder and the number of people with big egos who *could* fill a slot was way more than the number of slots. And having that feeling at the end of each day that she wasn't really anything but a punching bag for the other executives and a mommy for her own people.

And then Dad was always *so* proud of her, but was that just because he hadn't gone too far up the ladder in his own career? Maybe he was getting too *much* vicarious satisfaction out of hers?

She didn't even want to think about what they'd say at

3Com. "What? You want to be a grunt again? Why would you want *that?*" She'd never been an engineer there so they had no idea she could even do it.

Finally, did she even want this? Being a manager had always made her feel grown up and trusted. If she gave it up now, would she feel like a failure?

So, It would be tough, and not just the technical part, although that was bad enough. She booted her PC.

14

THE BEATING HEART OF SILICON VALLEY

Everything was a struggle after she managed to get the Mosaic source code on her PC at home. That was the easy part, but the code was for Unix only, so far at least, not Windows, so it didn't really do her any good. She didn't have a Unix system at home.

They had them at work, of course, but how was she going to find any time for actual work, given that she only got 30 or so seconds between meetings, phone calls or her staff walking in on her?

"Get out of your cube!" was the only answer.. She walked down to Tony's cube. He and Margo were talking about Mosaic and the World Wide Web, apparently. Just the topic! She felt a little reticent about exposing her ignorance, but she went ahead and told them about how she'd gotten the source code on her home machine. Mercifully, they were supportive and didn't make fun of her. They asked her some questions about what equipment she had at home. Tony assumed she must have a whole cluster of machines, all connected by Ethernet, of course, with a leased line to headquarters. Like a boss *should* have.

She had to admit it was just a regular old 486-based

Windows PC with a modem. No Unix, no Ethernet. But they took it as a challenge: Margo asked if she could bring home another machine from work and run SCO Unix on it. Janet wasn't certain what that was and didn't know how to install it, but they both said if she brought over the machine, they'd install it for her. Janet said, "Well, if there's one thing I do know how to do, it's order a PC! I'll just say it's for the lab."

A few days later, some big cardboard boxes appeared in her cube. Tony came over with some CD-ROM's and spent a couple hours fiddling. Several times he had to go ask for help, and Janet got to meet a whole bunch of other engineers she'd never talked to. At the end of the day, Tony apologized and said he had to leave, but he'd be back tomorrow. Margo just laughed and said this was par for the course with PC's. Janet wondered how they ever got any work done, when the *obstacles* to doing work were so high.

At home, she didn't feel like telling Walt about this. He would probably wonder why this was *her* problem and not something she could just assign to one of her people. After all, they worked for her, didn't they?

They finally got SCO installed the next day and she brought the machine home. Walt helped her carry the stuff in from her car and set it up in the home office.

"Oh, no, those things are multiplying!" he said. "Or do you have to bring the old one back?"

"No, this is additional. I have a project I want to do."

She told him she was getting bored with this management business and wanted to get her hands dirty on something real.

"Oh, is this like that coffee table I built? Or the house we're going to build for your dad?"

"It's exactly like that, sweetie! Thanks for the help," she kissed him.

"Anytime. I guess I can't help you with *this* project, though!"

"Not unless you have some talents I wasn't aware of."

Janet could tell Walt had misgivings about her becoming a techie, but didn't say much about it the rest of the evening. He thought about that "pool party" she dragged him to once, with all those executive-types. He had to admit that not having to be around people like that anymore would be a *big* plus. But surely she couldn't just give up being a manager!

That night she tried some things with her new SCO Unix machine. No matter what it was, there was *some* obstacle she wasn't expecting! She needed to get the Mosaic source files on it: how was she going to do that? They were all on her Windows machine, but that wasn't doing her any good. She'd been working at 3Com almost 8 years, for God's sake; couldn't she just use Ethernet and transfer them over? Both the machines had an Ethernet card in them.

She didn't have any Ethernet cable at home, though. How about just fetching the source from the Internet again? Would SCO recognize her modem? She spent the rest of the evening trying to get that to work. Fortunately Margo and Tony were expecting her to come by tomorrow morning, and she did. They said she needed a "crossover cable" to connect the two machines directly with Ethernet. Neither of them had one, but they asked around and got her one. Then she told them about the trouble she'd had with the modem, and that problem wasn't quite as easy to solve. Neither of them had ever done that particular thing before, but they looked online, and it turned out she needed to go to Fry's to buy some cables. "Welcome to Engineering!" said Tony. "Where everything is possible and nothing is easy!" Janet smiled and thanked them.

Tony asked Margo, "How far do you think she'll get?"

Margo said, "You might be surprised. Janet can be pretty persistent."

"OK, this is going to be harder than I thought!" Janet said to herself. On Saturday morning, she asked Walt if he wanted to go to Fry's with her.

"Fry's? Why, what's there?"

"Oh, it's this electronics store in Sunnyvale. They sell everything, apparently."

Walt groaned, but said, "OK, I guess I can do that, *once*."

The Fry's parking lot was almost full. The store had a whole section on the right where you could return stuff, and a bunch of security guards. There was someone playing a piano in the middle of the store, and 15 or 20 aisles full of gear that Walt had never heard of. In the back there were tables full of monitors, computers, and laptops, and sales people standing around waiting for questions. She asked one of them where to find the cables she needed, and he didn't know, but disappeared to look it up. As they were waiting, Dan Markunas walked up!

"Janet! Fancy meeting you here!"

"Hi Dan! How's Oracle?"

"Oh, it's oracling along. What are you doing here?"

She reminded him of her quest to work with Mosaic source code and now, her struggles with SCO Unix. He was sympathetic but didn't know much about that. He thought of something, though:

"Hey, aren't you coming up on your second sabbatical?"

She thought back to the first one: it was 1989! Oh my God, he was right: every four years.

"Oh, jeez, I didn't even think of that! Thanks."

"My pleasure. Hey, one more thing!" She looked expectantly.

"Porter and the gang have a regular lunch at Gordon-Biersch in Palo Alto on Fridays. You should come and catch up with the old Xeroids!"

She told him about the times years ago she'd met them all at the Dutch Goose. He said,

"Yeah, now it's at G-B. Better beer!"

Finally the sales person came back and told her which aisle to go to, and they went there.

Dan kept wandering around and saw a guy who looked

vaguely familiar. He had a sort of sleazy hairdo and sunglasses that rang a bell. *"How do I know this guy?"* he asked himself, but the guy recognized Dan first and shook hands with him. It was Stan, the guy he'd met in Santa Fe; the one who wanted to put porn on the Internet!

Stan reminded him of how they'd met, and Dan asked him how things were coming along for him. Stan said, "Oh, super, super! I've got my PC on the Internet and I'm trying as hard as I can to drum up interest for my projects!"

Dan didn't want to know what those projects were. "Great, how's that going?"

Stan was undaunted. "Well, it's a struggle, but this thing's going to be big! I know it is. These PC graphics cards do need some work, though. I'll be like a pioneer in the Old West! "

"And to think I knew you when!" Dan said, but the irony went over Stan's head. They exchanged some pleasantries, Dan wished him good luck and said he had to be somewhere.

"Porn on the Internet! Is that why we're doing all this?" he chuckled. He made a mental note to tell Matt about this on Monday.

While Janet was looking at the bags on the shelf and reading the packages, Cassie tapped her on the shoulder. Janet, Walt, and Cassie all hugged ecstatically. Janet said,

"So how's Palm coming along? We miss you!"

Cassie was surprised to see Janet here buying techie gear, and had lots of questions for her about why she needed all this. Walt said,

"So, do *all* the techies come to Fry's on Saturday morning?"

Cassie laughed. "Pretty much. Whatever you want, they have it here."

"I need a box of left-handed 7/16 inch wood screws. Do they have those?"

Cassie said, "Damn, I was just looking for those, but they were out!"

They all laughed. Janet said, "Well, I think we're out of here. Nice seeing you, Cassie!"

There was a long, long lane you had to pass through, with impulse-purchase items like batteries, Skittles, Snickers, and beef jerky, leading to about 25 cash registers. A staffer was standing there directing customers to the next free register. The cashiers had a light that they turned on when they finished with a customer.

Outside, Walt said, "Well, that was an experience. Now I can say I've been to Fry's."

"The beating heart of Silicon Valley. Now we've been there!" said Janet.

Then he thought of one more thing:

"What was that Dan said about a 'sabbatical'?"

Janet told him that after four years at 3Com, you got six weeks off with pay, in addition to your regular vacation. A lot of people stuck around just to get their sabbatical. Now she'd been there eight years, so she was due for another one.

"If I left for six weeks, my business would fall apart!"

She laughed. "We have a few people at 3Com just dying to take my place!"

"So given that I can't go anywhere, what are you going to do?"

She shrugged. When they got back home, she tried her new cables. Getting the machine to work with the modem and getting on the Internet consumed the rest of Saturday. Walt was already asleep when she finally finished, around 11:00 pm.

On Sunday, she thought she'd give Walt a break and not do any computer work today. He was always supportive of her, but she didn't want to push it.

15

THIS NEW THING

Walt's patience was wearing thin. Another Saturday afternoon and Janet was closeted in the home office with yet another of her work friends. He was watching a game on TV, but he'd rather have been hiking with Janet and Bernie, or doing chores, or really doing *anything* with her. This "getting hands dirty" thing seemed to take *way* longer in her line of work than it did in his.

A month ago he'd helped her carry the second computer in from the car, and she'd said she was itching to get her hands dirty again. He thought, "Hey, I can relate to that. I need to grab hold of a crescent wrench once in a while, too. Arguing with suppliers and subs does get old."

As long as he'd known her, she'd been a manager. It did bring in a *very* nice salary for them, usually way more than he made, unless it was a really big year for contractors. She looked good and dressed very nicely, so he felt like a major stud whenever he was out with her on his arm. All the people he worked with looked at him much more appreciatively whenever she paid him a visit. "*What's not to like about her job?*" he always wondered. "*So what if you have to deal with some obnoxious people! What else is new?*"

But he'd assumed getting her hands dirty would take a couple hours, at most. That was two months ago. Dan Markunas, who at least Walt liked, was at the house today, helping Janet do whatever it was she was doing. He'd tried sitting in there with them a couple times and asking some questions, and they were always happy to talk. But he usually gave up when they started explaining Windows and Unix and "TCP" and "drivers," whatever those were. Not like socket drivers, he was pretty sure.

He had to admit Janet seemed like a different person now. Sex was sensationally better, for one thing. He could feel himself blushing whenever he thought about it. *"Hey, we're married! What's the problem?"* he told himself. But this "getting hands dirty" thing was doing *something* for her, he had to admit that.

Around 3:00, she and Dan came out of the office for a break. They sat down on the sofa with him. He muted the sound and said,

"So how's things going in there?"

Dan answered with a sigh, "Everything is a struggle. Things that are supposed to work, don't, and you can't find any information anywhere."

She added, "So we always end up asking a question on the forums, and waiting half a day for someone to answer."

Dan looked at her and said, "If all else fails, as it usually does, I guess that's what we'll have to do."

She looked at Walt. "You see what high tech is like?"

Walt tried to relate that to his world, but he was puzzled.

"So why do you need to do this, whatever 'this' is? Is someone paying you for it?"

Dan looked at Janet for the answer. She hesitated before saying,

"Well, we don't *need* to. I mean, it's not for my work or his work."

Walt waited for the rest.

"It's fun, I guess. This World Wide Web thing is brand new. Lots of people all over the world are jumping on it."

"World-wide web? What the hell is that?" he asked.

Dan said, "So, you've heard of the Internet?" He shrugged.

"It's this network of computers that's been slowly, slowly growing over the last 20 years or so. Janet and I both went to a conference about it in Santa Fe a couple years ago."

"Oh, yeah, I remember you went off to Santa Fe" he said to Janet. "So it's that thing? I think you tried to explain it to me, but I forgot what you said."

She put a hand on his thigh. "Dan said it: it's been an academic thing forever, but now it's been approved for commercial use."

"So, if you have a computer you can use it? OK, we have a computer, or I guess two now, but most people don't have *any*."

They both realized that conjuring up a future where lots of people were on the Internet was not going to work on Walt. In his profession, massive changes like that weren't routine.

Dan thought Janet should handle this. She squeezed his thigh extra hard.

"I'm just enjoying it, hon. After all these years of sitting in meetings, it's a nice change to be really *doing* something."

He got her meaning.

"OK, well, I'm glad, then. Maybe next weekend I'll go up and see your Dad. We'll see how that guest house is coming along."

"That's a great idea. We haven't heard much from him lately."

Then, to Dan, she said, "Well, shall we give it one more try?" They trudged back into the office. Walt turned back to the TV and unmuted it.

≈

THE NEXT WEEK, Walt drove up to the cabin in the Sierras where Janet's dad Len was staying. He got there late Friday night, and they sat around drinking Scotch for an hour or so. This house was so familiar to Walt! He'd always loved coming up here with his mom and brothers when he was a teenager. He was never quite sure how Mom had ended up with it in the divorce. Dad must have tried for it, but somehow or other she got it, giving up God knows what, and she'd never talk about it afterwards. She must have been determined to keep that bit of family memory for herself and the boys. Now Walt had it, and he was letting his father-in-law retire there. It was perfect!

They went out fishing together on Saturday, and Walt noticed that Len didn't have as many fish stories as someone who fished daily would have. Maybe he didn't, really?

The new house hadn't made much progress, either. Len seemed to get a lot of phone calls and they sounded business-y. Finally, Walt's curiosity got the better of him. While they were watching TV that evening, he said,

"So, Dad: what are you occupying your time with these days? I get the feeling it's not fishing!"

Len shifted in his chair. "Well... I guess I wasn't really ready to get put out to pasture, after all. I thought I was."

"No?"

"I still have some fight left in me. I'm doing some financial work for some of the little businesses up here, which is what all those phone calls were about. And I'm starting a little private investment business, sort of a mutual fund for just a few 'sophisticated investors', as the SEC likes to put it."

Walt thought that answered *some* of his questions. Len continued,

"You can see all this paperwork on the desk here. Even though it's still private, I have to file what's called a Private Placement Memorandum with the government, and naturally you need a lawyer for that."

"Wow, I'm surprised. I thought we had you all set up here!"

Len was apologetic. "You and Janet have been great, Walt. I couldn't ask for a better son-in-law!"

"Hey, no need to apologize, Dad! We just want you to be happy."

Len smiled and they didn't talk much for a while. He got up and went to the computer and fiddled with it, then turned to Walt.

"Come here. I want to show you what I've been doing."

Walt walked over and squinted at the screen. "So what am I looking at here?"

"This is an investing forum on America Online. I spend an ungodly amount of time debating with these people about stocks. That's how this 'mutual fund' thing got started. Some rich guys kept asking me to run some money for them. Me! A poor kid from Detroit. Imagine that."

"Stocks, like investing, you mean? I've always stayed away from that stuff. Too risky for me."

"Well, it can be. When I was at Chrysler in Finance, we had a lot of restrictions on what we could invest in, plus I had to put Janet through MIT. But now, hey, I'm retired and she makes more money than I ever dreamed of! It's kind of a hobby for me. I understand it pretty well, after all. And I'm not risking a whole lot of my own money on it."

"Wow. You're braver than I am."

Len shrugged.

"So you guys just swap tips and news and stuff?"

"Oh, it's *way* more than that. There's this software you can get that downloads the data, analyzes it, graphs it, and does all sorts of comparisons for you. You can spend 100% of your time on this stuff if you want."

Walt had nothing to say about that.

"So now you know why my phone is always busy."

"We did notice that, actually. We just thought you'd made some friends up here!"

"Well, I have, but most of it is, I'm online."

"If it makes you happy, Dad, then we're happy, that's all I've got to say."

Len fiddled around some more, and switched to a window with nothing but text in it.

"And this, Walt, is The Internet you've heard so much about!"

Walt put his hands over his ears. "Gah! There's that word again! I came up here to get away from that stuff."

Len laughed. "It can't be in *your* business, can it? Not yet, anyway."

Walt told him the whole story of Janet's coding efforts. Len listened appreciatively.

"Well, I guess I'm partly responsible for all that, so I'm sorry, Walt!"

"You? How so?"

Len explained that Cassie had asked him about something called "Mosaic" which he'd never heard of, and he'd asked Janet about it. But he never thought she was going to spend all her time on it, when it wasn't even her job! My God, 3Com was paying her enough already to do her regular work, and now she was working for free as well?

Len and Walt were now seeing eye to eye on this. Who the hell works for nothing in this day and age? Especially when you have a husband at home who loves you, sitting by himself in the living room?

On Sunday they worked on the guest house after Len got back from church. He apologized as he left, saying that going to church was kind of expected up here, plus he met a lot of people who turned into bookkeeping clients.

"Oh, and I do the church's books, too!"

"I bet that's fascinating," said Walt, with a smile.

"You'd be surprised, young man. I'm tracking down some

suspicious-looking invoices for their nonprofit right now, which was what some of those calls were about."

"Uh-oh," said Walt. Len didn't go any further.

JANET WAS SPRAWLED on the couch watching TV when Walt got home. She looked exhausted. Walt was concerned.

"Hey, you look like you were out digging ditches all weekend or something."

"We had the worst bug in the world today." He waited for more..

"It was the kind where nothing happens!"

"I guess you're going to explain that to me?"

"Well, if something crashes, at least you can get some idea when or where it went wrong."

"OK…"

"But when something was supposed to happen but didn't, you have nothing to go on."

"So you had a big nothing?"

"Exactly. We spent the entire day figuring out why it *didn't* happen!"

"But you found it?"

"Finally. Yes."

He kissed her. "I'm glad, even though I have no idea what you're talking about."

She pulled him down on top of her. "Oh, Walt! I missed you so much."

"Not as much as I've been missing you this last month."

"I know, I know. I'm sorry, hon. I just get so wrapped up in all this stuff. I'll make it up to you, I swear."

They just leaned against each other the rest of the evening. She didn't think this was the right time to tell him she was going to a conference about the Web in Cambridge in July.

16

WHERE'S THE MONEY, HONEY?

After Walt left on Sunday night, Len felt terrible that he'd turned him into a Computer Widower. He was the one who asked Janet about this "Mosaic" thing, and now she was spending all her time on it. Poor Walt had to come up to the mountains to have someone to talk to.

He was also wondering how Cassie was faring in her efforts to become a single mother. It still seemed nuts to him, but she did ask him to be the godfather, so he had a legitimate reason to call her. And she was the one who told him about Mosaic, too. So he called.

"Hi, Mr. Saunders! How nice to hear from you." Len gave up on getting her to call him by his first name. She was from the generation that respected its elders; you had to give her that.

"Hello, young lady, I was just wondering when I'm going to be a godfather! I have to line up some murders and so forth, so I need some lead time."

She laughed out loud. "Oh, no need to go to any extra trouble for me, Mr. Saunders. Unless, you know, you wanted to kill them anyway."

He waited.

"Yeah, I did go to some meetings at the adoption agency, but I'm at a new job now, and it's just crazy. I have no time. We're launching our product in June and the hardware partners are insane about bugs. People are practically sleeping at the office."

"Wow. The overtime bills must be off the scale for that."

"Overtime?" She laughed ironically. Len was from a different world, where you couldn't make people stay after quitting time without paying them time-and-a-half.

"You know, 'overtime.' Where you actually pay people extra for keeping them late."

"This is Silicon Valley, Mr. Saunders. Maybe Janet told you?"

"OK, OK, I think I heard about that. Anyhow, I wanted to thank you for asking me about this 'Mosaic' thing. Now Janet's spending all her time on it, and her poor husband just spent the weekend with me to get away!"

Cassie had to think back to when she'd mentioned that to him.

"Oh, yeah, Mosaic. Why, what's Janet doing? I haven't talked to her in a while."

Len told her about Janet getting back into coding, and how he was feeling bad that he was the cause of it.

"Janet's writing code? That's fantastic! I have to call her. I guess you don't know what she's doing?"

He didn't, of course. They exchanged pleasantries and hung up.

Cassie was home only because it was Sunday night. Everyone at Palm was exhausted and catching a few Z's before another week of grinding. The Consumer Electronics Show in Chicago was coming up and the old truism "trade shows are the cause of all technological progress" was manifesting itself yet again. You can tell your boss the software's late and they grumble but accept it. But a trade show happens whether or not you're ready. You have to be ready.

They were showing their handheld organizer, the Zoomer, with hardware partners Tandy and Casio. Casio sold tons of small electronic devices and this was just one more doohickey for them, whereas it was Palm's entire life. Casio expected bug-free software, and for a simple thing like a calculator, that was doable. They weren't used to large software systems where there are *always* bugs, and if you tried to fix them all, you'd never ship anything.

The software was "burned" into read-only memory (ROM) on their little devices, so replacing the ROM after the device was in the field was *really* expensive. Thus, every single bug was a Red Alert for Casio, which meant it was a Red Alert for Cassie, too. Sigh. At work the next day, she called Janet for a lark and offered her a job coding at Palm. Janet laughed ruefully.

"So I'd be working for *you*? No, thanks! I heard your management training was pretty subpar."

Cassie said she'd talked to Janet's father and heard Janet was spending all her time working on Mosaic. Janet didn't know about the godfather thing. It was a good laugh for both of them. Cassie remembered that Janet had worked for Apple, and asked her if she knew any of the Newton people, "Newton" being their handheld device that did handwriting recognition. Janet wasn't sure anymore who worked at Apple.

Cassie's phone rang as soon as she hung up, with yet another frantic call from Casio. Back at it again. The Palm team was working maniacally despite knowing that Apple would be at the show too, with Newton. Apple's marketing machine had been hyping this thing forever, and of course *their* demo would have a hundred times more glitz than Palm's. On the minus side, the press had been hearing their hype for a long time, so it was "put up or shut up" time now. The tech industry had been talking about handheld computers for years now as the Next Big Thing, but no one had a decent one yet.

The reporters weren't going to roll over and reprint their press releases anymore.

On top of that, there was the ever-present threat from General Magic, the highly-overhyped company with Sony, Motorola, Matsushita, Philips and AT&T as its partners. It had Andy Herzfeld and Bill Atkinson, heroes of the Macintosh, and for a while they *thought* they had Apple's backing, too. After all, they'd *come* from Apple! Didn't that count for something?

"*Not where CEOs' egos are concerned*", they realized, when John Sculley stabbed them in the back by announcing Apple's own device, the Newton.

The Zoomer was pretty slow. They were all discouraged by that, but they realized that no one else had anything faster. One of the team even took to sleeping in the motel across El Camino, rather than driving home to San Francisco late at night only to drive right back in the morning. It was an insane time for all of them.

One night, Cassie went to Draeger's, the extremely upscale supermarket in Los Altos, after work. On these crazy days it gave her at least *some* comfort to have a nice breakfast with good coffee before heading back to work. While she was looking over the fresh cherries, Dan Markunas spotted her.

"Cassie? Is that you?"

She turned around and was overjoyed. He hadn't changed a bit! They hugged.

"Dan! So good to see you? What are you doing up here? Don't you live down near Cupertino?"

"Oh, some days I come home from Oracle along Woodside Road and then 280. How about you? How's Palm?"

Her haggard look answered for her. "Busy. We have CES coming up in a week. I shouldn't even be here."

"I guess that's a big deal, huh? I'm not even following that. Where is it this year?"

"Chicago. McCormick Place. Aren't you from there?"

"I'll say. Janet and I were there with Xerox to introduce the Star, way back when!"

"How the time does fly. Hey, I just talked to her, and she's thinking of going back into programming!"

"Yeah, I've been helping her, but I didn't know how serious she was! Janet's giving up being a mucky-muck?"

"Hard to believe, isn't it?"

Dan remembered back to when the two of them worked on a feature for the Star together.

"Well, she used to be good at it, as I recall. Good for her!"

"How about you? How's Oracle?"

"Oh, it's pretty good. You knew Matt was there now, didn't you?"

"Matt Feingold? Oh wait, I guess I did know that. He gave up on this handheld thing at the right time, I'm starting to think."

Dan remembered how GO was going, no pun intended. Was Palm yet another victim of the handheld hype?

"Well, someone's going to get it right someday. Might as well be you guys. I'm pulling for you."

She looked at her watch. "Well, thanks, Dan, and say Hi to Matt for me. I gotta run."

Dan and Matt were at Oracle, a nice, sane, big company whose stock was rising steadily. Janet was at a boring company that was going nowhere, but at least she got home at a reasonable hour. Here Cassie was, working seven days a week in a teensy little company that might go out of business any time now.

But at least here, the people in charge, Dubinsky and Hawkins, had their heads on straight and she believed in them. Everyone was pulling in the same direction, and they needed her contribution and everyone else's. Unlike other places where Marketing was the enemy, in a startup you just looked at them as, *"they're working for me!"* Every time some visitor in a suit came to visit, it was comforting to think they were really working for *you*. If they got what they were after, your stock might be worth something.

Whether it would ever lead to any serious money — who the hell knew? But it was an experience you could tell your grandchildren about. Then she remembered, *"Wait, I have to have a kid first to have grandkids! Or else get married."*

That adoption plan was on hold for now. How could she possibly deal with caring for a child when she had a life like this?

The next day at Oracle, Dan told Matt about seeing Cassie.

"Oh, yeah, I think I did hear that. Palm, huh? Yet another attempt to do the impossible."

Dan sighed. "I didn't get much chance to talk to her. Apparently they're presenting at the Consumer Electronics Show, so everything's insane right now."

"Oh, God. Did she talk about the Newton?" Everyone had read the hype about Apple's new handheld. Dan shook his head.

"Well, good luck to them. And here we are, worrying about DNS config files."

Dan's and Matt's project involved using an Oracle database to configure computers for the Internet. That was traditionally a matter of editing text files, which was prone to error, so having a database and input forms was a Good Thing. Dan suddenly remembered a bug he had to fix, excused himself, and went back to his office.

That night, Matt made the mistake of telling Miriam about Cassie and Palm and the Consumer Electronics Show. Afterwards, he wondered why he did that, since she didn't even *know* Cassie. Conversation had gotten strained between them since he left GO, so maybe he was just reaching for something to talk about. Or *maybe* he subconsciously wanted to provoke her.

"Palm? What's that?"

"Oh, it's yet another handheld thingie that recognizes your handwriting. I don't know much about it."

Miriam's face darkened. "So are *they* going to succeed? What are they doing that GO didn't do?"

"I told you, I don't know too much about it. I didn't even realize I knew anyone there until today."

Miriam was a clinical psychologist, so she was trained in not revealing her feelings when hearing something upsetting. It was hard to do in your personal life, though. Matt could tell there was still something on her mind.

"So why aren't *you* there?" she finally asked.

"It's a small company, Miriam. No one asked me."

"Yeah, but… that was what you said about GO, too."

GO was a mistake that he was glad he was out of. The last thing he wanted was yet another startup with big competitors.

"I should have stuck with that answer. GO sucked. I'm glad I'm out of there."

"Oh, great. So when they go public, we're not getting anything!"

"They're not going public, Miriam. They'll get run into the ground by Microsoft. Or get smothered by AT&T. Or just run out of cash."

He added, "Anyway, I *am* partially vested, at least."

Now she was really irritated.

"How *the fuck* would you know what's going to happen with them? Were you in all those big meetings?"

Matt got up and went to the refrigerator, got a soda, and sat back down.

"Miriam, this isn't General Motors where you're off at a car plant in Topeka and don't know what's going on. We were right in the middle of it there. We *knew* those guys."

She sat down next to him and lowered her voice an octave.

"So, honey, how are we ever going to get out of this rat race, if you stick with these shitty big companies?"

"Shitty? We're up almost $50,000 already on my Oracle

stock. That's more than I made on stock in five years at 3Com."

"Fifty thousand isn't a downpayment on a downpayment in Portola Valley, Matt."

There it was again. They'd had this conversation before.

"Fuck Portola Valley, Miriam. Seriously, fuck Portola Valley. What's wrong with here?"

"Here?" she said, her voice back up in pitch. "Around all these shitty houses from the 1950's? Where we have to get in the car to go anywhere? Don't you want any more out of life than this?"

"I don't know, do I? Look, it beats the hell out of Minneapolis. Or Queens."

"Yeah, well, at least we were in the *high end* of Queens."

The boy from the wrong side of the tracks. She'd never let him forget it. "Before you married me, you mean."

"Come on, you know that's not what I meant."

He was not mollified. She thought for a while. Then:

"How can you stand to work for Larry Ellison? That guy's such a creep."

Matt laughed. "Yeah, so, what's your point?"

He had her there. She changed the subject.

"That time I visited you there, and people were pressing the Close Door button on the elevator instead of holding it for us. Yuck."

"It's capitalism inside and out, Miriam. No fake politeness. It's kind of refreshing, actually, after all that passive aggression at 3Com."

While she was figuring out what to say next, he added,

"Or at your clinic." Matt had visited her once at her psychological clinic, and thought they were just a bunch of neurotic phonies. He was on a roll now and didn't let her interrupt.

"Or that fundraiser that your boss Abigail and her hoity-toity husband hosted that time. My god, those people made me puke. It figures 3Com's marketing VP Patrick was there. Brown-nosing his way to the top!"

"Oh, so I'm passive-aggressive now? And Patrick Logan was a real gentleman!"

"Come on, I didn't say that."

She was about to say, *"As if you even know what that means!"* but thought better of it. Instead, just "I'm going to bed now." He thought sleeping on the couch might be a good idea tonight. Bernie was confused but stayed on the floor in the living room with him.

17

BIG DECISION

J anet broke the news to Walt: she was taking her second sabbatical from 3Com, and she was going to spend it coding. Even worse, she was going to a conference in Cambridge, Massachusetts in July about this "web" stuff, *at her own expense.*

Walt was surprised, and not at all in a good way:

"You have six weeks off with pay, and *this* is what you're doing with it?"

She detected something underneath his usual reserve there. Maybe this required a little more diplomacy. She sat down and patted the couch beside her. He sat down.

"Honey, I know I've been leaving you alone a lot lately, and I *am* sorry. I miss spending time with you, too."

"But…?" he prompted.

"But…" she started. "But as long as you've known me, I've been a manager, right?" He nodded.

"I always thought that was what I wanted to do with my life, and I was getting pretty good at it. It's what Dad did, too."

"I guess you must be good. They seem to keep promoting you, anyway."

"Yeah. I don't do anything but act like a robot grownup, and they love it."

Walt laughed. "Robot grownup. That's good!"

Janet laughed, and moved her arms up and down stiffly like a robot and intoned. "Prioritize! Strategize! Incentivize!"

"Now I understand what you do all day!" he chuckled.

"So can you understand how it gets old?"

"Well, it's a job, right? That's why they call it 'work' . I mean, shit, I hate my job half the time, too."

"*How do you answer that without being self-indulgent?*" she asked herself.

"What if you could make good money and *not* hate your job?"

Walt laughed. "Well, then you'd really have something, wouldn't you? I haven't figured that one out yet!"

She still didn't know what to say. Finally, he spoke again:

"So you think giving up everything you've worked for is going to make things better?"

"I don't know, honey. I really don't."

She didn't want to make some sappy speech that would just sound stupid later. Finally, Walt said,

"Well, what if you just go away somewhere by yourself for a week or two and think things over? I could shut down for a while and join you later if you want."

She leaned on his shoulder. "Hmm, that does sound nice," thinking, "*Sometimes winning the argument isn't the most important thing.*"

That weekend, she didn't do any coding. They went on a hike at Windy Hill with Bernie. In his younger days, he showed more interest in other dogs, but now that he was older, he was pretty indifferent to them. At least half the *people* they met wanted to pet him, though, which Bernie loved. The weather was beautiful, but what else was new? The hills were still green from the rain.

When they were eating their lunch, she asked him, "What

did you want to be when you were a kid? I think you told me once."

He thought about it and said, "An astronaut! Or sometimes a fireman. How about you?"

"Well, I didn't see myself as a mom, that's for sure."

"No?"

"Nah. I looked up to my dad. I didn't look up to Mom."

Walt thought back to when he met her. He had to admit, she did seem a little stiff.

"It's hard for me to judge. I only met her that one time. She *was* a little cold, I'd have to say."

Janet laughed. "You think? The stories I could tell."

Walt thought there was probably more, so he just waited.

"There was one Christmas... well, I could *always* tell which one of them bought which present for me. I got a chemistry set, and a brand new dress. Not hard to figure those out."

"That was nice of Betty to get you that chemistry set! How did she know that was what you wanted?" Walt ducked as she pretended to hit him.

"Then one time, there was a summer weekend class on astronomy, I wanted to go, and she told me that it was just for boys. Dad took me anyway."

"And were you the only girl?"

"Well, yeah, but I was used to that!" He laughed.

"Do you think your dad really wanted a boy?"

"Maybe. But he never made me feel that way."

Walt had just spent the weekend with Len a few weeks ago. "Speaking of Len: did you know he's starting a little business up there, instead of fishing?"

"I guess I sorta knew that. How's he doing, do you think?"

"I don't know, I think he's itching to get back in the saddle again, but I don't know as what. He seems to be involved with ferreting out some shady bookkeeping, from what I can tell. Some big time crime up there! I had no idea."

This made Janet pause.

"Shady dealings: he always used to tell these stories about the bad guys he caught, before he worked at Chrysler."

"I never heard those. What was he, a cop or something?"

"No, no. He was an auditor, but I guess he liked it when there were embezzlers to catch!"

Walt smiled again. "A second career for Dad. Good for him. Maybe he should move down here!"

Janet looked alarmed at that idea. "It's so expensive here. What would he do for money?"

"You wouldn't want him to live with us, I guess?"

"God, no. He'd go nuts. He's used to living by himself, since I went to college." She was imagining him hanging around the house and giving her career advice.

Walt was pensive. "Yeah, I guess I can see that. He *is* kinda independent."

She agreed. The thought of Dad wanting to go back to work again was a new worry for her. She'd only ever known him as an auto company guy in an auto town.

Her second sabbatical came around and she did stay home coding. Walt didn't say anything about it. She went off to the Web conference in Cambridge in July, and found it incredibly exciting. She got to meet Tim Berners-Lee, which gave her some serious bragging rights for a *long* time. She met other people who were doing the same thing she was, namely, a Web browser for Windows, and they spent endless hours comparing approaches. When there was nothing interesting going on at the conference, she went down to the MIT campus and revisited places she'd lived or had classes.

How did she imagine her career 20 years ago? She walked by the building where she and Ken had their first "date," a Computer Science talk that made them feel self-consciously nerdy even at the time. But CS was *exciting* back then.

All she could think of as a goal then was being the head of a big data center, "having your own shop" as they called it.

This didn't really appeal to her even at the time, but there didn't seem to be anything else to aim for. Amazingly enough, now she had it, more or less. What was so great about it? You never got to do anything really interesting, and you dealt with stupid people all day long.

Computers were still the preserve of big business or aerospace back then. There *were* a lot of computer companies in the Boston area, the "Route 128" companies: like Digital Equipment and Data General, but going to California seemed more appealing. She and Ken both got jobs in the defense industry in the LA area; Janet at TRW and Ken at Hughes Aircraft. She threw herself into learning about satellite communications, and Ken became a PDP-10 systems programmer.

The LA area was dominated by defense companies, not entertainment — at least when you got out of the Beverly Hills - West LA - Santa Monica area. Ken and Janet didn't know anyone who worked in movies, TV, or music; everyone was at TRW, Northrup, Hughes, Rockwell, or General Dynamics. Ken saw nothing at all wrong with that, and fully intended to make his life in aerospace. When she went to work on the Xerox Star instead and didn't want to have kids with him… that's where it all went south.

Ken was remarried now with two kids, climbing the Hughes management ladder, and she was up here in Silicon Valley. She hadn't spoken to him in years. Her new husband, Walt, had no connection with high tech at all, and maybe that was what she liked about him. He loved her and supported her, and unlike Ken, he never pretended to have an authoritative opinion about her work.

She knew people her age who'd gotten into some startup that had IPO'ed, and now they were millionaires, probably. Most of them didn't flaunt it, at least around her, but she always felt like she'd missed out somewhere. When you join a startup, you work insanely hard and suffer the naked rivalries and unbearable claustrophobia of being around the same people all day every day. Dan Markunas had told her about the one he was in and it sounded horrible, and it was the same for Matt Feingold with GO. Was it even worth it? She could be a VP of Engineering of one of those if she wanted to be, but a job like that was even worse than hers.

Janet hated having to sell, whether it was selling a job to a candidate or a new service to the executive team. In a startup, that would be practically all she did: recruit a team, convince dubious engineers that your idea was going to work; talk to venture capitalists and get them to fund you; meet reporters and nudge them to write good stuff about you and not your competitors. All the time, it was giving the same spiel over and over.

She'd always been a middle manager and mercifully free of most of that. But startups don't have middle managers! There's one person in charge of all the engineers: the VP.

When engineers talked about being in a startup, they always made it seem so romantic: "No bureaucracy! Everyone is pulling in the same direction! No legacy code to deal with — you can start with a clean slate and do it *right*!" They were all so naive about it.

Walt and she had talked about that once. He thought it didn't sound like a bad deal, really — you still got your normal salary, and maybe you'd get rich! But he wasn't enthused about never seeing her because she was always working, and now he was getting a little sense of what that would be like.

Still, the enthusiasm that people seemed to have for the Internet! The "mature" execs at 3Com made fun of it: "Hey, they're just a bunch of kids." But now here she was in the middle of it, and it wasn't just networking geeks anymore. The Internet had always been restricted to government and research, but now it was officially OK to use it for commercial purposes. Dad seemed to think he knew better than all the

3Com execs that this thing was going to be *huge*! He spent his time trying to figure out how to invest in it.

Dad didn't have access to the Silicon Valley way to "invest": go to work in it. You got stock at $0.25 a share or something like that, and if it went public at $15, bang! You were rich. Your "risk" wasn't really the money you sunk into it; it was the two or three or four years you spent working there when you could have been somewhere better. And, of course, the much higher level of effort demanded of you. Most people like Dad or Walt didn't have the opportunity to do something like that.

Dad was so easy to thrill: she just had to tell him how many people she had under her. She just *knew* he bragged about his big executive daughter in Silicon Valley every chance he got. If she actually became a CEO sometime, he might die of happiness. To him, getting rich meant becoming a VP and making serious money on salary and stock options. A low-level or even middle-level person had no chance at that. But you still might get status: a nice office with your name on the door, a reserved parking spot, a chance to eat in the executive cafeteria. That was Dad's world at Chrysler.

She realized that being a programmer again had a lot going for it: she'd have a much easier time getting hired in one of those startups than she would as a manager. And most of all, as the conference made clear: it was *way* more fun. Dad and Walt wouldn't understand it at all, though.

Shortly after the plane reached cruising altitude, she'd made up her mind: she was going to tell 3Com management she wanted to be an engineer. If she was going to get hired at a startup as a programmer, it wouldn't be good enough to say, "I've been doing it in my spare time." That didn't count. She had to be doing it *for a living*.

She couldn't even say she wanted to be an engineer *again*, because she'd never been one there. What would they say and where would they put her? She had to figure that out. It had to be something that would sell her to the next company. Even if 3Com knew perfectly well what she was doing and why, she had enough credibility from eight years there that they had to let her.

She especially looked forward to talking to all these "women in tech" activist groups that always came and asked her what it was like to "crash through the glass ceiling." She'd say, "it sucks up there. I went back down."

OK, everything was settled, then! Janet slept very well on the rest of the flight home.

18

WHEN IT'S OVER

Dan's phone rang one day in September, 1993. It was Janet! She shared her big news: she wasn't managing anymore.

"Oh, my God. I thought you were going all the way to the corner office! Congratulations."

"Thanks. It was not easy, I gotta tell you. My dad had his heart set on his daughter becoming a CEO someday. He still hasn't gotten over it."

They chatted about what led up to this, and what she was doing now. It turned out that she was now a senior engineer on something related to Dan's old project: the network management station. It sort of fit, since "managing networks" *had* been her job, more or less, except that was people management and administration, not writing code. She was busy reading documents and learning all about network management on the Internet, which turned out to be exactly what Dan was doing, too! They were reunited again. He had an idea:

"Hey, you should come to Porter's Thursday lunch at Gordon-Biersch sometime! A lot of the old Xerox folks go. It's not at the Goose anymore." He told her some of the regular attendees that she might remember, and to bring lots of cash. Porter's algorithm for paying was, "Everyone throw $20's on it, until the bill is covered!"

Janet thought that sounded like fun. She hadn't seen most of those people since Xerox days, or maybe when she used to go to the Dutch Goose after she moved up here. It would be good to get back in circulation again. The Old Boy Network really was a reliable source of jobs, even if you weren't a boy.

At G-B on Thursday, she had a great time reconnecting with the old Xeroids she knew. They'd moved over there from the Goose because the beer was brewed onsite, but she wasn't much of a beer drinker anymore, especially in the middle of the day. The garlic fries were to die for, though.

A bunch of them worked at one of the three DEC research labs in Palo Alto, which had scooped up Xerox refugees all through the 80's. Porter himself had come from one of them, where he had pioneered the X-Windows system.

They all remembered Bob Metcalfe and asked if he was still at 3Com. Everyone had been on the Internet for years and years, so it was nothing new to them.

Porter asked Janet if she was interested in "visiting" Oracle. She knew that could easily turn into "interviewing," and it was somewhat appealing. She knew a bunch of people there, but Redwood Shores was a *long* way from Campbell where she lived. And it was yet another big company. After TRW, Xerox, Apple, and 3Com, maybe it was time to try a startup, just so she didn't become *too* much of a bureaucrat. She thanked him but was non-committal about coming up there.

JANET'S DAD, Len, was indeed brooding about her career switch. He'd always loved telling older people he met about his high-ranking executive daughter in Silicon Valley, especially when they bragged about their grandchildren. Now what was she? A programmer. Not quite as brag-worthy.

She did seem happier, though, he had to admit that. When he had a technical question about UseNet or AOL or the Internet, she actually knew the answer without having to ask Cassie. And she didn't have that guarded manner she used to adopt with him sometimes. That was nice. So OK, maybe she wasn't going to be a CEO someday after all.

Watching her now, she reminded him of the little girl he'd take to the library, and she'd ask him questions about the astronomy and physics books she brought home. Most of what he knew on those subjects, he'd learned by getting an Encyclopedia Britannica volume off their shelf and reading it with her.

Anyhow, back to investing. It seemed like everyone on his investing forums was chasing the big winners of the 80's: Home Depot, Circuit City, Coca-Cola, Merck. A lot of his friends were scarred by the boom-and-bust history of technology stocks and refused to have anything to do with them anymore. Companies in the early 80's used to have their IPO, have a big run, and then die. Who needed that?

Len had a daughter in high tech, though, and now he lived only a few hours away from the beating heart of it, so he had a different take. He thought that all those retail stocks everyone loved were yesterday's news. *"You can't go back in time and buy those!"* he used to say, until people got tired of hearing it.

He had a Dell computer himself, and Dell had had a great run in '90, '91, and '92, but this year it crashed. To all the tech skeptics, which included most of his online friends, this was just *deja vu* all over again. But the stock seemed to be coming back now. On their next weekly call, he asked Janet what she thought about it.

"Dell? Well, we're still ordering PC's from them. I heard

they hired a guy I knew at Xerox as a VP, and he's a really sharp guy. So it might be worth a flier."

"How about Sun Microsystems? Are they going to get wiped out by Microsoft?"

She thought about the Mosaic effort at 3Com, and her own work at home on SCO Unix.

"Well… they still have a pretty good toehold. Almost all the Internet work is getting done on Unix. Microsoft hasn't figured out why that's a problem yet."

"Thanks, I think I *will* buy some of that for the fund. Oh, wait, can I ask you one more?"

"Shoot."

"American Online, or AOL."

Janet laughed out loud. "The company that's buying up a quarter of all the CD's manufactured in the world? That one?"

Len said, "Don't laugh. Advertising works. Sometimes!"

"OK. We have enough drink coasters now to last us until 2020 or so."

"Yeah, well, I'm buying some of that, too, Miss Smartypants!"

"I'm sure you know what you're doing, Dad!"

"Anyhow, how's the programming going? Are you ready to go back to managing yet?"

She laughed. "Not yet, Dad. Maybe not ever."

He didn't really expect to win her over.

"Well, as long as you're happy."

"Thanks, Dad. I am."

They chatted about real estate prices in the Valley, which always amazed him. Janet was going to be a millionaire just from her house, without all the hassle of being a big-shot manager! This daughter of his really did have it together. Then he remembered something.

"Say, how's your friend Cassie doing? I haven't heard from her in a while."

Janet had finally found out the truth from Cassie: that she wanted to adopt a child, and Dad was going to be the godfather. He didn't know that she knew, though. She wanted to see if he'd tell her.

"Oh, last I heard, she was working 24-7 at Palm. Any particular reason you're asking?"

He figured out that she must know.

"Maybe she told you I was going to be the godfather of her child?"

"Oh, yeah, I think she did mention that. Any progress on that?"

"I haven't heard anything. I think her plans are on hold for now."

"Yeah, it would be pretty hard to have a new kid when you're in a startup."

"You Silicon Valley types! There's more to life than work, you know."

"I've heard rumors like that. But I do have a husband, you know."

Len said, "And a wonderful one, too. You're both welcome up here anytime!"

"Thanks, Dad. You're welcome down here anytime, too."

They chatted a little further and then hung up. Len thought maybe he should pay a visit down there. Maybe he'd get to see all her friends again, too.

MIRIAM DRAGGED Matt to another of Abigail's charity fundraisers, this time for TheatreWorks, the local "professional" theater company in Palo Alto, and he hated everything about it. They had a major fight about that. She started in the car on the way home.

"Wasn't that *wonderful?* I just love that we have real professional theater down here and you don't have to go to The City for it anymore."

"So what's their annual budget now? Why do they need even more money?"

She was tired of just ignoring him when he got this way.

"I have no idea, Matt. It costs money to hire professionals."

"Evidently. I guess it takes more than just developing your own talent."

She got more irritated.

"So what — we're supposed to have a bunch of community college graduates put on shows, because they're 'local'? I'd rather see something like we used to go to in New York."

"In New York there was this *excitement* about going to a show. Here it's… what? One more reason for rich old Menlo Park people to go out for the evening."

"We have to start somewhere, Matt. TheatreWorks is trying to start something down here."

"If they were actually 'starting something' we'd have lots of other high-toned theater companies springing up, wouldn't we? But we don't, because they're sucking up all the money."

"What is it with you, anyway? You're getting so… I don't know, *cranky* about everything lately."

Matt knew he should just ignore this, he realized, but he just couldn't help himself.

"I'm getting cranky? You're getting to be Little Miss Social Climber."

"I'm not going there with you, Matt. We're not doing this."

"Fine." They didn't speak any more that night.

Miriam was constantly on the phone asking people for donations to TheatreWorks, West Bay Opera, the local high schools, or some other Palo Alto-related cause. Fortunately, she didn't consider their house a suitable place for a fundraising event, so he was spared that much at least. But she seemed to be spending most of her time outside the house now. That asshole Patrick, the former VP of Marketing at 3Com, was always calling about some charity event or other, and he was *elaborately* polite to Matt whenever Matt picked up the phone.

Whenever there were marches about the Rodney King trial and the riots in LA, Miriam was always there. He just *knew* he was going to set her off when he brought that up, so he wasn't too surprised at how it turned out.

"So Miriam, you know there are a lot of black people in East Palo Alto. I haven't seen you being all that involved with helping *them*!"

She got a frozen smile on her face.

"Or you, either, Mr. Workingman's Hero. At least I'm doing *something*."

"Yeah, like trying to keep them from using '*our*' parks here!"

Matt was referring to a series of City Council meetings where the residents complained about poor people from East Palo Alto coming over and picnicking in Palo Alto parks because they didn't have any nice places in their own neighborhood.

"You know perfectly well what that was about," she said, stiffly.

Matt just sniffed. Miriam went into the bedroom for a half hour or so and talked on the phone to someone in a hushed voice. He knew this was probably not a good thing. She came back out.

"I think maybe we need to talk about a divorce, Matt. We got married in college and we're totally different people now."

They agreed that Matt would move out until the divorce was finalized. He finally got an apartment in Foster City, ironically a place he'd driven by every day when he worked at GO.

19

THE BEST THANKSGIVING EVER

L en thought it would be a great idea to come down to Janet and Walt's house for Thanksgiving, 1993. They didn't have any other family to invite, but maybe she could get her friends together, and make *them* bring food. As far as he knew, most of them didn't have family in the area either.

Janet thought that would be fun. They'd been having Thanksgiving dinner with Walt's family, whom she liked, but they could always do Christmas dinner instead this year. She called Walt's plumber friend Pete, and he and Barbara agreed immediately.

Cassie's mom was down in Simi Valley, only a six hour drive, but she was tired of I-5 and she'd be down there at Christmas anyway, so she was in. Dan and Matt were in, too. Janet wasn't too surprised when Matt said that Miriam wouldn't be coming.

Dan was assigned the salad, Cassie the biscuits, and Matt the wine, so they all had pretty easy cooking tasks. Barbara of course volunteered to bring her chocolate and strawberry cake, since that was such a hit the last time they'd had dinner.

Len brought some fish he'd caught and kept in the freezer.

This was not exactly a traditional Thanksgiving dish, but hey, they were in California, he explained. Janet said they'd have that on Friday instead of turkey leftovers, which made them all happy.

Janet called Walt's mom Lenore to ask her how to cook a turkey, since she'd never done it before. Lenore told her a 10-12 pound bird should be more than enough for eight people with plenty to spare if they got some last-minute drop-ins, so she bought one and put it in the fridge to defrost on Saturday. She wasn't sure if even Dad cared for all the traditional side dishes Mom used to make, so she skipped the green bean casserole and the sweet potatoes.

Thanksgiving arrived. Janet put the turkey in the oven around 10:30 am. Len was assigned the mashed potatoes, so he had plenty of time and sat in front of the TV watching football. Walt had the challenging task of opening the cans of cranberry sauce, and he fired up his chainsaw just to make Janet nervous.

Dan arrived first with his salad. Janet said,

"Oh, wow, what's that?"

"This is walnut, pear, and Gorgonzola salad from *The Savory Way*, which is a cookbook by Deborah Madison. She was a founder of *Greens* up in the City!"

"Oh, yeah, Walt and I went there once. It was wonderful. Didn't she write *The Greens Cookbook*?"

"Yeah, those are restaurant-level recipes. This book is more my speed."

"Jeez, I hope you're not a vegetarian, Dan!"

"No, no, no. I just took her class down at Esalen. It sounded fun."

"Well, it looks wonderful. Why don't you grab something to drink and go visit with Dad."

Dan took a beer from the fridge and joined Len on the couch. They shook hands.

"Dan, good to see you again! Are you keeping busy?"

"Trying to, Len. How are you and the Internet getting along?"

Len laughed. "It's a damn firehose, I always say. Once in a while I manage to get a drink from it."

They talked about the game, which featured Dan's team, the Bears, vs. Len's, the Lions. The Bears were winning, which Dan tactfully refrained from gloating about. They were both looking forward to the big game of the day, Miami vs. Dallas. It was freezing in Dallas *and* there was snow falling, so a fun game was expected.

Cassie arrived with some buttermilk biscuits that were *almost* fully baked, so they just needed another minute or two in the oven. Pete and Barbara came with the cake. Matt came with the wine, which Janet put in the fridge. They all gathered in the living room and watched the game absent-mindedly. Janet had nothing further to do in the kitchen for a while, so she joined them and said,

"Thank you all for joining us for Thanksgiving, everyone! All the food looks yummy. Does anyone need anything?" No one did.

Len raised his glass. "Let's drink to our hostess and her handsome husband for inviting us!" Everyone agreed.

Pete said, "I think the last time I saw all of you was at the wedding."

Walt answered, "Wait, how can *you* remember any of that? Didn't Barbara have to drive you home?"

Barbara said, "I think we poured him into the car." Everyone laughed.

Janet said, putting her arm around Walt, "Everyone here except for Dad had some part in getting Walt and me together. Actually, even Dad, in a way."

Len said, "Wait, what did I do?"

"You gave your approval, remember?"

Len didn't. Janet continued, "I don't think Dad's heard all this story before! Who wants to start?"

Pete said, "Well, I was the one who swerved the boat and threw them into each other's arms, so I get to go first! Or last."

Walt said, "Good thing you did, because I was about to punch you."

Barbara said to Pete, "Anyway, I was the one who called Cassie to set up that trip!"

"Wait, how did you two even know each other?"

"We didn't. I read her phone number off your notepad."

Cassie said, "Couldn't you just dial *69?"

"We didn't have that yet."

Pete said, "Anyway, if you hadn't messed up with Janet, it would have happened before at the dance lesson."

Janet said, "Hang on, what? What dance lesson?"

Cassie owned up, "At Cubberley. Pete was bringing Walt, and I was supposed to bring you. It was my fault."

Walt said, "That's it, you are never getting any work from me again, Pete!"

Pete raised his hands in surrender.

"Anyhow, you got to dance with Cassie all night, so it worked out."

Janet said, "Well, *this* is getting interesting. I'm not sure I want to hear all this."

Walt said, "She did teach me pretty good, you have to admit that."

Len had been taking all this in. Finally he jumped in,

"So Cassie had to teach you to dance, Walt? A grown man who doesn't know how to dance? Kids these days!"

Janet ignored that. "What I want to know is: how did all this start? I wasn't exactly begging for a fixup."

Matt, Dan, and Cassie all looked at each other. Finally Matt spoke up.

"I think Miriam and I might have had something to do with that."

At that name, Walt winced. Len just enjoyed the show.

"I'm sure Walt remembers our kitchen remodeling job."

Walt said, "As much as I try to forget it."

"It was not going well. My soon-to-be ex-wife and Walt were not on very good terms, let's just say."

Janet went into the kitchen to check on the turkey. Walt looked like he had something to say, but he stayed silent.

Matt continued, "Janet was the one who referred us to Walt, and she apparently was taking it all personally."

Dan added, "A little *too* personally!"

Janet yelled back from the kitchen, "I heard that!"

Cassie laughed out loud. Len said,

"Now *this* I haven't heard before. Walt, was this before or after I met you at that hardware store?"

Walt had no idea.

"So it was yet another Remodeling Job from Hell that we have to thank for all this?"

Dan said, "I guess when one door closes, another door opens. As it were."

Len ignored him and asked Matt, "And then what happened?"

Matt said, "You mean about the remodeling, or about Janet?"

"Both, I guess, but mostly Janet."

"Well, Miriam fired Walt and I paid him what we owed. She wanted to sue, and she never forgave me for that. You notice I called her my 'soon-to-be' ex-wife. "

Walt *really* looked like he was holding back something.

Cassie said, "We had the idea of getting them together at a dance lesson, since Walt was going to be Best Man at Pete's wedding and he'd need to dance at the reception."

Barbara grabbed Pete's arm at the memory of their wedding.

Len was confused now. "But wait. How would *you* know Pete? Did he work on your house, too, Matt?"

"No, but Dan knew him."

Janet put the turkey on the table and said, "I hate to break this up, but dinner's ready!"

Walt said, "To be continued. Never." They all sat down at the table.

The food was excellent. Everyone complimented Dan and Cassie for the salad and the biscuits. Barbara's chocolate-strawberry cake was fantastic, of course. As they were drinking coffee afterwards, Len said, "So, change of subject, if you're not all sick of work talk?"

No one was. He continued, "So has anyone changed jobs since I saw you last? It's so hard to keep track of you techie types."

Walt said, "Not me. Same old shit here."

Cassie said, "I went to Palm, but I've talked to you since then."

Janet said, "I gave up managing, but I think you all heard about that."

Matt replied, "Oh yeah, how's that going? How do you like the life of a peon?"

"It's such a relief. I come home, and I know what I accomplished today."

Cassie sighed. "Once in a while I have that. Usually it's someone else who gets that feeling."

Len asked, "Why's that?"

"Oh, I get a bug report, try and reproduce it, give it to the right engineer, and *maybe* eventually they fix it. Then I mark it fixed, and I might even call back Casio or Tandy if it's a high priority bug. Rinse and repeat."

Len said, "That's it? That's your job?"

Pete roused himself and said, "That's why they get the big bucks, Len, like I always say. You and I couldn't do that."

Dan said, "Or wouldn't want to."

Len continued, "And Matt and Dan? Still at Oracle?"

Dan answered for both of them. "Yup. It's nice to have one clear goal in life: make Larry Ellison richer."

Cassie said, "So is it really as much of a sweatshop as we're always hearing?"

"Nah. Maybe some parts of it are. It depends who your VP is."

Matt nodded. "Porter was pretty cool, and that carries over even after he's gone." No one but Janet knew who Porter was, so she explained it to them.

They all cleared the table, threw out the scraps, rinsed the dishes, put them in the dishwasher, and then retired to the living room. Len put the TV on, and the Dallas-Miami game was at halftime. Dan said, "What's that white stuff? Is there something wrong with your TV?"

Pete said, "I believe that's called 'snow', Dan. I think I read about that once."

Len said, "I didn't get to hear the whole story of this boat trip, or whatever it was. Finish it, Janet!" Dan and Matt agreed enthusiastically, since they hadn't been there, either.

She muted the TV and was about to start, when Cassie patted the couch for Bernie to jump up. He sat on her lap and engulfed her, and Janet laughed and said, "I remember when Bernie kept Cassie and me warm, just like that!"

Barbara said, "We stopped, fished for a while, caught nothing, and Walt moved the boat again, and then we *all* started catching fish."

Pete agreed, "That *was* a pretty good spot, wasn't it?"

Walt remembered, "I think we all caught our limits within a half hour, didn't we?"

Pete said, "I took the helm as we headed back in, so you two could be alone, I remember that part. We were sneaky, we were."

Cassie looked around Bernie and laughed at the memory. "Barbara yanked me over to the other end of the boat."

"I didn't *yank*!" Barbara objected. "I *encouraged* you."

Pete continued, "I kept an eye on the two of them, and we

were *almost* back in port. Then something happened, I don't know what... "

Janet looked embarrassed.

"But suddenly Walt looked at me and started walking towards the cabin, like he was going to punch me out or something. I had to think fast."

Len asked, "Are we coming to the good part?"

Janet just smiled.

"So I cut the engine and turned the rudder hard right. Everything on the boat that wasn't tied down went flying."

Finally Janet decided to spare Walt any more embarrassment and took over.

"As luck would have it, he fell right into my arms."

Len said, "Aw. My little girl knew just what to do?"

Walt said, "And I'm glad she did." They hugged. Pete had a cassette in his pocket, and he put it in the tape player. *The Way You Look Tonight*, the Sinatra version, came on, and Walt and Janet started the foxtrot.

Pete took Barbara's hand and the two of them joined in. Cassie got Bernie off her lap with some effort, and grabbed Dan's hand. She said, "Come on, I want to see if you still remember what I taught you." Dan groaned but stood up, and she went limp in his arms. She'd taught him how to lead by acting like a sack of potatoes, and it all came back to him.

Matt and Len looked at each other. Len said, "I guess you and I are stag tonight, Matt." Matt moved over to the couch alongside Len.

After the song was over, Janet and her father danced. Len held back tears with some effort. Cassie and Matt took their turn.

Meanwhile, Dan watched the football game, and he went over and grabbed Len, who looked annoyed at first. Dan said, "It's 14-13 Dallas with two minutes left, and Miami has the ball."

Len excused himself and unmuted the TV. The field was

covered in snow and Miami was practically on their own goal line. Pete stopped dancing and joined them, and Barbara said, "So they're playing in the snow? Where is this, Buffalo or something?"

Pete laughed, "Dallas, dear. There's only two minutes left, and it's Dallas 14, Miami 13. That's Miami in the green."

Barbara said, "It snows in Dallas? Why don't they just postpone the game?"

Pete answered without taking his eyes off the screen, "It's football, dear. They play no matter what."

The excitement got to her and she sat down to watch. Janet and Walt noticed and came over and sat down in front of the TV, too. Dan explained to Walt, "Dallas just missed a field goal. Miami has to at least get within field goal range."

Janet asked Walt, "Who are we rooting for here?" He said, "Miami, of course. No one likes Dallas." Dan agreed, "No one."

Steve DeBerg, the Miami quarterback, completed some short passes. Then it was 4th and 1, deep in Miami territory. They couldn't possibly punt; they had to go for it. Everyone held their breath, and DeBerg completed a very short pass, the receiver was tackled immediately, and the announcer said, "Byars is drilled! Did he get a yard?" He did. First down.

DeBerg completed another pass, down to the Miami 41-yard line. Leon Letts for Dallas *almost* intercepted a pass, which would have ended the game. 1:03 left in the game, and they were still too far for a field goal. Janet squeezed Walt's thigh.

Another pass completed, to the Dallas 49. Then an incomplete pass, which stopped the clock. Pete Stoyanovich, their field goal kicker, warmed up on the sidelines for a chance at the game-winning kick. They were still too far away. They completed another pass, down to the 30-yard line, and called time out. With 21 seconds left, DeBerg completed another pass to Byars, who ran out of bounds at the 23-yard line to stop the clock. Stoyanovich came on to kick the field goal.

Pete said to Barbara, "If he makes this, Miami wins." Janet said, "I usually don't like football, but this… wow."

The kick was blocked. The announcers said, "The Cowboys will win!" Jerry Jones, the Dallas owner, was shown triumphantly raising his arms. The stadium rocked.

But then: "Wait a minute, wait a minute!" Did Miami recover the ball in the Dallas endzone?

The announcer said, "A Dallas player touched the ball, and then the Dolphins went on and recovered it!"

Len said, "Holy shit. Holy shit." Then he caught himself. "Pardon my French, Janet."

On the replay, they saw all the Dallas players waving each other off, since the ball was dead at that point. But Leon Lett, the same guy who'd dropped the interception earlier, slipped on the snow and touched it, which made it a live ball again! Miami recovered it on the 1-yard line. There were three seconds left. While the referees conferred, the Miami players cleared the ice off the patch of field where the ball would be held for the second field goal attempt. Finally, Stoyanovich kicked the field goal, and the Dolphins won.

They all looked at each other. Dan said, "I don't think I've *ever* seen anything like that before." Len said, slowly, "What. A. Game. What. A. Game."

After they'd watched the replay a few dozen times, Janet turned off the TV. Everyone gathered up the dishes they brought. Janet tried without success to give away some turkey leftovers.

Cassie hugged Janet. "Thanks, Janet and Walt. This was the best Thanksgiving ever!" Everyone agreed.

20

DETECTIVE WORK, FOR REAL

Len couldn't wait to get home after Thanksgiving and solve the mystery that Rev. Collins had brought him: his nonprofit's money had been flowing out faster than he expected, and they sure didn't have any money to waste! If someone really *needed* help, of course, the charity, the churches, and their parishioners would step up, because that's what Christians do. But just taking it — that's cheating someone who needs it.

Len dug and dug into the books for Sierra Helpers, and it was tedious work. They had a surprisingly large number of transactions for such a small organization. Harold, who *had* been doing the bookkeeping up until 1991 or so, apparently had never heard of computers, so it was all on paper. Since then, the two ladies Helen and Dorothy, who did the books, had used two different accounting programs, which of course didn't talk to each other. The Reverend never thought about money, except to raise more, and just trusted Harold, Helen, and Dorothy to handle it. So at first he wasn't even sure how much was missing, or how long this had been going on. They'd never had an audit.

Len got a warm feeling of *deja vu* from all this: it reminded him of the fraud audits he used to do back in the early 50's. Nobody has any clue what's going wrong, but Len Saunders is on the job now, so the bad guys better lawyer up! He knew that embezzlers often find some way of generating fake invoices and paying themselves, and then try to cover it up with some scheme they think is clever. Len had seen it all, but he was afraid maybe the bad guys had upped their game in the 40 years since he'd done this stuff.

Usually the jobs he used to do were for a medium-sized company at least, not a small nonprofit like Sierra Helpers, and then he could demand all their original paperwork. For this one, if they even *had* paperwork, it was in boxes in their storage locker. So off to the storage place he went. He brought home the boxes for 1990, 1991, and 1992, and started entering the invoices and checks by hand. Nowadays at least he had a computer to help with the job, whereas back in the 50's it was all on paper.

After he had all the original invoices and checks for the last five years in Lotus 1-2-3, he started comparing the expense totals to the tax returns they'd filed. Things matched up, more or less. Then he sent postcards to everyone who'd received money from Sierra Helpers and asked them to verify it. Most of the cards got ignored, which he expected, so he had to call the people, and sometimes even that didn't work, so he visited in person. Day after day, driving to some business that Sierra Helpers had supposedly paid, and asking if they really did.

While all this was going on, Dan Markunas came up to visit, as he'd been doing regularly since the last boat trip. Dan had had a summer job in college at a stock brokerage, and doing the "audits" had been the task they saved up for him, so he got a bang out of hearing about this. Stock brokerages all get audited once a year, and the auditors would send out a postcard to every correspondent of the brokerage with a state-ment of each stock's "position" (long or short), and they'd be asked to check it and verify it. Naturally, no one wanted to spend time answering these, so they left them for the summer guy: Dan.

Dan wasn't an accountant, of course, but he still didn't think Len's work was boring, unlike Janet and almost everyone Len knew. He asked a lot of questions about the detective work and Len showed him what was going on. Len was thrilled to have *anyone* taking an interest.

"Dan, if I had a son, I'm sure he'd be just like you!" Len used to say. Dan would roll his eyes and say "Aw, shucks, Dad!"

Dan looked at the bank statements for the last few years. There seemed to be cash withdrawals or transfers almost every week and some weeks there were several, and he asked Len what those were. They were usually $250 or $500, and Len had noticed them, of course.

"Yeah, I already asked the Reverend what those were, and he said he does use cash for a lot of stuff, including slipping a $20 to a needy person now and then. Once in a while, he'll just have the bank transfer money to someone's account."

"So, every week?"

Len looked helpless. "He's not sure."

"Great. This adds up to a lot of money, doesn't it?"

"It sure does. I don't know how we're going to track this down."

Dan thought for a bit. "Maybe the bank has records? Photos of who's using the ATM?"

"Yeah, I thought of that. I'm not the cops, so they're not going to show that stuff to me, if they even have it."

"Does anyone besides the Reverend have an ATM card?"

"I asked him that, too. He's pretty sure no one does."

"Maybe he lends the card to his bookkeepers?"

"No, he doesn't. Way ahead of you, here, Dan!"

Len thought again that Dan was the son he never had. A guy who actually thought chasing down fraud was fun.

They turned off the computer and went out for a walk with the dogs. Besides Mickey, the Labrador, Len had adopted a retired K-9 dog, Gretchen, from the local police. Gretchen was getting old, so her days of running down bad guys were in the distant past. Now she slept on the floor next to Mickey, who spent a lot of time licking her ears. Gretchen walked stiffly, but she still loved to go with them. The two of them ran ahead and sniffed everything, even if they'd just been there yesterday.

They were silent as they walked. Dan couldn't stop thinking about the money withdrawals.

"So, Len, does the Reverend use the computer to access the bank?"

"The computer? I don't think he even knows how."

"Is his bank on the Internet?"

"The Internet? Good God, I hope not. Why?"

"I don't know. Just wondering. It's a new thing, so there's bound to be criminals trying to exploit it, sooner or later."

Len just laughed. "People up here can barely use a calculator, Dan! That's why they moved here — to get away from that stuff."

Dan didn't have anywhere to go with this topic. They changed the subject. After another mile or so they turned around and headed back home. Dan said,

"You know, my Dad can never give up on the newspaper crossword puzzle. He'll get disgusted and put it down, and then a half hour later he'll pick it up again and work on it some more. This can go on all day sometimes. I think I take after him: I'm stubborn."

"Your Dad and I would get along, I think. You're still thinking about the money, aren't you?"

Instead of answering directly, Dan said, "I bet if you and the Reverend went to the bank and talked to a VP, they'd help us out. Maybe not give us *all* their data, but anything would help. It *is* an important nonprofit up here, isn't it?"

Len pondered that. Getting the Rev to go to the bank with him — ok, he could probably do that.

The next Friday, Len called Dan.

"Well, Dan, I *think* you had a good idea there. The Rev and I went to the bank and talked to a nice young lady named Heather with "VP" in her title."

"They're all VP's at the bank. Anyhow, what did they say?"

"Well, she gave us some printouts of all the cash withdrawals and transfers."

"And?"

"The Rev got confused and didn't recognize some of them. But he really wasn't sure about them."

Dan thought, *"Another obstacle! It's just another day for the crime-fighting team of Len and Dan!"*

"Great. Now what do we do?"

"Good question. I'm looking at the questionable ones now."

"OK. Anything stand out?"

"Yeah, not sure. They're all over the place. Different days and times, different amounts…"

Dan was getting more interested. Detective work!

"Well, I can't come up this weekend. Maybe next, if you haven't found it by then!"

"You don't need to go to any trouble for me, Dan. I took this one on, so it's my burden. And what else do I have to do with my time?"

"It's no trouble, Len. I told you I'm stubborn."

"Yeah, you sure did. It's a curse, isn't it? Well, maybe I'll see you next weekend, then."

Len stared at the stack of paper and cursed. He paged through it, looking again for *some* kind of pattern, in vain. He decided to enter the data into Lotus 1-2-3 so he could send it to Dan, at least. That took most of the weekend. He attached it to an email and sent it to Dan's work address on Sunday night.

Monday morning at Oracle, Dan looked at the data and loaded it into a database. He knew this was overkill for just a few hundred records, but hey, this was Oracle, and Len and the Reverend would be impressed, anyway. He had to restrain himself from working on it all day, but after 6:00 pm he figured he was off the clock, so what the hell.

After messing around with that, he realized there were PC programs that were a hell of a lot easier than Oracle, and he switched to Excel on his PC. He sorted the expenses by time, by amount, and by which ATM machine was used, to see if any patterns turned up. While he was doing this, his buddy Matt dropped by on his way out the door. Matt was living by himself just a few miles away, now that he was getting a divorce, so he didn't need to hurry home to a wife. Dan explained the problem to him.

"Anything jumping out at you?" Matt asked.

"Well… there seem to be a lot on Thursdays," Dan said, pointing at the screen. "Different amounts, though, and different ATM's."

Matt stared. "Is there anything special about Thursdays?"

"Don't know. I've never met the Reverend. Maybe Len can ask him."

"Let's see…a lot of $250 withdrawals on Thursday." Matt said.

"I wonder what's special about $250," Dan mused.

"Is that the daily limit for that bank?"

"Good question. I don't know that, either."

Matt had an idea. "So if they took out $250, it can't be all in $20's, right?"

"Yeah, probably $50's. So?"

"So $50 bills aren't all that common, right? Maybe they're taking them somewhere and changing them into smaller bills!"

"Great, so we just have to go to every establishment in the

Sierras and ask them if anyone comes in with $50's a lot! That should be easy."

Matt wasn't willing to abandon this idea quite yet.

"Maybe not *every* establishment!"

"What do you mean?"

"Well, it would probably be some place near the ATM, right?"

"Maybe. Not necessarily, though."

Matt had to admit Dan was right.

"Maybe it's someone with a gambling problem, and they go straight to a casino?"

Dan liked that idea.

"Now we're getting somewhere. I don't know where you'd go to gamble up there. And Reno's not that far, so there's still a lot of possibilities."

Matt said, "OK, I'll have to think about this. See you tomorrow." and headed out the door. Dan called Len with their ideas.

Len was impressed that the big brains of Silicon Valley were on the case. He knew the Reverend would be thrilled, too. He decided to go to his office and ask him about the Thursday thing, and also the $250.

The Reverend wasn't much help. He *thought* he sometimes took out $250, and it might be on a Thursday sometimes, but he really had no clue. Helen was in the office when he came by, and he took the opportunity to chat and ask her what she knew about the money. She knew a lot, of course, since she and Dorothy handled it for the Reverend. Dorothy was out that day.

Helen was a slightly overweight lady in her 50's, Len guessed, who'd lived here in the mountains all her life. She had photos of her husband and family on her desk, and she belonged to the Seventh Day Adventists. She had some odd-looking objects on the chair behind her, and Len made the mistake of asking her what they were. Helen launched into a lengthy lecture on the healing power of magnets, and how these were helping her with her back pain. The Church didn't approve of drugs, so painkillers were out. She offered to sell him a magnet, which he politely declined.

Helen was concerned about the money, and listened closely as Len and the Reverend talked. When she excused herself for a few minutes, Len looked over her desk again, and noticed a yellow Sticky note stuck to her monitor. "Ah-hah!" he thought. "Someone can't remember their password, so they put it on a Sticky note! Case closed."

His time on embezzlement cases had taught him something, though: don't tell anyone what you're thinking. Everyone's a suspect until proven innocent. He didn't say anything about it, and couldn't wait to call Dan that night and tell him.

Dan was disappointed. He'd hoped it would be some sophisticated theft involving the Internet, but no, it was just a stupid password thing. Len said,

"Hang on there, cowboy. We don't know who's *using* that password, do we? We can't just change it and close the case!"

"No? The Rev just wants the problem to go away, doesn't he?"

Len thought, "*Who cares what he wants? We're on the case now!*"

"Aw, Dan, that's not what *we* want, though! We want to catch the bad guy. Or girl."

Dan thought this sounded like *real* detective work, not computer stuff.

"I guess. How are we going to do that?"

"I'm not sure. Let me work on that."

Len liked to watch detective shows on TV. They were always way more glamorous than real life, he figured, and now he was sure of it. *Someone* was probably using the bank account password, since it was right out there on Helen's monitor. But it might not be Helen!

While he was thinking, Dan called.

"Hey, Len, I thought of something!"

"You're letting this get to you, Dan. Anyhow, shoot."

"Let's get the bank to disable the account temporarily, with some kind of bullshit excuse."

"OK. Why?"

"The bad guy might call their Customer Support number to see what's wrong!"

Len said, "Oh, come on. Why would they be that stupid?"

Dan laughed. "Weren't you the one who said people up there can barely use a calculator?"

"Yeah, but… OK, we can try that. What happens if they do call?"

Dan asked if the bank had Caller ID on their phone. Len didn't know, of course, but he understood the point immediately, and he said he'd check on that, too, when he talked to Heather at the bank again. Honestly, would anyone be dumb enough to call Customer Support on their home phone? Well, no harm in trying.

He went to the bank on Thursday and talked to Heather again. She said she didn't have the authority to do that, and he almost asked, "Wait, aren't you a Vice President?" but he remembered what Dan had said about banks. He waited while Heather went to talk to her boss.

Her boss was a middle-aged man, Mr. Ambrose, who Len thought just *looked* like a bank vice president. Mr. Ambrose said that he was sorry but he'd need a signature from an officer of Sierra Helpers or an order from law enforcement to do something like that. Len thanked him and drove down to the police station.

21

A FREE GIFT FOR YOU

L en spent all afternoon at the police station. He had to tell his story at least five times, as one detective would listen and then get interrupted and sent out on a call, and a new guy would come in and make him say it all again. They were used to listening to citizens who were off their rockers, so he had to overcome that suspicion, too.

Finally, he met an older detective who seemed to be on desk duty, Frank Griffiths, who knew Rev. Collins and his bookkeeper Helen, and was familiar with Sierra Helpers. Frank was sympathetic but had reservations.

"I'd like to help with this if I can, since Sierra Helpers does a lot of good work up here. The problem I have, though, Mr. Saunders, is that I don't see a crime yet. The Reverend has *suspicions* that money is disappearing, but you can't point to any."

"Yeah," said Len. "That's the problem I'm having, too. He does handle a lot of cash. There are all these cash withdrawals and transfers, but as far as the Rev knows, any of them *could* be legit." Frank looked over the printout again.

"I *do* see a lot of $250 transfers on Thursdays. Are you sure those are all kosher?"

Len told him about the sticky note with the password on it on Helen's monitor. To Frank, this was it: Case Closed!

"So is there a reason why you don't just change the password and tell her not to post it on her monitor anymore?"

"Oh, come on, detective! We want to catch the perp, not just stop the crime, don't we?"

This was the wrong thing to say, and Len realized it from Frank's reaction right away. Real life cops must be tired of citizens using TV cop lingo. He corrected himself.

"Sorry, Detective, guess I've been watching too many cop shows."

"That's OK, Mr. Saunders. We're used to it. Anyway, I'm not sure what I can do for you right now. Thanks for coming in." Frank got up from his chair. "I have to get home and drive my mother-in-law to the church for bingo night tonight."

Len stayed seated. "One more thing: we did have this idea that I need your help for, Detective." He explained the idea about disabling the account temporarily and that he needed the police to request it.

Frank was tired of this conversation, but he thought as long as it was just a phone call, what the hell. He agreed to call the bank, and showed Len out.

When Len got home, he called Mr. Ambrose at the bank, and told him to expect a call from Detective Griffiths.

"Thank you, Mr. Saunders. What do you want us to do when someone calls about it?"

"Just write down the time and the phone number it's from. Heather tells me you have Caller ID now."

"OK, got it. Should we re-enable the account then?"

Len pondered that. He wanted to gather as much information as possible.

"How about after the *second* call, not the first?"

That night, Len called Dan and gave him an update.

"OK, son, now we just have to wait. Unless you have some other ideas?"

Dan didn't. He thought it was funny that Len had talked about "the perp" to a real-life detective, though.

"So did Detective Griffiths make a face when you told him you wanted to get the perp?"

"Yeah, it was subtle, but it was there. Then he said he had to leave to take his mother to bingo night or something. People have busy social schedules up here."

"Sounds like it. OK, well, keep me posted." He went back to watching *Seinfeld*.

Next Monday afternoon, Heather called Len.

"Mr. Saunders, we did have a couple calls for customer support on that account. Do you have a pencil ready?" She proceeded to give him the times and phone numbers of the callers.

"I re-enabled the account as you asked. Is there anything else I can do for you?"

"Not right now, Heather. Thank you for your help!" and hung up.

"*Now what do I do?*" he asked himself. "*Who do these numbers belong to? I guess I could just call them and see who answers.*"

A moment's reflection told him that might just alert them. Anyhow, this whole thing was Dan's idea, so he decided to call him and see what the bright boy wanted to do *now*.

Dan said, "Hmm… Hmm… There *is* such a thing as a reverse phone directory, where you start with the phone number and it tells you who owns it. I'm guessing you don't have one of those, though."

"Darn, no, I sure don't, Dan."

"Well, we could go to a private detective. They have all kinds of sources."

"That's going to cost some money, though, right?" Dan conceded that point. He offered to check on the Internet, just in case those phone numbers appeared anywhere, but wasn't optimistic that he would find anything. Len said, "Sure, go ahead," but then said,

"Hey, I have an idea for something *you* can do!!"

"Ooh, I'm all a-tingle!" Dan said.

"They won't know *your* voice, right? So what if you call them and wheedle their name and address out of them?"

"Oh, God. How would I do that?"

"I don't know, Dan. This was your idea, if you remember. You'll figure something out." He gave him the phone numbers.

Dan said, "OK, well, can you send me the regular phone book? That might help if I just get a name."

Sitting around later watching TV, Len ruminated on everything that happened today. Something Detective Griffiths said suddenly came back to him: "I have to get home and drive my mother-in-law to the church for bingo night tonight."

"Wait, what day did I see the detective? It was Thursday."

Bingo on Thursday night, and a lot of the money transfers happen on Thursday. Was this just a coincidence? Probably. Still, it wouldn't hurt to check it out. *"Where do they play bingo?"* he wondered. *"He said it was a church."*

He called Dan back and told him about the "bingo" idea. Dan thought maybe he could find a bingo game up in the mountains! But really, were the people up there going to announce their bingo games on the Internet? Maybe someday. Not now.

The next day Len walked through downtown Placerville, looking for a likely person to talk to. Finally, he dropped into a few of the antique stores, since they seemed to be empty and run by older people who were probably desperate for conversation. This was a weekday and there were no tourists, so his main problem turned out to be *exiting* the conversation, not starting it.

Len was an older person himself, so he had no difficulty convincing them that he really did want to play bingo. They all said the First Reformed church off Highway 49 had a regular bingo night every Thursday. It was all for charity, of course, they assured him.

In his last antique store, he had an inspiration: he told Horace, the man running it, that his wife's sister wanted to find a Seventh Day Adventist group up here. Wow, did that ever set off a gusher of invective! Horace went on for twenty minutes about the Adventists in this area, and how holier-than-thou they were. Horace was a Presbyterian with no patience for these extreme sects. Finally, Len looked at his watch and said he had to get home to his wife.

As Len was leaving, Horace continued his rant with, "These pious, holy people aren't supposed to do gambling, but I happen to know you can find some of them every week at that bingo game you were asking about!"

Len smiled, thanked Horace for his time, and closed the door before he could go on any further. Then he kicked himself, *"I said 'my wife' but I'm not wearing a ring! Oh, well."*

DAN THOUGHT he ought to tell Janet what was going on with Len. After all, it was her Dad! She was only a little bit amused.

"He wants you to call a random number, pretend to be someone else, and get their personal information? I think this hobby of his is getting out of hand! Let me call him."

Walt overheard this and chuckled.

"What's Dad up to now, hon?"

She told him about the embezzling scheme, if that was even what it was, and how he and Dan were playing *Matlock* over it. Or maybe they were doing *Murder, She Wrote*. Walt thought it was the funniest thing he'd heard all day. This irritated her.

"Hey, it's not funny. He could get hurt messing around like that."

"What, someone's going to run him over with their

walker? He does have a German Shepherd to protect him now, doesn't he?"

"Yeah, a retired police dog who can hardly walk."

She called Len. They argued for a long time, but she finally gave up and just told him to *please* be careful. She was not happy afterwards and she and Walt didn't discuss it any further.

DAN CALLED CASSIE and asked if she wanted to help with his phone scam. She agreed immediately. He went over to her apartment on Saturday morning. She was taking a script off the printer.

"Wow, you're really getting into this detective thing, aren't you? Do you have lines for me, too?"

Cassie looked excited. "You're playing the mark. Let's rehearse this scene before we do the show."

Dan read the script. "Ooh, you're using cop lingo, too." He gave her a nod. She tried to look officious and held her little finger to her mouth and her thumb to her ear.

Cassie said, "Hello, I'm calling from Volcano Telephone. To whom am I speaking, please?"

Dan said, "Who wants to know? Who are you, again?"

"I'm sorry, my name is Heather McCracken with the Volcano Telephone Company. We're conducting a quality check in your local office, and your number came up on my screen."

"OK, Heather McCracken, we get a lot of these unsolicited phone calls and our son tells us to just ignore them. So I'm hanging up now." He slammed down his hand.

He laughed, "How'd I do?"

She said, "Let's try that again. Hello, I'm calling from Volcano Telephone. To whom am I speaking, please?"

Dan said, "Who wants to know? Who are you, again?"

"I'm sorry, sir, my name is Heather McCracken, with the Volcano Telephone Company. I realize you haven't reported any problems, sir, and if you'll just give me a minute of your time, I'll let you go on with your day."

"OK. What can I do for you, Heather McCracken?"

"Can you give me your name and address, please?"

"Our son tells us to just ignore people calling us like this. So I'm hanging up now."

She said, "Once more. Hello, I'm calling from Volcano Telephone. To whom am I speaking, please?"

Dan said, "Who wants to know? Who are you, again?"

"I'm sorry, sir, my name is Heather McCracken, with the Volcano Telephone Company. I realize you haven't reported any problems, sir, and if you'll just give me a minute of your time, I'll let you go on with your day."

"OK. What can I do for you, Heather McCracken?"

"I have a very old directory here that says you are James Harper at 466 Canal Street, Placerville. Is that correct?"

Dan hung up the phone. "OK, that might work. People can't stand to hear themselves misidentified." She said, "Hah! Thanks, Dan. Are you ready?"

He gave her a thumbs up and she dialed the first number. He put his ear next to the phone. On the fourth ring, an answering machine picked up.

"Hello, you have reached the home of Fred and Delores Robinson. We are unable to come to the phone right now…" Cassie hung up.

Dan picked up his phone book and thumbed to the R's. "Great, there are only about a hundred Robinsons." He found "Fred" and checked the phone number. It matched. "Got it! Now the next one."

For the second number, someone picked up. They gave each other the thumbs-up.

"Hello?" said a male voice.

"Hello, I'm calling from Volcano Telephone. To whom am I speaking, please?"

"This is Harry. Who did you want?"

Dan tried to keep a straight face as she said, "I'm sorry, sir, my name is Heather McCracken, with the Volcano Telephone Company. I realize you haven't reported any problems, sir, and if you'll just give me a minute of your time, I'll let you go on with your day."

"OK, what do you want?"

"Thank you so much. I have a very old directory here that says you are James Harper at 466 Canal Street, Placerville. I guess that's not correct?"

"James who? No, I *told* you my name is Harry. Harry Redding."

She had him spell that, then got his address. Cassie heard a voice in the background saying, "Who is it, Harry?"

Cassie said, "OK, thank you so much for your time, Mr. Redding."

Dan motioned for her to give him the phone. She looked puzzled, but said, "Just a minute, Mr. Redding. My supervisor Mr. Densmore wants to thank you, too." and handed it to him.

"Good morning, Mr. Redding, thank you very much for helping us out. May we send you a free $10 gift coupon for a local business as a token of our sincere appreciation?"

This time Cassie suppressed a giggle.

Dan verified the address again and then thanked him and hung up.

Success! They high-fived each other. Dan said, "Hey, do you want to call Len?" She dialed him.

"Hello, Mr. Saunders. I have Dan here with me. We have some names for you!"

"Well, hello, Cassie and Dan, my little assistants! What have you ferreted out for me?" She gave him the names and addresses.

"Helen Robinson: that's the Reverend's bookkeeper. I

don't know this other person."

"This was fun. Let me put Dan on." and handed him the phone.

"Hi, Len. We got it, thanks to Cassie's persuasive voice here!"

"Wow, you two are amazing. Now I have to figure out who these 'Redding' people are."

Len told Dan about the Thursday bingo games. Dan told him about the $50 bill hypothesis. After some small talk, Dan and Cassie high-fived again and Dan left. Back home, he used his home computer to look up "Redding" in various places on the Internet. Unfortunately, he got back mostly mentions of the city of Redding in California. But he did find a couple bulletin board posts by a guy named James Redding. This guy seemed to be a Computer Science grad student at the Davis campus of the University of California. He read the posts, which were mostly just stuff about local restaurants and bicycling, but he decided to follow up on this guy. Maybe he was Harry's son, or something?

He concocted an identity for himself and joined that bulletin board. After a couple messages to establish himself as someone who lived in Davis, he tried asking some questions about bicycling up there, claiming his parents were planning to retire there and wondering if it was just too hilly to ride a bike.

Score! James responded. They conversed for a while, and James said his parents lived in that area, too. Dan asked him what there was to do besides enjoying the beautiful scenery, and James said they were devoted to playing bingo! He didn't understand what the attraction was, but for his mom, it was the center of her social life. Dan sympathized.

He called Len and told them that the Reddings were definitely their prime suspects. This was getting exciting.

22

BINGO

Now they had a name, Harry Redding or probably his wife, plus a possible co-conspirator, Helen Robinson, the bookkeeper. What was the connection?

"I can't talk to the Rev, or to Helen yet. They might alert the others or cover their tracks." he figured. *"Who is this Redding person?"*

He decided to go to the bingo game this Thursday. He'd probably attract attention as a newcomer, but he *was* an older person, after all, so he had an excuse. He decided not to make up a cover story for himself, though, since some of them might know who he really was. He'd read that the CIA called a fake life like that a "legend" and he really wanted to have one, but this was a small community. Sigh.

At the church's social hall, he did indeed stand out as a stranger, which was good, in a way. It gave him a chance to socialize and meet lots of people before the game started. None of them were named Redding, though. He watched, inconspicuously he hoped, as people paid their money for the bingo cards. One lady gave a $50 bill, but he didn't get her name. He tried to sit near her but didn't get any more information about her.

She got up to leave after the bingo was over. Her husband came to pick her up, and he walked around chatting with the other players. Len went over to meet him. "Harry Redding" – got it! Now he had his perps. What to do?

He thought of going to see Detective Griffiths again, but already thought Len was a crazy old guy trying to play cop. The detective probably wouldn't want to bust two old ladies for stealing small amounts of money to play bingo, anyway. That wouldn't look good for the County Sheriff in his re-election campaign.

Dan came up to visit that weekend, and the two of them war-gamed it all out while they were fishing.

"So what would the Rev do if you told him?"

"I don't know, he'd probably just give Helen a good talking-to. Maybe he'd fire her, maybe not."

Dan didn't think that was sufficient, considering how much work he and Len had put in.

"And if you told that detective about it?"

"Hell, pardon my French, that guy's just coasting to his pension. He doesn't want a bust of some old ladies' bingo ring on his record."

Dan giggled and repeated "bingo ring." They didn't talk about it for the rest of the weekend. When he got back home, he called Cassie and told her how their phone scam had turned out.

"Oh my God, Dan, is Mr. Saunders going to the police now?"

Dan explained the complications around that.

"So how does the bookkeeper explain those transfers to this 'Redding' lady?"

Dan didn't know that, either. He didn't think the Rev ever checked the books anyway.

Cassie couldn't wait to tell Janet, who was not happy.

"Oh, God. I told him to be careful!" She thanked Cassie

for telling her, but they agreed that a couple of little old ladies probably weren't going to whack him.

The next time she and Len talked, she asked him, "So what's happening with the bingo ring?"

"'The bingo ring' " he repeated, chuckling. "I'm still wondering what to do about it. If I just tell the Reverend, he probably won't do anything but tell Helen to stop. That just doesn't sit right with me. Or Dan."

"Well, maybe you can find some way for *him* to find out on his own, or someone else to find out! Anyway, you did what he asked you to do, right? You found out who was stealing from him. So now you're done!" Janet was hoping she could just close the book on this little adventure of Dad's.

"Yeah…" he said, not quite buying it. She was still a little worried when they hung up.

The next couple of weeks, Len mulled over what to do. He really wanted those two ladies to face *some* consequences, but he wasn't sure what should happen, or how to cause it. The cops sure weren't going to bust them. Finally, he just told the Rev that he'd found the source of the funds' leak! The Rev was delighted and thanked him profusely.

"If it's OK to ask: what are you planning to do about it?" Len asked.

"Well, I really hate to have to fire Helen, but I do have a responsibility to the poor and needy up here, and after all, it was *their* money she was stealing."

Len didn't hear any more about it. There was nothing in the paper about any arrests, so he figured the Rev didn't go to the police, and Detective Griffiths had filed him in his "nut-case citizen" file. Janet relaxed and hoped Len's crime-fighting days were over.

~

THE NEXT WEDNESDAY, he went to visit one of his best clients, a B&B outside of Placerville, and left wondering if he'd forgotten to shower that morning. Dotty, the woman who ran the place, kept him waiting for a half hour, and then with a frozen face, gave him a check for her outstanding balance and said they weren't going to be using him anymore. She said, "Thank you for your work, Mr. Saunders." She'd usually called him Len, so he noticed the "Mr." particularly. Then she got up and left the room.

Over the next three weeks, almost half of his clients canceled. They offered various excuses, but after the fourth he stopped hearing what they said. It seemed pretty clear that he was *persona non grata* up here. It *must* be because of the Helen business, he figured, but hell, she was stealing from a charity! She was the one who deserved to be shunned, not him.

Several times when he was walking around in town, he noticed people on the other side of the street huddling and trying to look inconspicuous as they pointed him out. Something was up. He went to visit the Reverend and they sat down in his private office.

"Reverend Collins, after we found out about the embezzling scheme, what happened, exactly?"

The Reverend folded his hands on the desk. "Well, I dealt with the problem, as I told you. Why? Is something wrong?"

Len told him about all the weird behavior he was seeing, and how half of his clients had deserted him. The Reverend expressed his sympathy. This wasn't getting anywhere, so Len tried a different tack.

"Do you have any idea why they're mad at *me*, and not Helen?"

The Rev sat back and tried to compose a suitably gnomic answer.

"Len, the mountains are like a small town. Helen has lived here all her life. You're an outsider."

Len felt annoyed, but he suppressed it, since anger

wouldn't get him anywhere. Maybe he could draw the Rev out a little:

"You mean Helen has a lot of friends who just blame me?"

"I wouldn't say they *blame* you, but maybe they don't think what she was doing was that bad. And it *had* been going on for a long time."

Len wanted to argue, but that wouldn't accomplish anything.

"I see, I see. So now she's out of a job and I'm the one who did it to her."

The Reverend smiled and sat back. "Actually, I was the one who fired her, but you're the outsider here."

"Got it. I just did what you asked me to do, but now I'm the bad guy?"

"Yeah, I'm sorry if I put you in that position. Tell me again: how did you figure out it was her? Was it your Silicon Valley daughter and her high tech tricks?"

Len went over the way he and Dan got Helen and her friend to expose themselves, leaving out a few of more unsavory details. The Reverend listened intently.

"So you and the high tech folks used some deception; is that it? Do you think that was fair?"

Now Len was beginning to grasp what was going on: the folks up here didn't like him deceiving them. He didn't see anything wrong with it, but arguing wasn't going to get him anywhere. Nor would reminding the Rev that he was the one who asked Len to look into it.

"I see your point, Reverend. It's the methods we used?"

Reverend Collins looked at his watch and stood up. "Something like that, Len. I have to get to an appointment now. Thanks again for helping us out here."

Len brooded on that for weeks. He and Dan did lie to these people, he had to be honest about that. But jeez: they were uncovering a criminal conspiracy! How else were you supposed to do that; wiretap them?"

He called Dan and told him about the unexpected blow-back he was getting. Dan was unable to resist a good joke when it occurred to him:

"I think this is a reverse *Wizard of Oz*, Len!"

Len had no idea what he was talking about.

"I have a feeling we *are* in Kansas!"

"I'm kinda slow here, Dan. Explain?"

"Bad joke, never mind. Something about the rural mindset of people up there."

"Ah. Yeah. Anyhow, I think we stepped over a line some-where, Dan. All that matters is, it's us versus a local, and we're not *from* here."

"Yeah, I guess so. Well, you're retired, so you don't have to care, right?"

Len agreed without much enthusiasm. He knew he *should* look at it that way, but this area was like a big small town. Having everyone hating him was not the way he envisioned his retirement.

Dan came up to visit and cheer him up. Len took him for dinner to a place near Placerville on Saturday night. They went to a historic old place, the Smith Flat House, that was built in 1853 during the gold rush. As they were eating, Len noticed an elderly guy at the next table glancing over at them repeatedly. He looked familiar. "*Oh my god!*" He thought. It was Harry Redding!

"*It really is a small town up here!*" he thought.

Dan came over and Len introduced him as his nephew Dan Markunas. Harry and his wife smiled politely and they all went back to their dinner.

Harry leaned over to his wife and whispered, "That voice! I think I've heard it before!" She just looked annoyed when he told her who Len was.

The next day, they came back to town for lunch. This time

they brought the dogs, since they were going to be eating outside, Len with Mickey, and Dan holding Gretchen, who was gamely limping along, trying to keep up the pace.

As they were walking down Main Street, Harry Redding suddenly stood in front of them and blocked their path. He looked at Dan and said, "Well, well, well. It's Mr. Densmore from the phone company!"

Dan tried to remember the name Cassie had used when he pretended to be from the phone company, and he had a sick feeling that she'd unconsciously picked the name of the drummer from The Doors. As he tried hard to think of something to say, Harry continued,

"You know, the phone company said they don't *have* a "Mr. Densmore!" And I never got that 'free gift' you promised me, either. We don't like people from the flats coming up here and lying to us!"

Len tried to defuse the situation, but Harry wasn't paying any attention to him.

Gretchen's ears went back and she started growling softly. Harry lifted his cane and swung it at Dan's head. Dan tried to duck and put his hands up, but the cane bounced off the top of his head. He went down on one knee.

Gretchen leaped at Harry and they both went down. She grabbed his sleeve and yanked it back and forth. Harry screamed as Len knelt down and yelled "Off! Off!", and Mickey pulled loose. Mickey backed up a few steps and barked furiously.

Gretchen continued to shake her head with Harry's sleeve in her mouth. Dan grabbed Gretchen's collar and tried to pull her off.

A police car arrived, lights flashing. One cop that Len didn't know and his old friend Detective Griffiths got out. The detective yelled, "Gretchen! *Halt!*"

Gretchen let go immediately at the German word *halt* and

came and sat down in the "alert" position next to the detective, who said, "good girl!"

The other cop helped Harry, Len, and Dan to their feet and asked them if they were OK. He radioed for an ambulance.

The detective said, "Does anyone want to tell me what happened here? Sir…" he said, looking at Dan, "you look like you got hit in the head. How about if you start?"

Harry said, "This vicious dog attacked me…" but Griffiths shushed him. Dan told him about the cane attack, with Harry attempting over and over to interrupt him.

Finally, the detective turned to Len and asked if he agreed with that account. He said he did. At that point the ambulance arrived. The medical team got out and the other cop directed them to Dan, who got into the ambulance. Len said he'd ride with them, if it was OK. They told him that Mickey couldn't ride with them, but Detective Griffiths quickly said he'd bring the dogs to the police station with him.

The detective said to Harry, "Sir, I'm placing you under arrest. I *will* handcuff you if you make any attempt at all to resist or run away. Will you go peacefully?" Harry said, "Yes, officer."

He read Harry his Miranda rights and stuffed him in the back seat. The police car drove away, with Detective Griffiths remaining on the sidewalk with the dogs.

He bent down on one knee and put his arm over Gretchen's shoulder. She wagged her tail.

"Good girl, Gretchen! I guess you've still got some fight left in you, huh? Maybe we shouldn't have retired you!" He radioed for another police car to take them all back to the station.

23

THE DYNAMIC DUO

J anet answered the phone. An official-sounding voice asked,

"May I speak to Mrs. Janet Saunders, please."

"This is she" she said, her fright level rising. The voice explained that her father had been admitted to the emergency room in Placerville after an altercation, and he'd named her as his emergency contact.

"Oh my God. Is he OK?"

They tried to assure her that this was just a precaution, and Mr. Saunders was in good condition. He had a friend with him who was also injured, a Mr. Markunas. She thanked them and hung up.

Walt could tell something was wrong. She told him the story, and he went into the garage and got his shotgun. He said, "I'll kill him, whoever it is. Let's go!" and got in his truck. Janet screamed but got in, followed by Bernie. They hardly spoke at all while they drove up to the hospital. Walt refused to talk.

At the hospital, the front desk told them that Mr. Saunders and his friend had been treated and released. They drove to the cabin. A police car was parked outside. Inside, Len and

Dan were sitting with Detective Griffiths, who had Gretchen's head on his lap. Dan had a Band-Aid on his forehead. Len and Dan were drinking Scotch, while the detective sipped from a glass of iced tea.

Janet ran in and hugged Len. After a while, she said, "So, Dad, are you sure you're OK?"

"I'm fine, sweetie. You should have seen the other guy!"

"And you, Dan! How are you?" Dan assured her he was fine, too. Len introduced her to the detective. He and Walt already knew each other from way back, since Walt had been coming up here since he was a boy.

They all sat down. The dogs all wagged their tails and sniffed each other ecstatically.

Detective Griffiths stood up and said, "I think you're in good hands now, Mr. Saunders. I'd better get back to work." Gretchen looked like she really wanted to go with him.

Walt said, "Before you go, Frank: can you tell us what happened?"

"Well, Walt, you know I can't talk about ongoing criminal cases. But just between us: Mr. and Mrs. Redding were pretty upset about what happened to Helen. The whole town is, actually."

Janet said, "Upset about what happened? She was stealing from a charity, for God's sake. And she didn't even get arrested!"

He put up his hands. "It wasn't really about her getting fired, as I understand it."

They all looked at him quizzically and waited for the explanation.

"Helen got kicked out of her church group for helping someone gamble. The Seventh Day Adventists take a pretty dim view of gambling." He added quickly, "And stealing, too, of course."

Janet said, "Playing bingo? That's 'gambling' to them?" The detective just shrugged and turned to go. Mickey ran over to him, and he bent down and scratched his ears. "Bye, bye, brave boy!"

Len smiled. Walt asked, "Why, what did Mickey do when all this was going on?"

Dan laughed. "Mickey was right there, helping, weren't you, boy?" Mickey wagged his tail.

Len said, "Mickey's a lover, not a fighter!" Everyone laughed, and Mickey made the rounds getting petted. The detective left.

They told the story over and over and then Walt went out and got a pizza for them. Janet offered to drive Dan home in Dan's car if he wasn't up to driving. Dan said he was all sobered up now, so he'd be fine. Janet and Walt both had to go to work on Monday, so they left, too, after Janet told Len to ease off on his crime-busting activities. Len said he'd learned his lesson.

Later that night, a reporter from the local newspaper called him, having seen the case on the police blotter. She seemed particularly interested in the Silicon Valley "angle," although Len didn't quite see why that was such a big deal. He told her how his daughter's friend Dan had used his software tools at Oracle to help figure out where the money was going, and tried the Internet, but really, Len could have done it himself; it was just sorting a few hundred records. He didn't tell her about any of the sneaky stuff they'd done. Len emphasized that the important thing was the great work that Sierra Helpers was doing, and how some people were stealing from them.

She said, "Got it. So, this Dan Markunas friend of your daughter: he's involved in the Internet, somehow?"

"Yeah, I guess he is, but that had nothing to do with this case."

"And your daughter, Janet, is, too?"

She asked some more questions, and then thanked him and said she'd call back if she needed anything more. Len had a queasy feeling that her story wasn't going to be *quite* what he would have written.

MATT AND MIRIAM's lawyers were in constant contact about the divorce settlement. Matt was thankful he could afford that service: at least he didn't have to deal with her directly. He wanted to get it over with as soon as possible, so if he happened to join a startup, she wouldn't get any of the stock. Fortunately, she also apparently wanted to marry this Patrick jerk, since *he* seemed to be going places. "*Unlike a loser like me, who's only getting options in a hot company like Oracle!*" Matt had heard through the grapevine that Patrick was at Microsoft now.

So Miriam had to be mentally computing how much money Patrick was going to make with all his Microsoft stock. Plus, Seattle was cheaper than Silicon Valley, so they could get a *much* better house up there. "*It's easy!*" she used to tell him. "*Why the hell can't you do it?*"

He was glad he didn't have to listen to that shit anymore. Oracle stock was rising steadily. It wasn't as spectacular as an IPO, but most people outside the business only hear about startup success stories. All the startups that flame out or never even launch a product just get swept under the rug and forgotten. Meantime, the unlucky people who went to work there sweated 24x7 and dealt with naked egos, sociopathic executives, and vulture capitalists. Oracle was a nice, stable company that wasn't going out of business anytime soon. And they had a fitness center on site and a good cafeteria.

She'd brought up this startup thing several times, before they split up. He was sick of explaining to her that great ideas were a dime a dozen, and it was *executing* them that was hard. She didn't want to hear it. Everyone she met in her psychological practice had tons of money or at least pretended to, and dammit: she was going to get some, too!

Cassie was trying hard and mostly succeeding in keeping a stiff upper lip about work at Palm, despite the fact that the Zoomer sales were disappointing. Her work level had settled back to something like normal, at least. The engineering team was hard at work speeding up the Zoomer and fixing the problems that had trickled in.

Jeff and Donna were relentlessly positive, though. They were holding the company together purely by force of personality. Everyone seemed to trust them to figure *something* out, and if they didn't — well, it was still a positive experience that they'd all enjoyed. Actually, she felt closer to the group than she had when they were in a big push. Now their real personalities were coming out, and she discovered she really liked these people.

She thought all the time about adopting a child. Before the Zoomer launched, it was "I'm so busy, how would I have time to raise a kid?" Now it was, "What if the company goes under and I'm an unemployed single mom?" Her mom was no help at all; she just thought Cassie should get married and then the problems would go away.

The men in high tech were mostly jerks. She couldn't stomach the thought of tying herself to one of those. Maybe she should do like Janet and marry a solid, blue-collar guy, who didn't think he knew how to do her job better than she did. The problem was, she didn't know any of those. Maybe Walt could fix her up? *"Now there's an idea,"* she woke up one morning thinking. It would be embarrassing, for sure.

On Tuesday morning, Matt got in early and was scrolling through the newsgroups when he saw a story:

Internet Crime Fighters on the Job!

A local man busted an embezzling ring with help from some Internet wizards, and was hospitalized for his trouble yesterday. A retired police dog, Gretchen, played a heroic role in the altercation.

[*It went to explain how two Oracle employees had deployed the power of the database and the Internet to figure out who was stealing money from a local charity, and how Len Saunders had been assaulted in the streets for it. The story named Dan, but not Matt.*]

He ran down to Dan's office, but he hadn't come in yet, so he just sent him an email about it. His friend Mike came by and asked if he'd seen the news yet. They were talking about it when Dan walked in.

"Oh, my God, Matt, we're famous! This must be our fifteen minutes. I've been waiting for that."

"You mean *you're* famous! It didn't even mention me." said Matt.

"Yeah, well, it's a cruel business, this 'fame' thing, Matt."

Mike said, "So have you hired a press agent yet, Dan?"

Dan pretended to take a notebook out of his pocket and jot down that idea.

Mike asked, "Give us the lowdown, guys. What really happened? Did the press get it all garbled yet again?"

Matt said, "Yeah, Dan. Is that Band-Aid on your forehead just for show, or what?"

Dan told them the whole story, putting particular emphasis on Gretchen, the retired K-9 dog, who'd behaved so heroically. Matt enjoyed recounting his sleuthing with Dan. A small crowd had gathered as they talked.

Sarah, a tech writer whose entire job often consisted of getting information out of engineers, finally said,

"So the whole 'Internet' connection was that this guy up

there emailed you an attachment, and you hunted around? Is that it, or have I missed something?"

Matt said, "That's pretty much it, Sarah."

"And the 'high-tech tools' you used to crack the case were: you sorted some records in Excel?"

Dan said to Matt, "Can't put anything past *her*, can we?"

Dan left to call Len, whose phone was busy for most of the morning. Finally he sent him an email asking him to call.

Then Janet called, and she was in a panic. Her dad was suddenly a celebrity, and everyone at work was asking her about it.

"Oh, God, Dan, why did you get him into this?"

"Why did *I* get him into it?" he objected. "Your dad got *himself* into it. He was already hip-deep when I got in."

"Yeah, I know, Dan, I'm sorry. I just feel so bad with him up there and reporters calling him non-stop. I bet they're camped outside his door by now."

Dan sympathized. He hadn't been able to talk to Len either so he didn't know what was going on up there. They hung up. Matt came by, and he was excited.

"Hey, Dan, do you see the opportunity here?"

"No, Matt. Opportunity for what?"

"You and Len are now celebrities in the brand new field of Internet crime busting! You can fucking *own* it."

Dan laughed out loud. "Internet crime busting. By emailing attachments around?"

"Hey, read the press. They make it look like you're Sherlock Holmes and Watson for the network age."

Dan just shook his head. "Actually, I was thinking more Batman and Robin."

"These imbecile reporters," he said to himself. *"If the facts don't fit the legend, print the legend."*

While he was thinking about reporters, his phone rang, and it was someone from Press Relations at Oracle. She warned him not to talk to reporters *at all*, since the story said he had used Oracle resources to track down this case. He didn't try to argue with her; he just got her phone number and said he'd pass it on to any reporters who called him. She also reminded him of the policies on using corporate resources for non-Oracle work.

LEN'S PHONE rang early that morning. This was unusual, since he didn't have many clients anymore.

"Hello, is this Len Saunders?" the voice asked. "This is he" he answered.

"Mr. Saunders, my name is Jennifer Mauger and I'm calling from the Associated Press."

"The Associated Press! Are you sure you have the right number?"

"You're the Len Saunders who was assaulted yesterday for busting up an embezzling ring?"

He laughed. "An 'embezzling ring'? Two older ladies stealing some money to play bingo? That's what you're calling an embezzling ring?"

Jennifer didn't want to argue about his characterization of the story. She pressed on.

"There's a story in a Sacramento newspaper about this incident, Mr. Saunders. Would you care to comment on it?"

Len said he hadn't seen the story, so she read it to him. It seemed to lean heavily on the high-tech connection between him and Dan, Dan's use of the Internet and on his executive daughter, and especially on whether this signaled a new trend in using the Internet to solve crimes. The story explained, for the benefit of readers who'd never heard of it, that "the Internet" was a brand new thing that was starting to break out of the closed academic world it had grown up in.

Len thought back to the conversation with the reporter on Sunday night. He hadn't thought much about it since then, and figured this was going to be a Page 10 story, if it even got printed. He recalled that the reporter did ask him a lot of questions about the Internet, but he told her it was not a big deal. He decided to call her and set her straight again.

Before he could find her number, the phone rang again. It was another reporter, who said he was from UPI. He patiently answered that guy's questions, which seemed to be even more stupid than the previous one's. This guy was also not much interested in Len's downplaying of the incident.

Then it was another reporter, and another. For one call, he had to put the phone down because a reporter and a cameraman were knocking on his door. He politely told them he had no comment for them and closed the door.

This was getting ridiculous. He decided to take the dogs, get out of the house, and go somewhere they couldn't find him.

24

THE TV STAR

Whan Len went into town for lunch and sat at an outside table with the dogs, people in the restaurant all looked out the window at him. Jeez, he should have just made a sandwich and gone out into the woods somewhere. Oh well. No one interrupted his lunch, at least.

When he got home, there were 23 messages on his machine. He ignored them and called Janet.

She was relieved. "My God, your phone was busy all morning! How are you handling it?"

"Well, it's a new experience being famous, honey. I'm not sure what to think about it."

"Yeah, I've had people asking me about you all morning, too. But you probably have it much worse."

Len gathered his thoughts.

"How long is this 'fame' thing going to last, do you think?"

"I have no idea, Dad. You could live with us for a while to get away from it."

"Hmm. I might do that. We'll see."

"Dad, can I ask you something?"

"Shoot."

"What do you really want to *do* in your retirement? We thought fishing was it, but I guess we were wrong."

Len was used to asking *her* questions like that. They never had that conversation about *him*.

"You know, I've been asking myself that a lot lately!"

She laughed. "And...?"

"And, I guess I still want to use my brain for something. And I don't mean crossword puzzles."

"Something that doesn't land you in the ER, I hope!"

"Right. And doesn't feature reporters calling me!"

Janet didn't know what else to say. Len went on,

"You know, honey, I feel so envious of you sometimes. I always had to worry about keeping a roof over our heads and putting you through school. But we did it, and now you kids are doing exactly what you want and keeping up with all the latest technology. I just think I was born too early."

She had tears in her eyes. "Oh, Dad. What would you *want* to do? I'll help you!"

"Thank you, sweetheart." Len had tears in his eyes, too, but then he collected himself.

"Well, I better start returning these phone messages. I don't want to be one of those temperamental celebrities!"

She called Walt, but he was out on a job, so she left a message and tried to go back to work.

Len called back the reporters, and ignored all the hate messages on his machine. Most of them were just like the first reporter, asking if he had any comment and looking for some angle the others hadn't covered yet.

One of them was kind of intriguing, though. It was an invitation from a public television show called *Computers This Week* in the Bay Area to come on and talk about how he and Dan had *really* cracked the case. Dan was invited, too. They were going to devote the whole show to him, so it wasn't going to be just some generic questions and then a commercial break.

He called Janet to ask her about it, since he'd never seen the show. Janet was horrified at first, but then she remembered the conversation about his retirement. *"Well, if this is what he wants to do with his life, I'm going to support him."* So she just told him it was a good show and they'd probably be straight with him. He could stay with her and Walt when he came down to do the show, of course.

A couple hours later Dan called to tell her he was going on TV with her dad! He was so excited. They didn't know yet when it was going to be taped, let alone when it would air.

The show's producers really wanted to talk with Len, but his phone was always busy, so Dan got to be the one to find out what they wanted. It turned out to be the Internet angle, and mainly what this case portended for the future. The producer, Molly, asked him whether there would be new kinds of fraud coming along. Perfect! Molly knew about Dan's involvement in the Internet Engineering Task Force, and he told her all about that.

She didn't really know much about the case except what was in the press, so Dan filled her in. He sensed that when he got to the "bingo" and "elderly" parts, she started losing interest, and when he told her what he'd actually done to find the perps, she was *really* tuning out. He had to think fast: this was Len's big chance! If they played this right, he'd have himself a prime job in Silicon Valley, which Dan sensed was what he really wanted, even if he didn't know it himself yet.

Molly said, "Thank you so much, Dan. Is there anything more you want to tell me about this?"

Dan had one of those moments of inspiration he could tell his grandchildren about (if he just had some kids first):

"Well, just that Len has a long background in ferreting out embezzlement, but he was used to doing it with pencil and paper in his accounting days. He put some guys in prison a long time ago."

This intrigued Molly a little.

"Can you tell me about that, if you know any more?"

"Well, I don't know too much about it, but on this one, he figured out how to use the computer and the Internet to find the guilty parties. I never would have thought of that."

"OK, but how much did the Internet really do for you?.."

"I was able to confirm the identity of that guy who attacked us. That would have been pretty hard without the Internet."

Quickly pivoting, Dan added,

"Len's also been spending a lot of time on Usenet investing groups, talking about how to make money in the coming Internet boom. He has some theories that are pretty unconventional."

Dan wasn't too sure what ideas Len had, but he'd get plenty of time to think of some before the show.

"Really? I'll have to ask him about those, if I ever manage to talk to him."

Just for good measure, he threw in one more.

"I've had a couple talks with a guy who's planning to do pornography on the Internet. Pretty wild. He came to the Internet Engineering Task Force meeting back in 1991, even!"

"*Pornography on the Internet! What TV producer can resist that?*" Dan congratulated himself for that one, and as a bonus, it was even true!

Dan realized that he and Cassie had, let's say, *skirted* a few laws in getting information, and he told them they couldn't talk about that. Also, any talk about his work at Oracle was out of bounds. Amazingly, Molly was fine with all that.

When they hung up, Dan called Janet and told her all about it.

∾

Janet told Walt about Len and Dan going on TV. He laughed.

"My father-in-law is going to be a TV star! When is it on? We'll set the VCR."

She didn't know. She told him what Dan had done to sell Len as an Internet expert and an embezzlement specialist.

"Your dad did all that stuff in his youth? You never told me this!"

"Probably because it was a long, long time ago. Now I'm worried they'll ask him a question about it and he'll just plead forgetfulness."

"We better tell him to do his homework, then!"

She thought she'd better talk to Len before the producers got to him, so she called. He grumbled, but she reminded him of what he'd said about still wanting to use his mind. This was his big chance!

After he and Janet hung up, Len thought about it the rest of the week. This living up in the mountains was getting a little old. It seemed like half the people here had worked in Silicon Valley and then retired to the mountains. No one ever went in the other direction! They came here to get *away* from the rat race.

But hey, Janet had done something nobody expected, either — she crashed through the glass ceiling in the other direction! People just assumed that once you got on the management track, you stayed on it until retirement. Not Janet. Maybe she was showing him how to listen to yourself and not to everyone else.

This whole "embezzling" thing: he didn't need to take that on. He could have just put off the Reverend and told him that when he got a concrete idea how much money was missing, Len would look into it. After all, why should he take on some ill-defined task like this? *"I just feel like the money's going out too fast!"* the Rev had said. Why didn't Len just smile and move on? Dan wouldn't have a bandage on his forehead that way.

It was fun, though. It was like *being* a detective instead of watching them on TV. He was actually helping someone in a way that no one else could have done. And having Dan to help him do it — that part was terrific! The two of them weren't just going fishing and hanging out; they were accomplishing something together.

He hadn't thought for a long time about his months in New York trying to find out what happened to his brother. Len just smiled, thinking of himself as a 17-year-old alone in a big city. How did he sleep? How did he eat? He could barely remember any of it anymore. There were some very kind strangers who took him in and fed him, but often they'd try to send him back to Detroit and he'd have to move again.

He sold newspapers some of the time. Besides that, he had no trouble finding employment, with the war on and all the men off fighting. Usually all he had to do was show up and be willing to get his hands dirty, and they'd hire him and pay him in cash. He was used to working after school anyway, so anyone could tell he was reliable. All that time, though, his real goal was to figure out where Jack had gone. He used to tell everyone he met about his brother, and a few people thought Jack might have enlisted in the British or Canadian armed forces. Chasing those ideas down took up weeks and led nowhere.

Finally, he thought about why Jack had left home: he was obsessed with the battle of Stalingrad destroying the factory he'd spent so much time building. Maybe he remembered all the Russian people he'd known there, and thought about how much they were suffering. What he imagined he could *do* about it, Len had no idea, but anyway: how would he try to get to Russia? There was a war on. You couldn't just buy a ticket on an ocean liner!

In a bar he met a guy named Bart who worked in the Merchant Marine, and Bart had been on a ship carrying trucks to Murmansk. Len had never heard of the Merchant Marine, and didn't even know where Murmansk was, but Bart told him all about the U-boats in the North Atlantic, and how a couple ships in his convoy had been sunk. Suddenly Len realized that *must* be what Jack did. He started going down to the Merchant Marine office, and finally he found out the real story. When he got home and told his parents how Jack had died, they kept insisting that he shouldn't have gone off to New York on a wild goose chase like that and left them in the dark. But he just kept telling them it wasn't a *chase*; he caught the goose! He knew his Dad was secretly proud of him although he'd never admit it.

Fortunately for his parents, his war job was Stateside, so he wasn't being shot at. He didn't tell them about the shady jeep parts manufacturer who was inflating his costs and hinted that Len would be a lot *safer* if he just accepted the occasional $20 bill to look the other way.

After he got out of college and started doing those fraud audits, he had some of that same feeling of having a mission, not just doing a job. People think accountants are dull, but Len always used to tell Janet, "*The bad guys always slip up and leave some trace somewhere, unless they're Mafia or something. When you find that trace and know you've got 'em, that's the best feeling in the world.*" He would have been thrilled if that made *her* want to be an accountant, but oh, well. She was doing pretty well as she was.

All those years at Chrysler, he put that stuff out of his mind as something kids fantasized about. He'd never thought about it much until now, when he'd actually caught a criminal. "*Even if it was just a couple of old ladies!*" he chuckled.

He and Dan did use a computer and (sort of) the Internet to solve the crime. Len *was* on the Internet himself, which made him unique for someone his age. Most people in their

60's didn't even know how to use a computer. But that might not be enough for the TV show. How about the future? What did he expect the investment landscape to be like once the Internet took off? And how was the Internet going to change the world of crime and law enforcement?

Len had to laugh: who was *he* to parade around as The Expert on this stuff? He was just a retired financial analyst who happened to piss off some old people and get in the news. He called Dan to chat about all this.

Dan was encouraging. He said it didn't matter if they *deserved* to be on TV getting interviewed as "experts." The TV show didn't care. They gave Len and Dan this opportunity, so what did Len want to do with it?

Len had a hard time accepting this. It seemed so cynical. "*Why me?*" kept going through his head.

He and his investing buddies on AOL and Usenet *had*, in fact, been musing about the coming boom in the Internet and how to play it. He decided to really get serious about this now. Maybe he wouldn't get a chance to say it on TV, but it wouldn't hurt to be ready.

25

THERE'S REALITY, AND THEN THERE'S TV

L en racked his brain: what should he say on *Computers This Week* that would make someone hire him? He was doing OK with his little "mutual fund" and bookkeeping work, not to mention the pension and Social Security, but it wasn't Silicon Valley-scale money.

Preferably, someone with big bucks would hire him! He'd heard all about "vulture capitalists" from Janet and her friends, and those people *had* to have a lot of money to throw around. So did mutual funds and other investment services. But why would they want *him*?

"*Probably to keep from getting ripped off!*" he thought. But those guys all thought they already knew how to read a business plan, so they didn't need his help for that. He did have a background in corporate finance, so that had to be worth something. His fund was doing great, but it was private and he couldn't advertise it legally. His angle had to be the Internet!

He watched *Computers This Week* to get some idea what it was about. It opened with the host, Jerry Althouse, in front of a room full of computers, lights flashing and electronic music playing. Jerry introduced this week's topic and his guests, with some kind of cute video. He was very good at asking the basic questions the audience would want an answer to. So what would he ask him and Dan? But more to the point: what did *they* want to get asked? If Jerry asked him the wrong question, Len and Dan would have to just ignore it and answer the one they wanted, like politicians do. The question Len really wanted was, *"Why should a mutual fund specializing in Internet stocks hire you?"* But they'd probably ask *"how will law enforcement use computers and the Internet to solve crimes?"* He had to figure out how to segue from that into the question he wanted.

Janet was really into this Mosaic thing. He tried it when he was at her house, and he had to admit, it was impressive. *Computers This Week* had already done a show about that, though. They'd done several shows on the Internet already.

The taping was next Tuesday, so he made arrangements to stay with Janet and Walt the night before.

～

CASSIE AND EVERYONE at Palm had had a low-level depression since the failure of the Zoomer. But then in May, everything changed! They were going to build the hardware themselves, not depend on a half-hearted effort from some gadget company. Good grief, they were really going for broke here.

They all felt like they were at the top of the roller coaster and heading down to the *really* big thrills. Jeff Hawkins had made a balsa wood model of the Touchdown (as they were calling it), with a whittled-down chopstick serving as a "stylus" and he carried it everywhere. He could keep it in his shirt pocket, which you certainly couldn't do with the Apple Newton. They looked at this hunk of wood as if it were real, and thought, *"OK, this probably IS what the world really wants in a handheld."*

She felt a thrill like she'd never had at work, like she was part of the moon mission team or something. Even when her job didn't require her to be at design meetings, she found she *wanted* to be, and once in a while she had some ideas to contribute.

Product meetings at 3Com had usually been numbingly boring endurance fests where the product manager came in with a list of features that he'd copied out of the technical press, and they were ranked from 1 to 4, where 1 was "gotta have", 2 was "should have", 3 was "could do without" and 4 was "don't need." People would argue interminably about the ratings, always trying to *raise* the priority of their favorite feature. Then the Engineering group would try to design the product, they'd leave out some features as not feasible, and everyone would argue about *that*. "Release 2.0" would be the usual resolution, meaning, "maybe we'll do that someday." Just saying "No" was generally seen as hurting people's feelings and not being a team player. If a manager said No to your feature, you'd appeal to higher authority and try to gather allies. It was depressing.

Every startup trying to make a handheld up to then had succumbed to what engineers called "feature-itis." Someone insists on a feature, so it's in. It has to have wireless communication? OK, that's in. It has to have an email program? OK, that's in. It has to recognize cursive handwriting? That one, in particular, seemed to be the death of Momenta, Newton, and GO. She thought back to what Matt had said about GO and their friend Mike about Momenta: they just assumed no one would use the product unless it recognized their handwriting, but then they couldn't get that to work.

For the Touchdown, it felt so exhilarating to discard all that crap. It had to sell for $299, it had to fit in your shirt pocket, it had to be fast, it had to have decent battery life, and *that was it*! If someone walked in with a pet feature idea, Jeff would apply those tests, and usually he'd shoot down that feature. Jeff was the person that the other startups all lacked: a person who could say No and make it stick. Everyone got good at killing features after a while, but Jeff's insistence on his guidelines did get a little wearisome.

It was industry wisdom that users wouldn't learn a new system of gestures if they couldn't type. "You *have* to recognize their handwriting!" the conventional wisdom said. But no, the Touchdown was going to use Grafiti, a system of simple one-stroke gestures. The "manual" fit on a little sticker on the back of the device. Would users accept that? No one was sure.

Lastly, industry wisdom had been that you had to have wireless communication. The Touchdown wasn't going to have that, either! It would just have a little cradle you could attach to your PC, so you could synchronize your data.

They were discarding *all* the industry gospel! Palm was really shooting the moon.

Cassie thought about the child adoption idea all the time. Realistically, she couldn't be a part of this effort with a young child at home. To her mom, it was no contest — of course family came first! She wondered, *"What will I think when the kid is successfully raised and in college? Will I wish I'd stayed at Palm, if it's a runaway success?"*

She knew the Hollywood answer: "children are the greatest gift." But if there's no biological clock ticking, i.e. she wasn't going to get pregnant, then she could wait. This was way fun. And maybe she'd make some money and have an easier time with a kid.

LEN DIDN'T WANT to rehearse for the TV interview. He thought it would just make him nervous, and who knew what questions they'd ask, anyway? Janet and Walt didn't know how to broach the topic, so they just avoided it. He went to Dan's house and they drove up to San Mateo together. On the way, Dan told him what the producers had told him: they were, indeed, going to ask about law enforcement and the Internet.

Great minds think alike. They both realized that they could just say, "we can't talk about an ongoing criminal case" and switch to related topics. Dan said he'd already told them that, more or less, so he was ready with that diversion.

Jerry had an assistant, Molly, who met them and took them to Makeup, which they both got a kick out of. The makeup artist explained that she was just applying a little bit of foundation so their faces wouldn't be shiny under the lights. Then Jerry came in and shook hands with them, and said that he didn't like to spend too much time with his guests beforehand, since it ruined the spontaneity. He also told them that they didn't usually do retakes, unless something really bad happened, like spilling a drink or dropping something. Gulp! One take and that's it. Here we go.

Molly led them into the "studio" which they recognized from TV. Naturally, it was mostly facade, and there were lights and other studio equipment behind the computers. Molly explained that in the actual show there would be introductions, commercials (except they didn't call them 'commercials'), and other stuff, but for the taping they were going to skip right to the interview part. Dan got his computer ready, and Len got *his* ready with the investing software he used. They signaled "ready" to Molly, Jerry stood across the table from them, and they were rolling.

Jerry led off with, "I have with me Len Saunders and Dan Markunas, who were in the news lately for an altercation with an embezzler that they caught, using computers and the Internet. Do you want to tell us what you can about that, either of you?"

Len said, "That's right, Jerry. I live up in the Sierras and Dan here is my daughter Janet's friend from way back."

"I'm going to interrupt you here for a second, Len. Janet is an engineer working on the Internet at 3Com, isn't that right?"

"That's right, Jerry, sorry. Janet and her husband Walt own

this cabin in the mountains and they let me retire there. But she wasn't involved in this case at all."

"OK, sorry, continue."

"Anyhow, I've been doing some bookkeeping work up there, as well as running my 'mutual fund'" he made the air-quotes around those words, "and a charity asked me to look into some funds that they thought might be getting stolen."

"So you got on your computer and figured it all out via the Internet?" Jerry prompted with a smile.

"If only it were that easy! Maybe someday it will be, as Dan's going to show you. Anyhow, it was a lot of hard work, and since it's an ongoing criminal case, we can't give too many real details about it."

"Understood," said Jerry. "Dan?"

"Hi, I'm Dan Markunas, and I work at Oracle now. I've been leading a group in the Internet Engineering Task Force on a new Internet standard for databases. Len's daughter Janet and I worked together on the Xerox Star and then again at 3Com."

"So you and networking go way back, is that what you're saying?"

Dan just smiled and nodded. Jerry continued, "We'd love to hear more about this new standard, but maybe another show. For now, what can you tell us about your embezzling case, if that's the right term?"

Dan said, "Well, as Len said, we can't step on the prosecution's case here. But anyhow, Len didn't have anything to go on at all! The head of the charity didn't even know how much money was missing, or when it disappeared!"

"Wow, so what did you do, Len?"

"Well, Jerry, way back at the beginning of my career, I used to work for Arthur Anderson and do what they called 'fraud audits,' or auditing a company where fraud was suspected."

"I'll bet it was a lot different back then, huh?"

Len smiled. "The work is on computers instead of pencil and paper now, but it's not all that much easier. It's still a hard slog. The bad guys like to pay money to fake companies that they control, so first you have to be sure all the invoices are legit."

"That sounds hard."

"Yeah, that part isn't really any different. It turns out the Reverend…"

Jerry interrupted, "That's the guy who runs the charity?"

"Right, sorry. Reverend Collins does a lot of his work in cash. If someone's really down on his luck, he might slip him a twenty or two. That made it much harder."

"Now I'm getting intrigued!" said Jerry. "So what did you do, and where does the Internet come in?"

Dan said, "Len got a list of all their bank account's cash withdrawals and bank transfers, and emailed them to me!"

"OK, you used Internet email. Len, you're on the Internet? That's pretty impressive all by itself!"

Len ignored the assumption that old people can't use the Internet. "Oh, I've been active online for several years now."

Dan continued, "I massaged the data in some ways I probably shouldn't talk about, and I found, let's say, some suspicious activity!"

Jerry laughed. "I guess we'll have to wait for the trial to find out what those were!"

Len said, "If there *is* a trial. I don't think the DA wants to put Mr. Redding in jail!"

Dan went on, "We got the bank to help us find out who was using their account."

Jerry said, "I'm going to interrupt you here for a break. When we come back, we'll find out the exciting conclusion!" He signaled "out" to Molly. Then he said to Len and Dan,

"This is going great! How do you feel about it?"

Molly signaled "ready." Jerry said, "We're back. Len, I

understand you run a mutual fund! Are you using the Internet to manage it?"

"I sure am, Jerry. See here on the screen is the 'MetaStock' program, which is one of the things I use. You can see here I can analyze the performance of Dell Computers, using data that I downloaded from the Net."

The camera zoomed in on the screen, and Jerry and Len went over the various aspects of MetaStock. Jerry said,

"We're looking at Dell here, which doesn't seem to be in the network sector. Does your fund have anything to do with the Internet?"

"It sure does. It's a private placement fund, just for sophisticated investors, that specializes in technology stocks. We think there are already ways to play the Internet, even though so far there aren't any stocks that are *pure* plays, as we like to call them."

He turned to Dan.

Dan said, "What we're looking at here is Mosaic, which I think you've featured on this show before. In one window here I have an interface to a database of Internet email addresses, and ways to search it. This isn't exactly what I did, but Mosaic is easy enough to use that you can imagine a person who doesn't know much about computers using it to follow a criminal's tracks!"

"So there will be no place to hide on the Internet!"

Dan laughed. "That's right, Jerry. Anyone can find you!"

"We've had Mosaic on the show before. Do you think this is going to revolutionize the Internet, like some people are predicting?"

Len said, "Absolutely, Jerry. Dan and my daughter Janet worked on the first graphical user interface, fifteen years ago, and I think this is going to be bigger than that!"

"And you have a mutual fund! How did that come about"

"Well, I'm pretty active in the online investing forums, and a few people trusted me to invest their money for them."

"And you said you were already investing in the Internet? How is that even possible?"

"We're looking for companies that are going to benefit from the Internet, rather than being put out of business by it. Also, being private, we can buy some things that the general public can't."

"Wow. This isn't 'Wall Street Week' so I won't ask you to name them! But I guess you've found a few?"

"More than a few!"

Jerry turned to Dan.

"And you've met a few people who want to put pornography on the Internet, I understand! I guess there's no avoiding it, is there?"

Dan and Len both laughed. Dan said, "They're working on it. I think they might actually be the first people to make money off the Internet!"

Molly signaled Jerry again.

"That's about all we have time for this week. I want to thank Len Saunders and Dan Markunas for some fascinating thoughts on investing in the Web!"

Molly came out. "That was great, guys! I'll let you know when the show is going to air." They shook hands with Molly and Jerry.

In the car back to Dan's house, they were in a daze. It all went by so fast.

Len said, "You did great, skipping over all the sneaky things you did!"

"What do you mean, the things *I* did? You're the one who thought of it all!"

Len put his finger to his lips, in the "ssshh!" gesture.

"Anyhow, I got to plug my mutual fund! We'll see if that turns up anything."

"Your mutual fund! We got Peter Lynch here."

He dropped off Dan and went to Janet and Walt's house.

Len was watching the nightly TV news when Janet got home.

"So how did it go? The big TV star!"

"Pretty good. They didn't ask about any of the sneaky things we did, and I got to plug my mutual fund."

"Your 'mutual fund'! Is that what you're calling it?"

"Hey. I have two million dollars under management now!"

"And those dangerous bingo players hitting you with their canes?"

"Somehow they didn't mention that, either. Let that be a lesson to you next time you see something on TV that you *don't* have personal knowledge of."

26

THE WATCH PARTY

L en drove back home the day after the taping. They said it would air in three weeks, so he had a long time to wait before there were any public reactions. His life settled back to normal up in the mountains: the local people still hated him. He kept busy watching his investments.

One Tuesday afternoon three weeks later, Janet's phone at work rang. That voice sounded so familiar! It was her old friend Grant Avery. The last time she'd seen him, he was living in Japan, married, and expecting his first kid, and she wasn't even *dating* Walt yet, let alone married to him.

Then, he was still at Xerox, and in California on business. But now, he was back living here, and he was divorced! He also had a new job.

"My God, you do have a lot of news!" she said.

"Yeah, you're married and I'm not. At least you haven't changed jobs, right?"

"Yes and no. I'm not managing anymore. I'm back to slinging code now."

"Good grief, how did that happen?" he said.

"Long story. I got tired of being the punching bag for everyone, for one thing."

"I can sympathize with that."

Then she had a thought.

"Hey, we're having a little watch party at my house on Thursday night. My father and Dan Markunas (you remember him?) were on *Computers This Week*, and we're going to watch it together. Why don't you come over?"

Grant agreed immediately and got directions to their house. He was back in Silicon Valley and divorced, so he needed to get back in circulation.

Janet's *father* was on television on a computer show? How the hell did that happen? He'd never even met the guy. Dan, he remembered vaguely from the Xerox Star days. She said she'd tell him all about it on Thursday.

Back in the day, he'd entertained fantasies of marrying her, but she didn't have much interest in him that way, and they became just friends. In 1981 he took an assignment with Fuji Xerox in Tokyo, and since he knew all about Xerox's new generation of laser printers, he filled a big need for them. Then he married Jun, who had gone to college in America, and her English was excellent.

They had two kids, she quit her job even though she didn't particularly want to, and he settled into the life of a *sararīman*, a salaried worker who takes the train to the office, goes out drinking with his co-workers after work, and generally devotes his entire career to one company. Jun's parents were as welcoming to him as he could possibly wish for, and they *loved* being grandparents.

In the 80's, life in Tokyo was frantic. The stock market was booming, property prices were skyrocketing, and it seemed like it would never end. His Japanese was getting better and better, or at least he *thought* it was. People always seemed surprised when he started speaking Japanese, and it seemed like he had to repeat himself no matter how clearly he spoke. He always wondered if it was him, or if they just couldn't handle a white guy speaking their language.

The bursting of the bubble at the beginning of 1992 was a big shock to everyone. The Nikkei stock market index had been in the tank for a year or more, but when the prices of land started plummeting too, it hurt. They'd gotten used to checking the value of their house and marveling at how rich they were getting, and now the wealth was evaporating.

It took him a long time to realize that he didn't really feel *at home* there, the way he eventually would in the States when he moved somewhere. He didn't grow up in Japan, didn't have family except for Jun's, and would never be Japanese no matter how well he spoke the language.

He's always assumed, even though they never talked about it, that Jun would be happy to move back to America some day. After all, she'd lived there for many years and always spoke happily about it. A few years in Japan, a few years in the US, maybe some in Europe — they could be a global family! But whenever he brought it up, she seemed to change the subject, and she'd speak of moving as a distant possibility. He might be a global citizen, but she was Japanese.

Finally one day in early 1993, the subject of divorce came up. He was never sure afterwards if *she* was the first to say the word or if she'd artfully gotten him to say it, but there it was. On his next business trip to California, he spoke to a few people at Xerox and arranged a transfer back to the States. He told them Jun would not be coming. There was no question of his getting custody of the kids; he knew that was never going to happen. Their grandparents were there, the kids could barely speak English, and they could come and visit with him sometimes. That was the hardest part. Coming back to America was the easy part.

After six months back in Silicon Valley with Xerox, he got the feeling that that story was coming to an end, too. Xerox had moved all of the Workstation people up to Sunnyvale and seemed to be ready to throw in the sponge on the whole experiment. He worked on printers now, not on workstations, but still, it was depressing. Back in the 70's, he thought Xerox was going to rule the world with their brand-new graphical user interface, the mouse, the laser printer, and the Ethernet. The copier people back in Rochester and Stamford never seemed to quite get it, and he had the particular job of explaining it all to those people. Still, he thought maybe they'd come around eventually. The lure of all that money — that would have to work its magic, wouldn't it? It didn't.

He thought, "*OK, new home, new country, new marital status, why not a new job as well?*" He knew that Apple and IBM had a joint venture to develop a new operating system, or something. Now it was called Taligent.

For years, Grant had been following the confused saga of "Apple after Jobs left" and "IBM after Microsoft split off from them," or *trying* to follow it in the trade press. In a way, it reminded him of his early years in Xerox, where he was constantly trying to mediate between the forward-thinking California technical people and the conservative East Coast people. He thought this must be similar, and maybe he could do a better job of it now.

Some of the Xerox people he knew had formed Metaphor Computer Systems, which got acquired by IBM in 1991, so he was able to use those contacts with IBM. He had some serious credibility as a high-level manager now, so the IBM guys thought he was just the person for that project! He'd have good relations with Apple, they hoped. He said goodbye to Xerox.

Taligent had some serious big-company politics every day. He loved it. He felt like he was making a difference.

He got to Janet's house a half hour before the show was coming on. It wasn't impressive by Dallas standards, but for Northern California it was pretty nice. For Tokyo it was unattainable.

Janet greeted him at the door with a hug. Len and Walt

were standing there, too. The dogs were excited. He handed her a bottle of sake as his gift.

"Grant! Welcome to our house. You haven't changed a bit! Let me introduce my husband, Walt and my dad, Len. And the dogs: Bernie, Mickey, and Gretchen."

They all shook hands and Walt offered to get him a drink. No one else had arrived yet, and they sat down in the living room.

Grant said, "Very nice house here, Walt and Janet! It's at least double the size of the one I had in Tokyo."

Janet said, "Oh, thanks, I give Walt the credit for that. He built at least half of it. Anyway, tell us about you! You moved back to the States. So are you back here to stay?"

"Yeah, it looks that way. I got divorced, as I told you on the phone, and I finally realized you can't *become* Japanese the way you can become American."

"Well, our life is pretty boring here, compared to yours. I'm writing code, Walt is building houses. Same old, same old."

"Sounds pretty good to me. Len, we haven't met before! I'm dying to hear about why you were on TV! Was it about that street fight up in the Sierras?"

Len laughed, took a deep breath, and was about to start, but just then, Dan arrived. He and Grant remembered each other from Xerox days, so they exchanged pleasantries. He said,

"I guess you came to see Len and me on TV! My fifteen minutes of fame, or I guess actually, thirty. Don't believe everything you hear on TV."

Grant said, "Now I'm *really* eager to hear about this. When did *Computers This Week* turn into Jerry Springer?"

They all laughed. Matt and Cassie arrived together. Janet and Dan exchanged quick glances.

Cassie said, "So, guys! You're famous. Can we still talk to you?"

Len said, "Our PR agent will get in touch with you."

Everyone there knew most of the story except for Grant. They filled him in on the details.

Walt said, "Don't forget to tell him about your hero dog, Gretchen, who almost tore the guy's arm off!"

At the mention of her name and everyone suddenly looking at her, Gretchen struggled to her feet and wagged her tail. Len patted her on the shoulder.

"Oh, you're exaggerating, isn't he, Gretchen? You just wanted to hold his sleeve until the police arrived!"

Dan said, "That's right. And Mickey was helping out, too!"

Now it was Mickey's turn for attention. Bernie felt left out.

The show came on, and they went silent.

It started with Jerry Althouse standing in front of the Wall Street bull. He said,

"You've heard of the Internet, but did you realize it can help you invest in the stock market? We have *two* guests today, one to tell us how he tracks investments on his PC, and another who's actually running an investment fund for the Internet! Today, on *Computers This Week*!"

Dan said, "Uh-oh. They didn't tell us about the other guy."

Then there was a brief commercial: "This program comes to you through the generosity of Intel Corporation" with a picture featuring the 'Intel inside' sticker," and then another Public Television sponsor video. Finally the camera showed some guy Rick van Beek whom they didn't know, with some investment software on the screen. Jerry and Rick went over what the software did, and how Rick was able to compare thousands of investments in a few seconds, something that would have been impossible before computers. They took a break for another sponsor video.

Grant said, "Well, so far I'm impressed with you two! They sure can work magic with makeup these days."

Len said, "Yeah, don't know what to tell you. They didn't say they were doing this."

The show returned. Len and Dan sitting at a table with computers in front of them, and Jerry holding the mic.

Everyone applauded and hooted. Janet said, "Who's that handsome man there?"

Len said, "Oh, that's Dan Markunas."

Jerry said, ""I have with me Len Saunders and Dan Markunas, who were in the news lately for an altercation with an embezzler that they caught, using computers and the Internet. We can't talk about that too much here, but Len, I understand you run a mutual fund! Are you using the Internet to manage it?"

In the living room, Len looked at Dan. "Is that what he said at the taping?"

Dan said, "Sort of. I *think*."

On the TV, Len said, "That's right, Jerry. I live up in the Sierras and Dan here is my daughter Janet's friend from way back."

"I'm going to interrupt you here for a second, Len. Janet is an engineer working on the Internet at 3Com, isn't that right?"

"That's right, Jerry, sorry. Janet and her husband Walt own this cabin in the mountains and they let me retire there."

In the living room, Janet said, "Woo-hoo!"

On TV, Len said, "Here on the screen is the 'MetaStock' program, which is one of the things I use. You can see here I can analyze the performance of Dell Computers, using data that I downloaded from the Net."

The camera zoomed in on the screen, and Jerry said, "Our previous guest Rick van Beek showed us some investing software, but it actually helps you run your fund?"

"It sure does."

He turned to Dan. "And you used the Internet in that embezzling case you were involved with?"

Dan said, "What we're looking at here is Mosaic, which I think you've featured on this show before. In one window here I have an interface to a database of Internet email addresses, and ways to search it. This isn't exactly what I did, but Mosaic is easy enough to use that you can imagine a person who doesn't know much about computers using it to follow a criminal's tracks!"

"So there will be no place to hide on the Internet!"

Dan laughed. "That's right, Jerry. Anyone can find you!"

"We've had Mosaic on the show before. Do you think this is going to revolutionize the Internet, like some people are predicting?"

Len said, "Absolutely, Jerry. Dan and my daughter Janet worked on the first graphical user interface, fifteen years ago, and I think this is going to be bigger than that!"

"And you have a mutual fund! How did that come about"

"Well, I'm pretty active in the online investing forums, and a few people trusted me to invest their money for them."

"And you said you were already investing in the Internet? How is that even possible?"

"We're looking for companies that are going to benefit from the Internet, rather than being put out of business by it. Also, being private, we can buy some things that the general public can't."

"Wow. This isn't 'Wall Street Week' so I won't ask you to name them! But I guess you've found a few?"

"More than a few!"

Jerry turned to Dan.

"And you've met a few people who want to put pornography on the Internet, I understand! I guess there's no avoiding it, is there?"

Dan and Len both laughed. Dan said, "They're working on it. I think they might actually be the first people to make money off the Internet!"

Molly signaled Jerry again.

"That's about all we have time for this week. I want to thank Len Saunders and Dan Markunas for some fascinating thoughts on investing in the Web!"

Then he talked about the next show, and there was an announcement about *Computers This Week* and which corporations brought it to you. Walt turned the TV off.

Grant said, "So, Dan, you're going to be the Porno King of the Internet?"

Dan said, "Not me, but I can put you in touch with the guy who is, if you want!"

Len said, "Wow, I had no idea they were going to change it all around like that! I thought the show was just about us."

Janet said, "Yeah, they barely mentioned the bingo ladies!"

Dan laughed, "And they made me look like Len's tech assistant!"

Len said, "And you were a darned good one, too!" Everyone laughed.

Grant said, "Well, I'm glad I got to hear the real story from *you* all first. We sure didn't hear it on TV!"

Walt said, "Yeah, two bingo ladies doesn't make for good TV, I guess."

Everyone took one of the little glasses Grant had put on the coffee table, and he poured them all some sake. He explained how this was a rare brand of sake and he'd brought it over from Japan himself. They all murmured appreciation even though no one knew much about sake.

Grant said, "So, Len, you're investing in the Internet? How is that even possible?"

Janet took his arm. "He's smart, my Dad!"

Len smiled and said, "Grant, the market anticipates things, so you just have to watch for stocks that are going up more than the public information would explain. Then, you ask yourself, 'If there *were* to be an Internet boom, would these companies benefit?' "

"Hmm," said Grant. "What if it's for some random reason you don't know about?"

"Well, if this were easy, everyone would be doing it!"

"So you don't start from the other end and figure out *who* is going to benefit. "What are some of these pre-boom stocks?"

"We got Louis Rukeyser here!" Len laughed. "Dan works for one of them: Oracle. I've been following them for a couple of years now. I figure, if everyone's going to be starting a website, they'll all need a database."

Then he added quickly, "And, of course, America Online!"

At that, everyone groaned. Walt threw one of their CD-ROMs at him.

"You laugh, but when Joe Average says, 'hey, how do I try out this Internet thing?' AOL is what he's going to try!"

Dan said, "Anyway, on databases: that's what Matt and I hope."

Grant explained what Taligent did, although Dan and Matt were constantly reading about it in the trade press, so they already knew most of it.. Then he said, "But won't there be a lot of companies that don't even exist yet?"

Len smiled. "Yep. I'm depending on you folks to tell me all about those."

"So your fund isn't public, huh?"

"No, it's called a Private Placement. I can only have 50 investors, and they all have to be 'sophisticated investors' which means they're rich and know what they're doing."

Cassie said, "That leaves me out, in a couple of ways!" They all agreed with her.

Grant said, "There are some people here I don't know: Matt, Cassie, what do you do?"

They explained what their connection with Janet was, and how they'd all conspired to bring Janet and Walt together. This was a well-worn tale by now, but everyone loved to relive it. Grant recounted how he suggested it to Janet before any of this happened and she just dismissed the idea. Janet didn't remember that at all. He didn't press the point.

Dan and Matt helped themselves to a little more sake. Janet asked if anyone needed anything from the kitchen.

Grant wasn't quite done picking Len's brain.

"So, Len, are there any companies that you're just *waiting* to spring into existence?"

"Oh, God, I'm not a computer guy. You all should tell *me* that!"

Dan said, "But how about from a business perspective? We're all too deep in the details."

"Well, that Mosaic program Janet showed me sure looks like a good thing. I don't know how you make money off it, though, if it's free."

Matt added, "And Microsoft would drive them out of business anyway, like they did with GO Corp."

Grant looked quizzical at that mention, and Matt said, "I used to work there. They're building a pen-based handheld computer."

Len thought everyone *might*, for a change, be willing to listen to one of his "In the old days" stories.

"When automobiles were just getting big in the 20's and 30's, it was the giant companies who made all the money. It was just too big a market for little players. They either sold out to the big guys or they went out of business."

Walt said, "General Motors, Ford, Chrysler, and then everyone else, right?"

"And American Motors, I guess. Later Packard and Studebaker, but they're gone now."

No one else had ever heard of those last two. Matt and Cassie got up and thanked Janet and Walt for having them over again. Grant said it was nice meeting them all. They exchanged more conversation on where they might be likely to see each other again.

27

VENTURES BIG AND SMALL

G rant had settled into his new job at Taligent. It felt like old times, but whereas at Xerox he dealt with two opposing cultures within *one* company, now he had three different companies to reconcile: IBM, Apple, and HP! Fortunately, the Apple and HP parts of it didn't require him to get on a plane, since they were both in Silicon Valley. For Apple, he could just walk over to their offices in Cupertino, while HP was close by in Santa Clara.

This was going to be the future of computing, he was positive. Microsoft was quaking in their boots, and the proof was all the vaporware they kept announcing to distract from it. It had started as an Apple effort codenamed "Pink" and even though that wasn't the official name anymore, people in Silicon Valley still called it that. After Steve Jobs left Apple and John Sculley took over, they became tabloid fodder as Sculley flailed about aimlessly. He would have denied he was doing that, but then there was the epic failure of the Newton.

The big question was, how would the Macintosh operating system evolve? Naturally, everyone at Apple had a strongly held opinion, and "object-oriented" became the trendy must-have. Pink was an "object-oriented operating system." Object oriented programming, or OOP, was something Grant had been familiar with since his Xerox days, and the Smalltalk language was still around and still venerated by OOP devotees.

But then IBM had joined up, and Apple and IBM had formed several joint ventures, including Taligent. Could *anyone* imagine Steve Jobs ever forming a joint venture with IBM? The sardonic joke at the time was "What do you get when you cross Apple with IBM?" The answer was "IBM."

In early 1994, Hewlett-Packard joined as well. With all this muscle behind it, how could it fail? Grant thought he was lucky to be a part of this. His phone was constantly ringing, and he was always being invited to give a presentation to someone or other. Since he'd lived in Japan and spoke fluent Japanese, he was automatically their guy whenever some big Japanese company wanted to hear about it, and that was often.

It was bittersweet to be back in Tokyo again so often, but at least he got to see his kids. Jun was very good about that. They still loved him and always asked if he was going to move back there again someday. It broke his heart, and sometimes he thought it might be better if they just forgot about him. Jun might get remarried and then they'd have a new stepfather who loved them, he hoped. He didn't want to promise them that they could come visit him in California without asking Jun first, and she was always non-committal about that. He figured when they grew up, they wouldn't need her permission.

One day in late 1994 he was planning to visit HP in Santa Clara on Kifer Road, and he realized that Janet worked just down the street, so he called her and they met for lunch. He'd never been to the 3Com cafeteria, and he had some vague hopes that he could recruit her to Taligent, but he didn't push it. They got their food and sat down. He said,

"Very nice cafeteria here, Janet! Better than ours, anyway."

"Thanks, I guess. Anyway, how's Taligent?"

"Giving the exact same PowerPoint preso, over and over. Fielding the same questions, over and over. It's a living."

"I don't know much about Taligent, other than what's in the press. So when are they going to set the world on fire?"

Grant was used to mock-skeptical questions like this from techies. Taligent had become something of a joke among Silicon Valley insiders. Nonetheless, he was being paid to believe in it and make other people believe in it, so he did.

"Well, where shall I start? Have you heard of the Grand Unifying Theory of Systems?" She shook her head.

"The Grand Unifying Theory of Systems, or GUTS, is a way of unifying all the nonsense about Mac and Windows and Unix into one overarching concept. It's built on the Mach kernel, which is a very small, fast operating system that connects directly to the hardware. There's an object-oriented interface to it, so that everything is objects."

She interrupted him. "So what happens to OS/2, and Windows NT, and all those things? We're developing on OS/2 right now, which I thought was the new IBM thing. I'm starting to have my doubts about that."

He was used to that, too.

"Those things are called 'personalities' under the Workplace OS. You can have a Windows personality, a Mac personality, an OS/2 personality, and so on. They all can coexist concurrently."

"Wow, that sounds hard."

Grant always projected an air of confidence when people asked him questions like that. His usual executive audiences tended to nod and take it at face value: "*Oh, they all run concurrently? Very nice!*"

He explained to her that the VP's and CEO's he talked to were always receptive to this talk. If he just dismissed

Windows and Mac as silly obsessions of the propellerheads, without using those exact words, they smiled and nodded. They hated having to care about that geeky stuff.

Janet admitted that she'd had almost no exposure to that world, even when she was in school. Her first job was in the defense industry at TRW, and then it was Xerox, Apple, and 3Com, none of which had anything to do with IBM mainframes. A lot of the customers who talked to her when she was in charge of the 3Com internal network did, actually, work in companies that used them, but even there, these were the people *outside* the IBM shop. The ones *inside* had only contempt for Ethernet.

He went on. These IBM bigots really felt in their hearts that Big Blue was going to handle all that stuff for them, and then they could get on with running their businesses. That's what IBM had done with their mainframes all through the 50's and 60's, and the natural order of things dictated that they would now do it again. Hell, they'd offered z/VSE since 1980, and they'd had the notion of a "hypervisor" since the 60's. They could run "guest operating systems" on their mainframe, so why did this have to be any different? He found that to be an easy sell for the audiences he spoke to.

Techies like Janet were always skeptical, as she was now. She was intimately familiar with how Mac, Windows, and OS/2 worked, and thankfully she was a real engineer so those were not abstractions to her. He could see she was dubious.

"We have the best engineers from Apple, IBM, and HP working on it, so I'm pretty confident they can pull it off!"

She didn't feel like arguing, so she changed the subject.

"Well, anyway, how are you liking being back in the US again, after all those years in Japan? Do you ever find yourself speaking Japanese and then catching yourself?"

He laughed. "Less and less. It's all the new stores around here now: I drive down El Camino and I hardly recognize any of the stores. At least Chef Chu's is still there!"

"Yeah, and the Fish Market! Remember, we had dinner there?"

"I do. I remember I said maybe you liked Walt more than you realized!"

"So you said at the watch party! I still don't remember that."

Grant said, "How's your dad getting along? Did his brush with fame permanently alter his life?"

"Oh, Dad is getting lots of calls from the financial types. He says they mostly just want to pick his brains for free, but he still hopes one of them will turn into something real. I have to admit, this isn't the retirement I pictured for him. I think he really just wants to be Jessica Fletcher and catch bad guys."

Grant was puzzled by that name, and she quickly added, "On Murder, She Wrote."

"So catching old people embezzling to play bingo didn't quite do it for him?"

She laughed. "The sheriff let her off with a warning, and the church forgave her, too, so I think all is neighborly again up there!"

He snickered. "Well, anyway, if you'd just give him some grandkids, then he'd have something more normal to do!"

"Yeah, there's this thing called the biological clock. Maybe you've heard of it?"

"Maybe once. Anyway, what about your other friends? Matt and Cassie, was that their names?"

"They both worked with me at 3Com for a while. I actually promoted Cassie to manager, and then she went and left me to work in Support. Oh well. That's what you're supposed to do: develop your people, right?"

"Very good! And now she's at Palm?"

Janet wondered if Grant wanted to ask Cassie out. She *could* tell him Cassie wanted to adopt a kid, but that probably wasn't her business to say.

"Yeah, she seems to be enjoying it. Everyone's been trying

to make a handheld computer and failing, so maybe Palm's got the answer. Who knows?"

"Are she and Matt an item? I noticed they came in together."

Janet thought her suspicions about Grant were confirmed now. She pleaded ignorance. He could find out for himself.

"I haven't talked to either of them lately. I know Matt was getting a divorce."

Grant didn't really expect her to tell him anything, but no harm in trying. He looked at his watch and said he had a meeting at HP to get to, so she walked him out. As they got to the sidewalk, she remembered something:

"Hey, remember Porter and the Dutch Goose?" He did remember the group of folks from Xerox, of course.

"Now they're meeting at Gordon-Biersch for lunch once a week. You should come!"

"That's a restaurant or something?"

"A brewpub. It's on Emerson in downtown Palo Alto."

Grant figured it couldn't hurt to reestablish some of his old contacts, so he agreed, and she said she'd email him.

MATT'S DIVORCE from Miriam finally became official. He was hoping this would change Cassie's attitude towards him. She'd been keeping him pretty arms-length, and he could tell that "I'm separated and I'm getting a divorce!" was a line she'd heard before. Half of those guys would get back together with their wives in the end, she knew.

Miriam was probably going to marry this Patrick jerk now. He couldn't stand the guy, so they deserved each other, he thought. Patrick was working at Microsoft now, which fit for an asshole like him. He wondered if she'd subconsciously identified with Microsoft after they'd basically killed GO

Corp! He didn't know what the guy was doing for the Beast from Redmond, and he hoped he'd never have to find out.

He asked himself if *he* should roll the dice and join a startup, now that Miriam wasn't going to get any of the stock. There were so many guys who *had* been rich, and then they got a divorce and the wife cleaned them out. At least that wasn't going to happen to him. His Oracle stock was going up steadily, so she got something, but any new options he got were all his.

Startups seemed like such a gamble. In the early 80's there were lots of startups going IPO, but lately not that many. And working at Oracle was so comfortable! Larry Ellison was a Great White Shark and you knew he'd find *some* way to make money for you.

He and Dan talked about this all the time. Dan had been scarred by his early 80's startup experience, which was crappy in every possible way. According to him, without all the rules of corporate good manners and with millions of dollars on the table, people turned into utter animals. This was something you don't hear about in those romantic myths of Silicon Valley startups, where everyone's like a family and they're all pulling together. In lots of real families, they all hate each other.

LEN'S BOOKKEEPING business had been slowly picking up again. His TV appearance had smoothed things out with folks up here, in some way he couldn't quite fathom. He hadn't talked about the bingo episode at all, but maybe people now saw him as a Guy On TV whom they should listen to, or something; he wasn't sure what they thought. Everyone asked him for investing advice now, for one thing. Or maybe it was just that he was a neighbor now.

He got calls and emails from various financial types almost

every day. They all seemed to want him to come down to the Valley or San Francisco, and give them some free advice. Or they wanted to place some money under his management. He always told them No, he wasn't legally allowed to have more than 50, and they all had to be "sophisticated investors." The latter was no problem for these folks, but the former was a barrier. He didn't even have to tell them what he really thought: "Besides, I don't know you and I don't want your money."

One Monday morning late in summer 1994, though, he got a call that was a little different from the others. It was from one of venture capital firms on Sand Hill Road in Menlo Park. Right away his interest perked up; "Sand Hill Road " was almost as famous as "Park Avenue" in Manhattan. He was a little curious just to see what it was like. They were pretty vague about what they wanted to talk to him about, but he thought, *"Hey, they're rich guys, it'll probably be good food anyway!"* He agreed to come by on Friday, and then he'd spend the weekend with Janet and Walt.

He got off 280 at Sand Hill and headed east. After all the hype, he was expecting big, impressive looking buildings, but actually, it probably looked about the same as it did 50 years ago. He had an address written down, and he kept looking on the left until he saw a low concrete barrier with a range of addresses on it, and a parking lot behind it, and then some two-story office buildings. *"Auspicious!"* he thought. *"I guess they don't need to flaunt their wealth."* He pulled in and parked.

The receptionist was extremely pleasant. She offered to get him coffee or water while he waited, and he sat down and took it all in. Everything was understated but tasteful. There were Oriental carpets on the hardwood floors, and modern art on the walls. The lighting was all indirect with no overhead fluorescents.

In a few minutes a tall, good-looking man in a blazer and open-collared dress shirt came out to meet him. He introduced himself as Brad and ushered Len back to a conference room, which already had four other guys, Jonathan, Tom, Mark, and Jim sitting at the table, all dressed the same as Brad. Mark had a Golden Retriever by his side, who seemed to know immediately that Len was a dog person and came right over to him.

Len nuzzled her and asked the group, "So did you all hear about the role my dogs played in that embezzlement thing?" No one had. "I'll tell you later."

Brad asked if Len was familiar with what their firm did, and he said he thought so.

"You know I used to be at Chrysler. We never had any contact with this stuff! It was like another world for us when Apple IPO'ed."

"Yeah, that's how we feel about Detroit. I'm sure we'd all love to hear all the nuts and bolts, if that's the right term."

Jonathan said, "*Literally* 'nuts and bolts' I guess!" Everyone chuckled.

Len said, "I used to be able to tell you exactly how many nuts and bolts went into a Chrysler LeBaron and what they cost us. But I'm afraid my memory isn't what it used to be."

Brad said, "None of ours are, either. But you're probably wondering why we brought you here!"

Len looked expectantly.

"We're getting an increasing number of what we call late-stage financing requests. Everyone thinks of venture capital as the initial investment for a startup, and that *is* most of what we do, but if we're lucky, some of those startups grow up and need more capital. A *lot* more capital."

"OK."

Brad continued, "Even aside from the financing, we sometimes feel like we need to be in closer touch with them than we can be. Eventually, they all need more money, which we call 'mezzanine round', and we get kinda worried that maybe they've gotten away from us."

Len still didn't see where this was going, but Mark jumped in.

"Really, we want you to be our eyes and ears there. Especially, and this doesn't happen very often, but we *have* to be sure they're all on the straight and narrow: marketing isn't spending like drunken sailors, the salesmen aren't padding their numbers, and so on. You know how all that works."

"I see, so you want some adult supervision, or something like that?"

"Exactly. The partners here are being stretched pretty thin, at this firm and actually most of the firms around here. I don't know of anyone else who's tried doing this, and to be honest we don't even know if it'll work. At Kleiner, Perkins they have John Doerr, who takes a very activist role in his companies…"

Len asked for the spelling of that name and wrote it down. Mark continued,

"But we think you might have the skills to help us out here, sort of a force-multiplier for us. None of us here are John Doerr, since he's one of a kind. It helps that your daughter's a tech veteran, too."

Len thought, "*And I don't have any ambitions, plus I'm too old to be a threat to any of you!*" but didn't say it.

Tom added, ""We've been burned once or twice with companies who, let's say, lost track of their mission. It was pretty embarrassing."

"So would I be your employee, or contractor, or what?"

Brad said, "We think we'd like to start it as temporary employment. We'd pay you per job, and then we can see where we go from there."

"OK, I guess it depends on how much time I'd have to do this, and how much access I'd get to their books and their employees. I don't know, right offhand, *how* I would do this. You know, at Arthur Andersen, we were the *auditors* and we could demand to see everything. This wouldn't be like that."

Brad said, "Definitely not! But you showed a lot of inge-nuity with that embezzlement case. We were all impressed!"

Len laughed, "Well, thanks. That *was* pretty fun." He asked, "Do you have a particular job in mind right now?"

"Glad you asked! Why don't we get some lunch, and then you and I can go back to my office?"

Len thought he was going to get to go to some fancy restaurant, but the receptionist brought in sandwiches, potato chips, soft drinks, and cookies. These guys didn't waste time on eating lunch.

While they were eating, he regaled them with the full story of the embezzlement case, including Gretchen the retired police dog violently shaking the guy's sleeve. They all laughed uproariously. Mark turned to his dog Missy and said, "You'd defend me if someone attacked, wouldn't you, Missy?"

Len said, "Well… I also have a Labrador, almost the same dog as Missy. Let's just say they're not fighting dogs."

28

THERE'S SOMETHING HAPPENING HERE

J anet was dying to hear how Dad's day with the VC's went.

"Did they take you to Buck's?"

"Buck's? What's that?"

"Oh, it's a restaurant in Woodside where all the deals get done, supposedly. I guess not."

"No, we just had sandwiches in the conference room. Real down to earth, those guys."

"Yeah, I bet. With their BMW's and their houses in Los Altos Hills."

"Anyhow, now you're not the only one in the family who can't talk about what they're doing at work!"

Walt said, "Whoa, jump back! Really?" She laughed.

"Yes sir, now I'm a card-carrying Vulture Capitalist Assistant!"

"Did they teach you the secret handshake, too?"

"They said after I finish the first job, they *might* show me that. Plus I'll get the decoder ring."

Len told them what he was going to be doing first, although he couldn't say what company it was. He couldn't resist telling them how much they were going to pay him for that, just to see their reaction. It was gratifying. Walt said, "I could almost build a wing on this house for that!"

Janet got nostalgic. He was not the old retired guy whom she had to worry about anymore. Now it was like he was her Dad again, with a real job. He told them he was taking *them* out to dinner, for a change.

Over dinner, Janet felt funny asking *him* about Silicon Valley instead of the other way around, but she went ahead anyway,

"So Dad, did any of your new vulture capitalist friends mention this company that Jim Clark started?"

"Jim Clark? No, I don't think so. Isn't he the guy who started Silicon Graphics?"

"That's him. Supposedly he's hired the guys who built Mosaic, and they're doing something with the Internet. John Doerr from Kleiner, Perkins is behind them."

Len perked up at that name.

"John Doerr? See, that's a name I *do* know!"

Len went on. "Mosaic, huh? You showed me that program. It seemed interesting, but it was free. How can they make a company out of that?"

"I don't know. Maybe you can find out."

Len laughed. "That's a new one: I find out something about Silicon Valley for *you*."

They didn't talk any more business that weekend.

CASSIE WAS LIVING with danger every day at Palm. It felt like they had a construction site on a river in the jungle, and any time now a lion pride might decide to have them for dinner. But for now, they kept on building that tourist resort that might someday make them all rich. Or not.

They had a great idea for a product, which they called the Touchdown, but they were running out of money. In a company that small, it was impossible to keep any secrets, and everyone knew that Jeff and Donna were calling every VC firm and every large company trying to raise more. The problem was that "handhelds" were a tainted product category; every VC firm had either lost money on it already, or if they hadn't, they were thanking their lucky stars.

VC's were a herd: they followed each other's direction. Their public image of being like John Wayne, the lone cowboy on the frontier, was a myth. They were more like the sheep.

"I'm not going to invest until *he* invests!" one would say, and then *that guy* would say,

"Well, I'm not investing unless *he* invests!"

And then the third guy would want to see a big corporate partner put up the marketing and manufacturing money that Palm needed. So Jeff and Donna would go off, hat in hand, to every big company they knew. For these people, there was never just one decision-maker; you'd have to meet with one group of middle managers, and then they'd pass you off to a different group. It was exhausting and dispiriting for Donna. Jeff had to stay relentlessly positive just to keep her in the game. Cassie really appreciated what those two were doing for everyone, more than she ever had with the top managers at 3Com.

Now that Matt's divorce was final, he was calling her more often. She liked him, but somehow, he just didn't do it for her. Although she didn't know what "it" was anymore. Were there *any* guys she could stand being with all the time? It didn't seem that way. Anyhow, Matt had been married for a long time, and he seemed like one of those guys who were just terrified of being single.

Adopting a kid: that prospect was always there in her head. Every time she did *anything* normal, she'd think, "How would this work if I had a child?" There weren't any good answers. Maybe she wanted to do it. Maybe she didn't. She wished she could decide.

GRANT AND JANET went to the weekly lunch at Gordon-Biersch most weeks. The first time, it was strange for Grant — he hadn't seen all these people in fifteen years or so. Most of them seemed to be at one of the DEC research labs that had sprung up in Palo Alto with the demise of PARC.

He remembered Porter Berwick from that time at The Goose. The two had hit it off over cars, working on them *and* driving them fast.

Porter had squinted at him when he arrived.

"Grant Avery! Can it be? We thought you were dead!"

"Close! Living in Japan. But now I'm back."

Everyone from the old Xerox days knew about Fuji Xerox, of course. They were all dying to hear how the Japanese language features of Star had been received over there ('politely,' Grant said). Back in the 70's, being able to type Kanji characters had seemed like a real game changer, and Fuji had sent over five or six of their engineers to help with the effort. It turned out that the Star was so expensive that it never really took off in Japan, either.

However, the laser printers had been a big, big hit, and that was what kept Grant over there for so long. As the American who knew all about these things, and who spoke Japanese besides, he was a big cheese there.

Grant got to hear what they were all doing. Porter wasn't at Oracle anymore, which somehow didn't surprise him. He didn't seem like the Oracle type. Supposedly he was thinking of running for Palo Alto City Council.

Porter said, "So I gather you're not at Mother Xerox anymore?"

"No, now I'm at Taligent. Maybe you've heard of it?"

Charles Green, another Palo Alto guy whom Grant vaguely remembered, said,

"Taligent! Are they still around?"

Grant remembered that this sort of good-natured ribbing was standard up here. No one in Japan would ever be that rude.

"Not only still around, but picking up partners right and left!"

This was too easy a target, so no one said anything overt. The conversation reverted to DEC's processor chips, bike-riding, sushi, what the old Xeroids were doing, and other perennial topics. All of them had been on the Internet for years and knew how to find everything they wanted on it, so they weren't too interested in whether the general public adopted it or not. Actually, they found the prospect amusing. Ordinary, non-computer people using the Internet? Yuck.

Janet asked the group,

"Does anyone know anything about Jim Clark and all those guys from Mosaic?"

Some of them knew the name from Silicon Graphics. They knew he hadn't left SGI on the friendliest of terms. The press had been all over it for a while, but that seemed to have tailed off.

Porter said, "No. They're over on Castro Street, right?"

"Supposedly. Do you think they're redoing it as a proprietary thing?"

Charles said, "I don't see how that would work. I mean, Mosaic is there, it works, it's free, who's going to pay for another one?"

No one had any good answer for that.

Porter said, "Besides, if they do, Bill Gates will just swoop in and clone it."

That was the end of that topic. "*Get the general public with their stupid Windows machines on the Internet, and Microsoft will just take it over and ruin it, like they do everything else"* pretty well summed up their attitude.

LEN WAS WORKING HARDER than he had since his very first days at Arthur Andersen. Brad at the VC firm spent a couple days tutoring him on the company he was going to babysit, especially all their financials. Brad was incredibly patient with him, but Len had to thank his lucky stars he'd spent so much time researching investments in these companies. Before he retired, he'd have had zero chance of understanding any of it. This was a company that was *very* early into the Internet; they'd been a for-profit company almost before anyone! They were an Internet Service Provider when no one even knew what that was. Their traffic was doubling every month, they claimed. The VC's were pleased, of course, but they were also a tad suspicious. "With great growth comes great opportunity for fuckups," Brad told him.

Finally, Brad took him to meet the folks at the company, NetsForAll. He introduced Len as his stand-in, with decades of financial experience and a director of a private mutual fund, all of which was true, more or less. The fact that Len had been on *Computers This Week* was a huge plus for him. They gave him a desk near the CFO, and his stories about the bingo embezzlement ring and his brave dog Gretchen made him an instant hit with the folks there. Len felt like he really had a second career now! He was old enough to be a grandfather to some of these folks, and it was so fun to be working with them.

The company, though: it lost money, and always had. They were focused on growth, which they were certainly getting, but not on profitability. Their leader Charlie Messner was a charismatic guy who'd been involved with the Internet for years and years, and had a vision of how big it was going to be. It almost seemed like a cult to Len. Everyone there had bought into the vision. When they had a company meeting, quite often the crowd chanted, "Char-LEE! Char-LEE!"

They had a thriving business selling Internet access to individuals, but that didn't "scale well," as they liked to say in Silicon Valley. If you wanted more customers, you needed more telephone lines, modems, and other equipment, and you needed more people to service them. Whereas selling to businesses — now that was a winner! Corporations paid their bills on time, and often didn't bat an eye if you raised prices. And if you had more expensive products to offer them, they were willing to listen. Business customers were where it was at. They had plans to sell off their individual customer division and just concentrate on the businesses.

Brad at the VC firm knew all this, of course. Len's job was to dig into it a little further and see if there were any skeletons in the closets. And also, just to be helpful and do what Brad would do if he were there.

This took some subtlety, which he hadn't needed when he was an auditor. He couldn't just demand to see every piece of paper. So he started by asking the CFO, David, what he could do to help out. That was a winner! Every CFO is, by nature, detail-oriented to a fault, and David could *never* get enough facts about his business. He also asked the VP of Marketing, Doreen, what she wished she could do more of, and "Customer Sat" (for "satisfaction") was something she was deeply curious about. They could get businesses who paid for Internet services, but maybe there was something holding them back from buying even more! Len could find out for her. Perfect! Len could visit the biggest customers, which was exactly what he wanted.

One of them, The Nerd Shop, sold computer and electronic components. They had a physical store near Fry's in Sunnyvale, which was where they made most of their money, but they were finding more and more that their customers demanded Internet shopping. The Nerd Shop shipped things all over the world, to people in locations with no access to most of their products. Once someone got on their "website" (he was learning the lingo), they could just search for what they wanted, provide their address and credit card information, and bingo, it was on its way! So The Nerd Shop was quite happy to pay a hefty monthly fee for a dedicated line that was up twenty-four hours a day.

Len found out that they got quite upset at *any* interruption in their service, and spent some time haranguing him on that. Once he got that issue out of the way, he started talking about what else they needed. He asked about advertising, and wow, did that ever get them talking. They knew there were a lot of businesses on the Web that could send *them* customers, and vice versa. And what if they could advertise specific *products* available on The Nerd Shop? Len thought there had to be a gold mine there.

He found a guy in Palo Alto who had two T-1 lines to his apartment, and he was running a travel site! You could book plane flights and hotel reservations. Amazing. This guy was getting calls from the phone company, asking why in God's name anyone needed *two* T-1 lines! He was getting free links from the various universities and research institutes who'd been on the Internet forever, but how big could that get? There were only just so many of them, and it seemed like every day, one of them got some new manager who clamped down on the free links.

He knew Charley was hoping to get rid of their individual users, but for now they still provided the bulk of the revenue, so he wanted to meet some of those. This had to be costing them a fortune compared to just using AOL or Prodigy, so what was in it for them?

One of them, Steve, used to be a student at Stanford and had gotten used to free Internet, and now he was marketing himself as an expert on it! He was making a decent income

selling contracting services to businesses who wanted to get on
the Web. Steve had skills that were pretty rare; he could show
you how to get a domain, put up a website, and connect it to
your database. He really needed to be on the Internet to
demonstrate that he knew how to do this. So paying a
monthly fee was just a cost of doing business.

Len was becoming an Internet evangelist!. He found that
Janet was fairly blasé about it, since she'd had it for so long.
When he talked about what it would be like if *everyone* was on
it, she just laughed. Even most businesses didn't use TCP/IP,
the Internet protocol, on their internal networks. How was
that ever going to happen?

He found that the people at NetsForAll were true believers
and didn't need *any* convincing. They were used to being
looked down on by the old guard of the computer companies,
who were too jaded and beaten down, they thought, and
couldn't see a giant opportunity when it was staring them right
in the face. As he walked around the offices, he noticed that
almost everyone was using Mosaic Netscape all the time.
There was a new company called Yahoo! that had a webpage
they all used, which gave you a directory of the Web. If you
wanted to find out who had travel information, they gave you
a list of those, including that guy in Palo Alto whom Len had
visited. You could just click your way to anything.

"*Yahoo!*" he thought. "*What real business would ever call themselves that?*" Still, it reminded him of the early days of cars in
Detroit: lots of crazy people setting up shop in a brand new
territory. Most of them were going to fail, of course, but that
was just the nature of things. Why the hell wasn't Janet in on
this?

Back at the VC firm, Brad was bemused by Len's enthusiasm. It seemed to him that everyone who looked at the
Internet business was either unimpressed, or absolutely bedaz-
zled. Len was definitely in the latter camp. He had to remind
Len that he was supposed to help *manage* the natives, not

marry them. So far, NetsForAll was growing like gangbusters, but they weren't making any money. This was not the story Brad wanted to sell to Wall Street: "*OK, it's not profitable, but look at those growth numbers!*"

When Len told him that Charley was seriously looking at acquiring another little Internet Service Provider to expand his geographical reach, Brad got really concerned. He thought that, all by itself, justified having Len there. He fired off a note to Charley saying, "Let's talk." Brad wanted Charley to turn NetsForAll profitable, not get even bigger and lose even more money.

Len was conflicted. Everything he'd ever done in his career was about *profit* and *cash flow*. Those words didn't even appear in Charley's vocabulary! All he seemed to care about was getting bigger. Was Charley nuts, or was Len?

One day he was back at the office, and the CFO's phone rang. Len couldn't help overhearing, and he could tell it was someone important by the way David acted. David was elaborately polite to the caller, saying, "I'm sorry, but I can't give you that information" and referring him to Brad if he wanted to talk further. Len was dying to ask David who it was and what they wanted, but he didn't want to be impertinent.

David turned to him and said, "Another big telecom sniffing around!" Len thought he *could* ask questions, but maybe David would just tell him, and later that day, he did.

"So that call this morning?" he began.

"The 'big telecom' call?"

"That one. Almost every week someone calls, hinting they might want to acquire us."

"Oh, yeah? Are they serious?"

"Well, who can tell? When I bring it up with Charley, he won't even talk about it. 'We're not for sale!' he always says."

"I can't say I'm surprised to hear that. He seems to be a man on a mission."

David didn't say any more. Len wondered what Brad

29

JANET JUMPS IN

It was winter 1995. At the weekly lunches at Gordon-Biersch, one of the guys, Vic, had joined Netscape. Janet really didn't know him too well, although they'd spoken a few times at Xerox. Vic seemed like the reckless type, and in response to everyone's questions, he just said, "It looks like a fun idea."

Porter asked him if it was true that they all slept on the floor there. Vic didn't exactly *deny* it, but he said those stories were exaggerated. Dan had gone to the University of Illinois where Andreesen and Bina were from, but those guys had barely been born then. The fact that they were from the NCSA, or National Center for Supercomputing Applications, certainly made sense, since "supercomputers" were Illinois' big thing, going back to the days of the Illiac IV. They'd been on ARPANET almost since the beginning. But microcomputer apps? That didn't seem to fit.

Janet asked Vic if they were doing Windows, and he said they were. She mentioned how she'd worked on the Windows port of Mosaic and even met Tim Berners-Lee! Vic was impressed.

"Well, you should come in and talk! We're not using *any* Mosaic code, though. That's an iron rule from the lawyers!"

She snapped her fingers in mock disappointment.

After lunch, Janet asked Dan what he thought about it.

"Netscape? I don't know. I had a bad experience with star-tups, after Xerox. I'm not sure I can handle another one."

"Yeah, me neither, and I've never even *been* in one!"

"You'd be in for a shock, I'm sure. Do you fancy having no life at all?"

Janet was silent at that.

LEN WAS TALKING to Brad at the VC firm every week. Brad kept mentioning that they didn't have a John Doerr there, so Len was filling in *part* of that role, helping them keep their companies on the straight and narrow path to a payout. Len finally asked him,

"So what is this superhuman person, 'John Doerr' doing now?"

"You know this is a small community here, right? We all find out what everyone's doing, sooner or later. John is backing Jim Clark's new company, Netscape."

"Really? They think they can make money off the Internet, other than by selling the hardware? When their software is free?"

Brad held his hands out, palms up. "Evidently. John's a smart guy, so I wouldn't put it past him."

Len thought about that. It just didn't add up. People seemed to be drawn to it like flies, yet there was no obvious way you could make money. Other than pornography, as Dan often reminded him. Dan was always telling him about his "friend" Stan, who'd been pursuing that avenue for years now.

That night at dinner, he told Janet about it. For a change, she wasn't dismissive.

"Really? One of the guys I used to work with at Xerox just

went there."

"Oh, yeah? What does *he* think about it?"

"I don't know. He didn't say."

"Maybe you should go interview there! Can't hurt to look around, right?"

Walt seemed concerned. He was imagining being a bachelor again and never seeing her. But he didn't want to say anything just yet. Silicon Valley people were always talking about moving around, he'd learned from hanging around with them. Most of the time it never came to anything.

A few days later, Janet got an email from Vic! He said he'd been talking to the guys on the Windows team, and a couple of them recognized her name from the Mosaic Windows port. He asked if she wanted to come by sometime and just "visit." Not an actual interview yet; just a get-acquainted to see if she liked the place. How could she say No to that?

She heard from a couple of her old Apple friends, and they told her that Terry, someone *else* they knew, had gone to Netscape. Now it was getting to be a trend. She went over there about 5:15 one Thursday.

The receptionist had gone home, but after Janet stood there for a while, someone came by and she told him who she wanted. Vic came out and led her back to his desk. The building seemed to have been designed by someone who'd watched a lot of *Star Trek*; there was a horizontal red stripe in the middle of the beige walls, and one of the cubes had camouflage netting hanging down from the ceiling around it. Not everyone even *had* a cubicle; some folks were just in a big bullpen. Janet had a flashback to her dorm at college. Everyone seemed so young! How would she fit in here?

Vic took her on a tour of the building, which didn't seem too out of the ordinary for Silicon Valley. Vending machines, common room, lots and lots of desks with stuffed toys, odd props, banners, and other decorations, but mostly just a lot of people working. Vic introduced her to the Windows team members, some of whom she remembered from her contributions to the Windows port. There were no big managers for her to meet, at least as far as she knew, which she was grateful for.

Fortunately, she remembered a few details from the Windows port of Mosaic, so she hesitantly mentioned them. This immediately struck a chord with the Windows guys; she could tell this was something they were intimately concerned with. They shook hands with her and went back to work.

Back at Vic's desk, they sat and talked, and Vic showed her the new version of Netscape he was working on. He didn't know much about what she was doing at 3Com, so she told him about all the network management stuff she was into. This didn't interest him too much, but when she happened to mention some of the Windows API's she had to deal with, his ears perked up. She asked him what the business prospects were for Netscape. He seemed to be restraining himself when he said, "Better than I could have expected! We've got businesses calling us constantly!"

"Really? For what?"

"As far as I can tell, they want to take site licenses, so they can give it to all their employees."

Janet had never thought about this. It made sense, from what she knew about installing software on the 3Com internal network.

"Wow. Everyone says, 'how can they make money when their software is free?' "

Vic pointed to his temple. "It's not free for *everyone!*"

Then he asked,

"So you used to be a big manager but you went back to coding?"

"Yeah, I went through the glass ceiling in the other direction!"

Vic laughed. "Excellent, excellent! How do you like it back down in the trenches?"

"Much better. Fewer asses to kiss, for one thing."

This was the right thing to say, she realized. She said goodbye to Vic, not knowing what was going to happen next.

That night, Dad and Walt both got the sense that if she got an offer from them, she was going to take it, so there was no point in arguing with her.

Things happened pretty fast. The next day they invited her in for a regular round of interviews. She'd already met the Windows team, or most of it, and her friend Terry from Apple was one of the interviewers. They made it clear she was not going to be managing, at least not initially, but the fact that she knew how to function in that job was a big plus. They'd much rather have people who could write code become their managers, rather than bringing in some faceless droids from outside. Terry apparently helped convince everyone that she really did have the respect of the engineers at Apple, and Vic did the same for Xerox. It was a done deal! All they wanted to know was, "When can you start?"

She gave her notice at 3Com, and they were sorry to see her go, of course, but ten years *was* a pretty long time to be at one place. No one else from 3Com had gone to Netscape yet, but they'd certainly heard of it. She called Cassie.

"Hey, guess who's going to a startup?"

"Not you! Which one?"

"Netscape! Maybe you've heard of it?"

"Heard of it? They're the hottest thing around! Congratulations! What are you going to be doing there?"

"Oh, working on their Windows version, I think. Not managing, thank God."

"Wow. I hear everyone there works 24x7."

"Yeah, I told them I'm too old for that, plus I have a husband. They seemed OK with it. We'll see. I think most of the time when someone's there all night, they're playing video games and goofing around anyway."

Cassie said, "Well, anyway, I'm so happy for you, Janet! Remember me when you're rich and retired!"

She laughed. "Right. Rich and retired. Or maybe just burned out."

They talked some more about how Palm was doing, and their other friends. Cassie hadn't heard about Len's new job, so she was really interested in that.

LEN AND BRAD huddled about NetsForAll. They both agreed that Charley would have to be replaced, one way or the other. Brad seemed to be leaning towards selling the company to one of the big telecoms, who were desperate to get into the Internet. Charley would probably quit after that in any case, if he even stayed through the acquisition.

Then Len told him the big news about Janet. Brad was pleased.

"Excellent! Now we have a window into what they're doing."

"Well, assuming she tells me anything. When she was on the Lisa project, she wouldn't even say what the price was going to be."

"Good employee. You'll have to worm it out of her. I hear they're doing a lot of business, amazingly enough."

"Really?" Len asked. "I thought it was all free!"

"That's what we want to find out. You work on that, Len!"

Len said he'd try.

MIRIAM'S HUSBAND, Patrick, was still down here in the Valley. He figured eventually Microsoft would move him up to Seattle, but for now, there was plenty to do here. One of the things he hoped he could do was to find out what was going on with the Internet. So far, the Redmond boys seemed to have their heads up their asses about it, as he kept telling Miriam. They had this "Microsoft Network," which was their idea of a walled garden that they would control completely. The notion of a wild-and-wooly Internet with no rules was just anathema to them.

Miriam had never been too close to Matt's friend Janet Saunders, but she was always hearing about her from Matt, and now she heard the news: Janet had gone to Netscape! There were no secrets in the Valley, really. She asked Patrick about it, and he was interested.

"Saunders? I remember that name from 3Com. She was a big manager, as I recall."

"You think they're making her the VP of Engineering or something?"

"Hmm. I doubt that. I'll ask around."

He tried calling her at work, but she claimed to be busy and said she'd call back. She never did, of course. Patrick tried once again to interest his contacts in Redmond in this Internet stuff. It was hard to tell if they were paying any attention or not. Windows 95 seemed to be all anyone ever talked about. He only heard about Bill Gates as someone you didn't want to mess with if you could help it. Did Bill even *know* about the Internet? Not that he could tell.

AT NETSCAPE, Janet felt like she'd jumped into the rapids on the Merced River, where she and Walt had gone rafting once. Except in this case, she didn't have a life jacket and there was no boat to pull her out. Everything was moving about ten times as fast as it had at 3Com or Apple. People were indeed working there late into the night, and while no one said anything *explicit* when she left at 8:00 pm, she was starting to feel that they noticed.

Contrary to her assumption, they were *not* goofing around and playing video games when they were there all night; they actually were working. Some of them really did sleep under their desks some of the time. There were no pep talks about how they were going to change the world, but that was because they didn't need them. The constant stream of reporters from national publications were all the reminder they needed, plus they were young and naive.

"Dethroning Bill Gates" was not a crazy idea to them. They all believed that, once there was a browser out there that ran on all the world's computers, there would be no more Microsoft and Apple monopolies. Now *that* was worth a few all-nighters, for sure.

Walt already wasn't happy when she got home at 8:30, and the thought of staying even later didn't thrill her. *Maybe* they'd make a lot of money and it would all be worth it, but how could you be sure? Len told them that companies usually went public only after a couple years of solid profitability, and Netscape wasn't even profitable yet.

The Windows version had to work on Windows 95, of course, and that wasn't out yet. Normally, Microsoft practically babied their outside developers, since having lots of applications was the whole reason PC's owned the market. They issued the new Application Program Interfaces, or API's, for any new release to all the developers as soon as they were ready. This wasn't out of the goodness of Bill Gates' heart, but so that when the new version came out the applications would all be available. It was just business.

Janet and the Windows team needed those API's, especially the ones that let you dial up your Internet Service Provider. Without those, they could not have their browser working when Windows 95 came out. But somehow, Microsoft kept dragging their feet. They'd tell the managers at Netscape about it, but no one seemed to have any clue what was going on.

At home, she told Dad about this. He was perplexed, too. The next day at NetsForAll, he asked Charley, the CEO, about their relationship with Microsoft. Charley seemed to tense up, although he tried to hide it.

"We have visits from them once in a while, yes."

Len thought this might be a sensitive topic. But hell, he'd brought it up, so might as well finish.

"Anything in particular they want from us? It doesn't seem like we'd be on their radar screen, but what do I know? They're into everything, I guess."

Charley realized that Len had the ear of Brad, their VC, so he couldn't just blow him off.

"The last time their guy, Patrick, was his name, I think, was asking me about Netscape."

"Netscape! My daughter is working there now."

Charley cracked a smile and relaxed a little. "Really! How does she like it?"

"I think they're working her harder than she expected!"

"That's what I hear, too. Anyhow, Patrick seemed concerned that I might give away the Netscape browser to our customers."

"Give it away? Isn't it free anyway?"

"For an individual, yes. He thought we might get a license to distribute it ourselves, so people wouldn't have to download it from Netscape. I guess."

"And were you going to do that?"

"Maybe. It was just something we've talked about now and then; no definite plans."

Len pondered that. First Janet tells him Microsoft is dragging its feet on the APIs, and now this.

The next time he saw Brad, he told him all this. Brad seemed to get very thoughtful.

"Microsoft. The Big Gorilla. Everyone's scared shitless of getting on Bill Gates' bad side."

"*How much is he going to tell me?*" Len thought. "*I don't want to overstep here.*"

"That's what my daughter and her friends always tell me.

Staying out of Gates' path is the only way to survive, they used to say."

Brad said, "Yep. We always have to factor their reaction into any investment we make."

"That's probably enough for now" Len thought. He remembered that time during the War when he caught one of the suppliers of jeep repair parts faking some invoices. This crook tried to hint that Len's life might get "difficult" if he made any trouble. On the other hand, Len might get lots of extra ration coupons for his family if he ignored it. He was careful not to say anything explicit.

"Who's getting hurt?" the crook said. "All the parts work. No one's getting killed over there."

Len just told him to void the invoices and he wouldn't say anything. He always wondered if he should have turned the guy in.

30

DID THE EARTH MOVE FOR YOU?

Miriam was getting impatient about when she and Patrick were going to move to Seattle. Wasn't that where everything was happening at Microsoft? How was he ever going to climb the corporate ladder down here?

Patrick had strict orders not to repeat company secrets, but eventually she wore him down.

"Look, you can't repeat this, OK?"

"Of course."

"Microsoft is developing their own Internet browser. I'm in charge of evangelizing it down here."

"These techies and their stupid words!" she thought. " '*Evangelizing*'!"

"A 'browser'? That's for using the Internet, right?"

He nodded. "Chairman Bill is worried they'll displace us with it, or something. He can't convince anyone else up there, but he's got a bug up his ass about it."

"Displace Microsoft? Isn't that ridiculous?"

"As I understand the concern, application writers could write to *Netscape's* interfaces instead of ours, and then their apps will run anywhere, not just on Windows."

Miriam didn't follow this at all. When Matt used to explain his business to her, it sounded like voodoo half the time, and this definitely did.

"So what do you do about it? Tell people Microsoft's browser is going to be better, or what?"

"That's a big part of it. Also pressing on some other leverage points."

This sounded mysterious to Miriam. "Leverage points? Like what?"

Patrick shifted in his seat. "Oh, different business deals and so forth." He didn't seem eager to get into the subject, so she dropped it.

LEN WAS HAVING his weekly meeting with Brad back at the VC in mid-June. Brad had some exciting news for him!

"Guess who's going public?"

"No clue. Who?"

"Your daughter's company, Netscape! We just heard on the grapevine."

Len was incredulous. "Already? How can they do that? They're not even profitable!"

Brad shrugged. "It's a new world, Len. Profits are just *so* old-fashioned!"

"So instead of profits, what do you have?"

"Growth, my friend, growth. Their revenue growth is off the scale. Not to mention the future potential."

Len tried to take this all in. His first thought was, *"Does Janet know this yet? And if not, can I tell her?"*

"Wow. What's their valuation going to be?"

Brad said, "A lot. The underwriters are going to set the share price when they see what the market will bear."

Len didn't know how all that worked, so Brad explained the "road show" and how Morgan Stanley would go out with

Barksdale, the CEO, talk to the big money guys, and see what their reaction was. He said,

"So your daughter's going to be very rich, Len! Are you ready for that?"

"My little girl, a millionaire! It *is* hard to take in."

"Well, you can be very proud, Len. You must have done *something* right raising her."

Len teared up and excused himself. He went to the bathroom and wiped his eyes. All those nights driving 12-year-old Janet to the library to check out books. All those astronomy classes where she was the only girl. All that tuition for Kingswood and then MIT. Who ever thought?

What would she and Walt do if they suddenly didn't have to work anymore for the rest of their lives? He honestly had no idea. *"Don't do anything rash!"* was the only advice he was going to give them right now.

Janet of course already knew about the IPO. Word spreads fast in Silicon Valley. A company-wide email went out, reminding everyone that there was a "lockup period" for employees in an initial public offering like this, which was customary to prevent company insiders from dumping their stock and splitting. Not that anyone would really do that, heh, heh.

There was also a "vesting" period for stock options, which was usually four years, 1/48 each month. Until your stock was vested, it still belonged to the company. "Fully vested" was something a senior engineer might boast to emphasize that, hey, he could cash in his stock and quit anytime.

Since she'd only been there a few months, almost none of it was vested, and it would be mid-1999 before she had all of it. So: no sudden riches! She wondered if Dad or Walt knew all that. There'd be some interesting conversations tonight.

She was always hearing about people who'd made a bundle and quit working in high tech. There was a guy who'd cashed in from 3Com's IPO and retired. He was now making music at his own studio up in Marin, pretty mediocre music as far as she could tell. Some other guys were hanging around in the Valley and goofing off all day, or else being junior philanthropists. One lady who'd retired was full-time in wine, that being her passion. She would set up a wine party for you and your friends, with some unusual wines from small vintners that you probably had never heard of. Janet thought, *"Meh. How exciting would that be, after a while?"*

Not having to work at all — that was everyone's dream, or so they claimed. But for the vast majority of folks that was all it would ever be. Now it was going to be a reality for her, *if* the stock price held up long enough for her to sell it. Who knows how that would go over the next four years? Microsoft certainly wasn't going to sit idly by while Netscape ate their lunch. Bill Gates was a mean, greedy bastard.

What would Walt think about it? He'd always done hard physical labor, so wasn't he going to get tired of it eventually? The thought of him sitting around the house and drinking all day wasn't a happy one, not that he was really a drinker now. Maybe it was really a good thing that she wasn't going to get a big rush of money all at once; they'd have plenty of time to think about it.

GRANT AVERY HEARD about the IPO and called Janet to congratulate her. He got sent to her voicemail, which he figured must mean she was getting a lot of calls today. He thought of asking if he could borrow a quarter million dollars until next year, but thought better of it.

Grant was bravely struggling to stay abreast of all the management changes at Taligent. The computer press had turned on them, since Apple's "next OS" story was becoming boring. John Sculley, who had pushed Steve Jobs out, had himself been ousted by the board, and Michael Spindler was now the CEO. How Apple's operating system was going to evolve was a long-running soap opera. Jobs was off doing his NeXT Computer company, making this über-cool black cube that no one was buying. It wasn't clear anymore if Apple would *ever* ship anything with Taligent's software.

"Object-oriented" had been the computing industry gospel for so long that people were beginning to doubt that it meant anything, except maybe on a single machine. However, that was not the ballgame anymore. "Distributed objects", where a program on one machine might have a "handle" to an object on another and be able to do things to it, was a whole other field of study. Legions of computer scientists and bureaucrats were working on that, and had been for years.

Still, IBM continued to put its massive weight behind Taligent, plus there was the Object Management Group (OMG), a multi-company consortium of Apple, IBM, Sun, Data General, HP, and some others, founded in 1989. OMG didn't release any software, but periodically they'd release a "standard" and maybe — *maybe* — some companies would release "OMG-compliant" tools. Grant had been appointed Taligent's representative to the OMG. It seemed inevitable that he would eventually be a fulltime employee of IBM. That seemed fine to Grant; IBM was a solid, lifetime company, their mainframes weren't going anywhere, and neither were their .big corporate customers. People used to joke that "IBM" stood for "I've Been Moved," and he figured they might move him somewhere else in the country, which would be fine with him.

He'd tried before to interest Netscape in Taligent or the OMG, and he got nowhere at all. He didn't know *what* these folks thought they were doing there, or how they expected to make any money from free software. "They'll make it up on volume!" was the joke he liked to tell.

Grant was now a divorced guy in his 40's, and wondered if he'd ever get married again. He still went bicycling with the Western Wheelers, and he even remembered some of the people from when he lived here before! But that was not a source of romantic attachments. He also went on hikes with the Sierra Club, something Janet and Dan had both told him about, back in the day. Once in a while he met someone and went out with her a few times.

～

THAT NIGHT, Janet and Walt were sitting on the couch when Len came home.

"Wow, do we ever have news for you!" she said.

"Netscape is going public?"

She snapped her fingers. "I should have known you'd hear."

"Yeah, we vulture capitalists know everything. Anyhow, congratulations, you two! I bet you didn't expect it so soon!"

"God, I'll say. I figured it'd be years."

They talked about how many shares she had, and about how vesting and lockups worked. What would the share price be when she could finally sell some? Len said all the VCs were trying to get some shares of the offering, so he didn't know if he'd even be able to buy any.

Janet said, "We're kinda discouraged from talking about it too much at work. People feel like it isn't real."

Walt said, "In my line of work, if this kind of thing happened everyone would disappear and never come back."

Len said, "It's a different world than we all grew up in, that's for sure."

No one felt like talking about it any more for now. They turned on the TV news for the latest in the O.J. Simpson trial. Len said, "He's gonna walk. I know it!"

Walt chimed in, "You really think so? With all that evidence?"

"Doesn't matter. He's black, the victims are white, the prosecutor is white, and no one likes her. Case closed."

~

THE INVESTMENT BANKERS, Jim Barksdale, and Marc Andreesen were off on the East Coast doing the "road show," where they presented Netscape to rooms full of sober-minded financial types in suits. From what people back in Mountain View were hearing, it was shocking how enthusiastic they were. The offering price was in flux up until the last minute. Usually a new stock came out at around $15 a share or so, which was a delicate choice for the underwriters: you didn't want it to drop right away because then the buyers would feel cheated. On the other hand, if you came out at $15 and it went to $25, that meant you could have gotten that extra $10 for the company. They had to gauge what was going to happen. The final offering price was set at $28.

August 9 was the magic day, and demand was so heavy that the opening of trading was delayed for two hours. People at Netscape were directed not to pay any attention to the stock price, but that was impossible. When the stock finally opened, the price was $71! It got as high as $74 before settling down for the day at $58. Janet knew she'd remember this day for the rest of her life.

If she multiplied the number of shares she had by $71, it was an unimaginably big number. What would she do with all that money? "*Oh well, it's not real. Yet.*" she thought. All the TV news shows led with the Netscape IPO. No one had ever seen anything like this. People who'd never even heard of "the Internet" were now issuing breathless proclamations that "this changes everything."

At work the next day, the excitement had worn off already, since no one had any cash in their accounts yet. The work schedule was harder than ever. Almost all of her tech friends were shaking their heads. The Internet had been around for years. Janet had gone to a conference about it almost four years ago. But now the world outside had heard about it, finally. Whereas before the joke had been, "How do you make money on the Internet? Porn!" now it was "How do you make money on the Internet? You start a company and include '.com' in the name!"

LEN WAS STRUCK by the change in atmosphere at the VC firm. Before it was kind of Quiet Big Money, like you were in the inner sanctum of some global-scale bank. Now everyone had a crazed look in their eyes. Was it the IPO?

Brad was busy in a meeting, and he had to wait in the lobby until it was a half hour past his meeting time with him. He was beaming when he came out to get Len, apologizing profusely for his lateness. On the way back to his office, he said,

"It's been absolutely crazy around here. We have random mom-and-pop investors calling and asking how they can get in on this Internet thing! Our receptionist has to tell them we're not a retail brokerage."

"Wow" said Len.

"Our chairman is asking us all to review our portfolios and see if we have anything we could take public, even if it's not profitable yet! Maybe even, *especially* if it's not profitable yet."

"I hope NetsForAll isn't one of them!"

"Well, actually… that's one of the things we have to talk about, Len. There's an old saying in investment circles: 'when the ducks are quacking, feed them.' "

"I take it that all those people calling on the phone would be considered 'ducks'?"

"And everyone who bid up the price to $74 yesterday!"

Brad continued, "I have some friends who *are* in the retail brokerage business. They said they've never seen anything like this: customers they haven't heard from in years, calling and asking if they can get some Netscape shares."

"I think my daughter is kinda tired of talking about it, actually."

"Yeah, I was wondering what it's like *inside* Netscape!"

"Oh, I think you'd be disappointed. These are computer nerds, Brad."

"God bless 'em!" Brad said. "Now let's figure out how to make money off them!" They sat down.

31

THE INTERNET GURU

Cassie had settled into a routine at Palm. She was testing the software and the hardware as much as she could, and she never got the feeling that she was just being a bureaucrat, like she sometimes did at 3Com.

They had their new device, the Touchdown, which everyone was excited about. There was still no money for manufacturing the thing, although they did have a manufacturing partner, at least. Flextronics was a Chinese company that a lot of Silicon Valley companies used for manufacturing. instead of having to build their own factories, which would have been hugely expensive. They had a lot of manufacturing expertise, too, which would have been impossible to duplicate quickly.

Flextronics was sending one of their engineers to Palm to review the design and make sure all of it could actually be built. So at least they knew it *could* be manufactured.

But it was still going to take a lot of money, plus the marketing costs of launching the thing, plus hiring enough sales people. They didn't have the money for all that. Selling software didn't take a lot of capital, but making hardware sure did.

Donna wasn't the type to lie about their prospects, which was one of things Cassie loved about her. She knew Jeff and Donna were out trying to raise money or recruit a partner, but there were no big announcements yet.

Her friend Janet had had the big IPO at Netscape on August 9. Cassie hadn't spoken to her since then, since she didn't want to be one of those people who suddenly discover they're your best friend when you have some success. Still, having your startup go IPO was the ultimate dream around here. Would Palm ever make it? There was one obstacle after another before they could achieve that. Palm didn't have any particular connection to the Internet, which was all anyone cared about since Netscape Day. Her friends seemed to be all looking around for the next hot Internet startup.

Then one day at the end of August, a special Comms meeting was called for a Thursday, not the usual Friday. They knew something was up. Donna was more serious than usual. She reviewed how Touchdown was a great product but they lacked the millions to properly launch and manufacture it. Everyone knew that, of course. Then she said they'd found an entity that was going to do it! Jeff took over and got right to the point: U.S. Robotics was going to acquire the company, paying $5 a share! There was no question anymore if their Palm shares were worth anything: they were going to be worth $5. Everyone mentally multiplied the number of shares they had by 5. This was not as big a payday as Netscape had, of course, but still, it wasn't bad.

Cassie was speechless. Everyone was. A *modem company*? Why them, and not someone like Compaq, which they'd assumed was their knight in shining armor? Did this mean they'd have to move to Chicago, land of awful weather? Was Donna getting replaced by some droid from USR? And what about their stock — sometimes when a company was acquired, all the stock options vested immediately. Was that happening here?

All the questions were answered: no one was moving to Chicago,, and in fact USR was thrilled to have a Silicon Valley presence. Yes, Donna was still going to be their CEO. No, their Palm options were not all vesting, but they *were* all getting some USR options in addition, with the amount to be determined. Their benefits would be at least as good as they had been, and in some cases, better.

Left unsaid was the company culture: they loved being part of a small company where they knew everyone. What was it going to be like to be a unit of a big company head-quartered somewhere else? It was obviously going to be differ-ent, and not everyone was happy about that. They'd just have to wait and find out what their new overlord was like.

For now, nothing changed. Everyone was focused on the Touchdown launch. Cassie asked for volunteers to help find and report bugs, and was gratified at how many people pitched in. Now Palm was going to have the funds to really launch this thing. "*Will anyone buy it, though?*" she wondered.

Cassie thought she might soon run out of excuses not to adopt a child: she'd have a steady job with a big company again and a large chunk of money from US Robotics stock, although not enough to quit working forever. Gulp.

Len's job at NetsForAll had finished. After the Netscape IPO, Charley, their CEO, became insistent that the VC's take him public, and they just didn't want to go on the road with him. Len didn't think an IPO was a good idea, either, even *with* the Internet frenzy.

Nor did the VC's fancy firing and replacing Charley. So they'd accepted a big buyout offer from a large East Coast telecom company; Brad called their insanely high offer "stupid money," but hey, that was just as green as *smart* money.

Charley had quit in a huff, and the acquirers didn't want him, anyway.

Brad told him, "Len, I can't thank you enough for all you've done for us! Right at the moment, we don't have another job for you, but *please* let us know if you get any other offers. We don't want to lose you."

Len *thought* this sounded sincere, but you could never tell with these rich guys. Anyhow, he moved out of Janet and Walt's house and went back to the mountains with Gretchen and Mickey. Janet told him, "Dad, we're going to miss you!"

"Well, I'm sure I'll be back down here again, but if not, it sure was nice. Now I can say I'm a Silicon Valley refugee like everyone else up there!"

He stayed busy keeping track of the Internet mania. All his investors thought he was a genius for getting onto this Internet thing before *anyone*. Then a month after Netscape Day, he got a phone call. It was some name he'd never heard of, Jim Something but the guy dropped a bunch of names of East Coast financial giants he certainly knew. He wanted Len to come down and talk to them. Len said,

"Jim, I'm really gratified, but it's a three-hour drive for me, and I'm just getting settled in up here again. Can you give me some idea what this is about?"

"Sure, Len, I know you're busy. I've been tasked by my company to boot up a new mutual fund out here specializing in the Internet. We might be interested in taking you on as one of our principals."

Len thought that sounded interesting. He wondered if this really meant becoming unretired! He asked some questions about the capitalization of the fund, what his responsibilities would be, whether he'd have to move down there, and so on. Jim was reasonably forthcoming, but he shied away from giving too much detail on the phone. Len finally agreed that he could come in next Friday. He called Janet.

"Hey, guess who has a job interview down there!"

"Wait, let me think! Is it Harry Redding, that guy who hit Dan with his cane?"

"No, clever girl, it's your old Dad! Some rich mucky-mucks want to talk to me about starting a mutual fund for the Internet!"

"Oh, my God, Dad, that's wonderful!" They talked about what the job would be, and most of all, if he was going to have to move down to the Valley. Of course he was welcome to stay with them again; in fact, they'd barely gotten used to him being gone.

The next Friday, he met Jim at Cafe Verona in Palo Alto. After the VC's lush offices on Sand Hill Road, this seemed odd, but Jim said they hadn't even rented office space down here yet. Len might even help them do that! Anyway, Cafe Verona was where Jim Clark and Marc Andreesen had first met to discuss starting a company, so it was kind of a holy place now. The cafe was full of people who were obviously doing business of some sort, or at least trying to look like they were.

Len was expecting a bunch of specific stock questions, because the other financial types were always asking him those, like "what's in your portfolio? How much money are you running? What do you think Microsoft is going to do?" But Jim's conversation was mercifully free of all that. Instead, it was about the financial firm he represented, and the other sector funds it ran. They did have a "computers" sector fund, but "Internet" was a brand new sector. They felt like they were behind already, and Len had been doing this for years!

Len thanked him, but demurred about his experience: he hadn't actually been "doing Internet" since there wasn't really any way to, before! But he did mention his time at NetsForAll, which was a bona fide Internet company. He realized that badmouthing yourself was okay up to a point, but you really shouldn't overdo it, so he also gave an abbreviated summary of his time at Chrysler, and the way he'd built up his private "mutual fund." The fact that people had come to Len, rather than him having to advertise, was impressive.

Len had never worked in an investment firm like this, of course, so he wanted to know what, exactly, they'd expect him to do. Was he going to make recommendations as part of a team, or have autonomy over some amount of money? Was he going to visit companies and ask them questions, give speeches at conferences, go to New York for meetings, write articles? Were other Wall Street giants doing something similar, and what were their prospects? Who was the competition in this space? Was his age going to be a problem? They spent a long time going over those questions, with "yes" the answer to most of the questions, except the "age" one.

Most importantly, would he get to go on *Wall Street Week*? This last one was a joke, of course, but Jim took it seriously. He'd seen Len on *Computers This Week*, so he knew Len could handle being on TV. The firm did like its managers to go out and represent it.

A bearded guy in jeans and a black T-shirt occupied the table right next to them. Jim noticed and realized the guy could probably overhear them, so he suggested they go out for a walk.

When they were out of earshot of everyone, Len brought up the question of compensation. Would he get a straight salary, or a percentage of his trading profits, or an annual bonus, or what? He apologized for not knowing what was customary for this kind of job. Jim explained that fund managers usually got a salary plus an annual bonus, where the bonus was obviously going to be heavily influenced by how well he did that year. That included not just trading profits, but public relations things, like Len had asked about: speaking, writing, helping other fund managers, and so forth. He was shocked at the salary: he'd never made that much money in his life. And the bonuses: who knew what those would be, but he got the distinct impression that they were *a lot*.

His last question: he knew the answer to this one. Yes, he *was* going to have to move down here from the mountains. Sigh. He wasn't fishing all that much anymore, and construction on the father-in-law house had been languishing for a while, too, so what the hell? Len figured he'd probably rent a place, since he didn't really know how long this thing would last. And staying with Janet and Len was always there as a backup.

When they parted, Len knew he had the job if he wanted it, and he told Jim he did. They agreed to talk in another week and meet some of the other people who were going to work in the Silicon Valley office.

Janet and Walt wanted to go out and celebrate, but Len cooled them down. He said, "Let's wait until I actually have an offer, at least! Many a slip between the cup and the lip, and all that." Still, it was a sweet moment for him *and* Janet. She always thought he was capable of more than he was doing at Chrysler. Was he sacrificing his chances to give her a stable existence? She didn't like to think so.

She felt a little guilty for pushing him to retire to a life of fishing up in the Sierras. That wasn't really what he wanted out of life, obviously! But he never said anything about wanting a second career. How was she supposed to know? Fortunately, he'd found one now.

In high school at Kingswood it seemed the other girls' fathers were all Vice Presidents and had a lot of money. She wasn't exactly *poor*, but she wasn't rich, either. Now she *was* going to be rich, and with any luck, Dad was, too! What would it be like to go to a class reunion *now*?

That thought only occupied her mind for a second or two. She still had her girlfriends from back then, and in fact she just saw them a couple years ago. Those were real friends, and who cared about the other bitches?

Janet, Walt, and Len were sitting watching the ten o'clock

news, and Walt got the distinct impression that they wanted a father-daughter talk, so he excused himself and went to bed.

They sat there for a while, and then Len turned off the TV.

"Well," he said.

"Well," she agreed.

"We both made it, it looks like, huh?"

"It does look that way."

"How do you feel?"

"I don't know," she said. "How about you?"

"I don't know how to be rich. I've always been middle class."

"Yeah. Me neither. Of course, we're not rich, yet."

"No, not really. But it does look pretty promising."

She agreed.

"Was this what you wanted from your retirement, Dad?"

"I guess it was. I didn't realize at first. I thought 'fishing every day' was going to be it."

"Yeah. I feel bad that we sorta pushed you into that!"

He grabbed her arm. "Hey, you didn't push me into anything. I'm the one who wanted it."

"OK. Anyhow, it looks like you found out what you really wanted."

"Yeah. In a roundabout way, I guess I did."

She leaned her head on his shoulder, and he put his arm over her.

"I always figured you were going to get rich by being a CEO. Not like this!"

"I disappointed you, you're saying?" she asked, mockingly.

Len laughed. "You always make me very, very proud, Janet. I think you got tired of hearing me say that a long time ago."

"Well, this time I'm proud of _you_! My dad started from nothing and now he's going to be an Internet guru!"

"An Internet guru!" he mused. "A couple years ago I

couldn't even spell it. Now because of these stupid bingo people I'm a celebrity."

"So how's it feel?"

"How's it feel? Like someone's going to unmask me any second now."

"That's how everyone feels, Dad. Just remember, those people don't know any more than you do."

Len didn't say anything. She continued,

"Dad, can I ask you something?"

"Sure."

"Did you ever feel like striking out on your own, when I was growing up?"

"Striking out on my own? What do you mean?"

"I don't know... switching jobs, going to a small company, something like that?"

Len thought about that. "Back in those days, if you had a good job with a big company, you held onto it. We didn't move around like you kids do."

She took that in.

"Besides, I had you to support! I couldn't take a risk of being unemployed with the mortgage and all those tuition bills to pay."

"Now you're making me feel guilty!" she said.

He squeezed her harder. "Never, honey. Never!"

They were both silent for a long time.

Finally, Len got up. "Well, I guess everything worked out in the end, huh?"

"Seems like it. Good night, Dad." He nodded.

32

THE FAMILY BUSINESS

Cassie had gone and done it! She'd adopted a kid, a two-year-old named Janine! Rather, she had "fost-adopted" Janine, which meant that she technically was just fostering her at first. After a year, when Cassie, Janine, and the agency all agreed that this was working, the adoption could proceed. Now it was finally a done deal: Cassie was a mom!

Janine was two when Cassie first took her home, which meant she was three now. It had been hell for Cassie at first. No matter how much she tried to prepare herself, read books, and talked to other mothers, there was nothing that could prepare her for this: a little kid who is always there. She always needed to be fed, clothed, washed, and watched to be sure she didn't kill herself. *"How does anyone do this?"* she wondered. Her own mother, Elaine, was dubious about this single mother-hood thing at first, but she melted when Cassie first showed her Janine. Now Cassie's problem was more *"how do I get rid of Mom?"* than *"how do I get some help with this?"* Elaine had stayed in Cassie's apartment with Janine at first, while Cassie was arranging day care for her. She was reluctant to leave, but she made Cassie promise that at *the least little problem* she could come back.

Cassie managed fine on her own, with Janine in daycare, except for when she had to fly to Singapore to visit Flextronics on an emergency visit. Some of the Palm Pilot units were dying, unpredictably, and this was an absolute showstopper. She ended up driving down to Simi Valley to leave Janine at her parents' house and flying out of LAX. But other than that, she did OK, although none of her friends ever saw her.

Since Janine was finally hers, Cassie decided to have her baptized, and called in her promise from Len to be the godfather. He'd forgotten, but a promise was a promise, plus he lived nearby in Sunnyvale now anyway. So the baptism was set for a Sunday a month away. She invited the whole 3Com gang: Janet, Walt, Dan, and Matt, plus Pete and Barbara, her co-conspirators from the infamous boat trip that got Janet and Walt together.

Dan asked Matt at work if he was going.

"Well, I'm Jewish, as you know, but hey, if they don't mind, I don't mind. I'm not going to promise to serve Jesus, though."

Dan thought of several jokes he could tell, but unusually for him, he resisted them.

"And here I thought I wasn't going to see you in a suit again until someone died!"

"I think Janet's wedding was the last time I wore it. Hope it still fits!"

Dan was a manager now, and finding out that you couldn't hire people in a big company anymore. Everyone wanted to join a startup and get rich. Startups were springing up like kudzu in Alabama.

It was hell. He finally transferred a woman from Oracle Ireland, who was making $35,000 a year, and he wanted to pay her $50,000, a fairly modest salary in the Valley. Larry

Ellison had to approve all engineering hires, and he scrawled a note on the request, "$15,000 is what percent raise??"

Nonetheless, it went through. Then he hired an Indian guy from a little company in Fremont whom he'd met in his IETF standards activities. The guy had an H1-B visa which restricted him to one company, but Oracle had an immigration lawyer who handled such things. It took a month and cost $10,000, and then when it came through and the guy turned in his notice, his company made him a counteroffer and he stayed.

Dan was so pissed he wrote to the guy's company and demanded they pay back the $10,000 Oracle had spent on him. To his shock and amazement, they sent him a check. He wasn't even sure what to do with it, since engineers never handle money like that.

Managing *really* sucked. This was the third time in his career he'd succumbed to it, and it'd probably be the third time he gave it up. On top of everything else, Oracle had bought one of those classic Vice President systems (meaning, no one but a Vice President would ever buy it), namely Clear-Case, a source control system. It meant that when you looked at what files you had, it would only show you the "correct" versions of those source files, not the ones you actually had in your file system. Everyone had to use it.

If this sounds complicated, it was, meaning it didn't really work. Yet, being the manager, Dan was still responsible for normal development, and all his people complained to *him* when the source control system didn't work. Who was he going to complain to?

Matt was busy climbing the management ladder at Oracle. He got invited to a yard party with a whole bunch of top management, which he understood to be his debutante coming-out. He hoped he passed. There was no big promotion immediately following, but he could tell by the new looks of respect the other VP's gave him that he was now a Made Man.

Janet had finally sold some of her Netscape stock, as soon as a year had passed since the IPO. Len told her *not* to just let it ride, but to take the money off the table as soon as she could. Working at Netscape had, if anything, gotten even harder since the IPO, not easier. She was getting tired of it and so was Walt, but at least they could mentally multiply 1/48 of her shares by the stock price every month, and figure out how much money she was *really* making.

The baptism took place at an Episcopal church in autumn, 1996, Len standing by the minister, Cassie, and Janine up near the front. Janine looked positively radiant in her little white dress. Cassie's mother Elaine sat in the front row. Matt and Dan sat side by side, with Matt watching Dan to figure out when to stand up and sit down. Dan had never been to an Episcopal baptism before, either, so he had to watch the other people. There was an awful lot of "and also with you" responses when the minister said, "the Lord be with you," which reminded Dan of the old Latin Mass *"Dominus vobiscum / Et cum spiritu tuo"* exchange.

Afterwards, the congregation filed outside for refreshments. Elaine said to Cassie, "I'll take Janine home so you can talk to your friends, sweetie." Janine very politely shook hands with all the grownups and thanked them for coming, which made Cassie more proud than she ever imagined she could be.

As she joined the group, all of them made a show of taking their Palm Pilots out of their pockets and crossing off their appointments for "Janine's baptism," which made Cassie laugh.

"So how *are* you all?" she said. "I'm sorry I haven't been around much lately, but I think you all know why."

Janet said, "Before we get into that: how are you making out as a single mom? It must be exhausting!"

Cassie said, "Yeah, it is. But it's *so* worth it."

No one had an answer for that. She was the only one of them who'd actually had a kid, and they all felt like maybe they'd missed something. But there was nowhere to go with that topic.

Finally Janet took the lead. She held up her Palm Pilot. "This is really a great device, Cassie. I don't know who's the busiest at work, actually, you, me, or Dad!"

Cassie said, "Thanks. Mr. Saunders, we're so glad to have you down here in the Valley full time now! How are you enjoying it? By the way, thanks for standing up for Janine."

"Oh, I enjoyed it. Arranging all those murders took some time, but hey, it's just settling the family business."

Dan said, "Oh please, not those Godfather jokes again! That was a Catholic ceremony in the movie, anyway."

He added, looking Len up and down, "Nice suit, by the way."

"Oh, thanks. We do need to clean up for the bankers, once in a while."

Janet put her arm around Len's waist. "Dad's a mutual fund manager now! Did you all know that?"

Matt did not. "Really? Wow, congratulations! Will we be seeing you on *Wall Street Week* sometime soon?"

"Don't laugh. The producers and I are trying to set up a time."

Len felt like changing the subject, so he asked Matt,

"Enough about me! How about you? What are you up to?"

"Me? Oh, same old same old. Working every day to make Larry Ellison richer."

Dan said, "We like that as our goal. It's nice and simple."

Pete jumped, "I can tell I've missed a whole lot of news with you techie folks! I thought you were retired and living in Walt's cabin in the Sierras, Len!"

Len looked stumped, but Dan answered for him. "Well, there was this money disappearing from a charity up there, and Len and I played detective, and… well, one thing led to another."

"And here I am!" said Len. Everyone laughed. Walt said, "I'll tell you the whole thing later, Pete."

Cassie said, "Janet, what's it like at Netscape these days? It seems like Bill Gates is trying to own the Internet for real now!"

Janet looked weary. Len felt protective and answered for her.

"Yeah, that's what the little jerk thinks. It's bigger than even him, though."

Dan said, "Oracle is actually partnering with Netscape. Matt and I are a little bit involved with that."

Len looked like he knew more than he could say. Walt put his arms around Dan and Matt and said, "Thanks for that, guys!" Everyone laughed.

Barbara said, "All this nerd talk! I think Pete and I will be taking off. Cassie, that was a beautiful ceremony and you have a beautiful little daughter!"

"Oh, thank you, Barbara. Thanks for coming, you two!"

Janet said, "Yeah, I think Walt and I will be leaving, too. Double what Barbara said, Cassie. I'm so happy for you!" They hugged.

Cassie's phone rang. She picked it up and listened, and said, "OK, I'll be home soon." and hung up. She turned to the others and said, "I'd better be getting home to my daughter, too. Thanks for coming, you guys, and especially you, Mr. Saunders!"

Now it was just Dan, Matt, and Len. Len looked at his watch and said,

"I guess I'll be getting along, too. You Oracle guys: you should know that you're not alone. That's all I'm saying for now."

Dan looked at Matt.

"Well, that's good to know. *I guess.* See you tomorrow."

33

CODA

L en went back to his rental house in Sunnyvale and changed out of his suit. Gretchen and Mickey were ecstatic to see him. He sat down to watch some football, Mickey jumping up to join him and Gretchen climbing up the ramp he'd bought for her, since she had trouble moving these days.

"A godfather. My life is complete now." he thought. *"I guess I have to go to church more often."*

All those years of working at Chrysler, keeping up with Janet's career, and not thinking about retirement very much at all, and here he was, 2000 miles away and living in Silicon Valley. Life sure throws you some curves.

Now his days were spent on the phone, meeting with bankers, tech executives, reporters, staff, and people from the parent fund company back East. Either that, or hunched over his Bloomberg terminal. He'd thought he was going to be playing golf and fishing when he retired, not running hundreds of millions of dollars.

The dogs were his best assistants. Almost everyone he met loved them, and he knew he could always regale them with the story of how Gretchen had taken down Harry Redding and clamped down on his sleeve like she'd been taught in K-9 Academy. He could tell she knew when he was talking about her.

Investing seemed so easy, too! A monkey throwing darts could probably pick stocks as well as he did — everything went up. Investors were throwing money at him. His bosses back in New York were kind of coy about what his bonus might be this year, but he had the distinct impression he was finally going to be able to buy a house here.

It was funny. A couple years ago, he would have thought that getting rich would be good because he could pass it all on to Janet when he died. Not that he ever entertained the thought of getting rich! After all, he was retired, so how would that even happen?

Now she didn't even need it! She'd gotten rich on her own. His ex-wife, thankfully, wouldn't get a cent of his money, since he'd made it all after the divorce.

There *was* a dark cloud over it all, though, and Janet and her friends had been telling him about it for years: Microsoft. The big bully in Redmond was intent on crushing Netscape, and they had the means to do it, too. Everyone he talked to about Netscape always led off with that topic: "*Isn't Internet Explorer going to crush them?*"

They were pulling out all the stops to do it. Apparently Bully Boy Gates was terrified that the browser would be the new operating system, and his stupid Windows would be nothing but "a set of buggy device drivers," as the Netscape kids liked to say.

As a fund manager, almost everyone in the Valley wanted to talk to him. Lately, he was picking up vibes that Microsoft was going beyond normal business competition, and starting to lean on everyone to not do business with Netscape. The Valley being a small place, Matt had told him that his ex-wife Miriam's new husband was one of Bill's Bully Boys, going around and threatening everyone in the computer business.

Len wasn't a lawyer, but from what he remembered about GM and Chrysler and the Feds, there are some things that you just can't do, according to the antitrust laws. Computer makers were being prohibited from including Netscape on their computers, for instance.

He would ask his lawyer friends about this, and they all told him that antitrust suits had gone out of style since the Republicans got into power, in 1980. The Feds had done the AT&T divestiture, and they'd settled with IBM (which, ironically, gave Microsoft the breathing room to become a monopoly themselves). There didn't seem to be much hope that even a Democratic administration would pursue Microsoft.

Still, he did hint to Janet's friends today that there *were* things going on, and indeed there were. Maybe, *maybe* Netscape's lawyers would get the ear of some of the lawyers in D.C. There was a white paper that he'd gotten hold of where they laid out the case for going after Microsoft. Would anyone in the Department of Justice pay any attention to it? And given how slowly the legal system moved, would anything happen before Janet's company got its oxygen cut off, as the Redmond bullies liked to say?

He always told her to sell her stock as soon as it vested. *"You never know what's going to happen, so get the cash!"* he said. He felt the same way about whatever money he made off this Internet thing: take the chips off the table, before the dealer takes them all back.

Now he had a goddaughter! He thought of little Janine in her white dress, shaking hands with all the grownups. My God, she was adorable. Did Cassie want him in their lives? Her real father never came up here with Elaine, and Cassie didn't talk about him much. He got the impression that her parents didn't get along too well, but he didn't want to pry.

Maybe she'd want him to babysit for Janine! Wow, that would be an adventure. At least she was toilet-trained, probably. He'd have to get used to answering a million "why?" questions again like he did for Janet when she was little.

The fund company was getting concerned about his age: did he have a "succession plan?" "*Yeah, I'll retire or die, and then someone else will take over!*" he always said. But they were insistent. Especially, they wanted him to have an up-to-date will. Was Janet going to end up as the manager of the fund if he died? They liked her but didn't think she was really up to *that* job, and she didn't, either. He had an appointment with an estate lawyer next week.

What about his personal assets? The default would be that Janet got everything, which would be fine if she actually needed it. But now he had an inspiration: "*I can direct some of it to Janine's college fund! That's something a godfather can do.*"

That felt good. He fell asleep watching the rest of the game. He didn't even need to tell Cassie this college fund existed, unless he wanted to establish it now.

He always read in bed, before turning out the light. Mickey took up most of the bed, but fortunately he always jumped off and went to his dog bed eventually. Then one of them would always come in and wake him up when they needed to go outside

Later that night when he was taking Gretchen out he had a sudden thought. He wasn't even sure where it came from, since he hadn't been dreaming about his brother Jack:

I could endow a permanent memorial to Jack Saunders at the Merchant Marine Memorial in Washington. It'll say,

"*He gave his life so that other sailors might live.*"

As he went back to sleep, Len thought, "I always wanted to catch bad guys. But this is pretty good, too."

"SPOILERS" FROM PREVIOUS BOOKS

This is a brief summary of what happened in the previous two books, *Inventing the Future* and *The Big Bucks*," for people who haven't read them and want to catch up. I tried to use some exposition in the text so reading this wouldn't be necessary, but one never knows.

If you *do* want to read those books now (and why wouldn't you?), then you may wish to skip this section, which is why I put it at the end rather than the beginning.

Book I: Inventing the Future

Dramatis Personae:

Dan Markunas: a young engineer who's had one previous job out of college. Joins Xerox El Segundo in early 1977, when the Star wasn't even called that yet. Dan is single. Dan is me.

Janet Saunders: a young engineer, also with one job out of college at TRW, which is right down the street from Xerox El Segundo. Janet is married to Ken, whom she met at MIT.

Grant Avery: a slightly older Xerox veteran, who's transferred to Palo Alto from Dallas. He's brought in to bring some seasoned management to the Office Information Systems project.

Other important characters who appear, but we don't get to see inside their heads. Some of them appear in later books; some not:

Ken: husband of Janet

Len: Janet's father, a financial analyst at Chrysler. Len lives in the Detroit area, where Janet grew up.

Mark Banks: project manager of Star in El Segundo

Tom Burnside: Dan's boss, a mild-mannered guy.

Brian Lerner: another engineer in El Segundo

Porter Berwick: "the Jerry Garcia of programming" in Palo Alto. Porter knows everyone and everything.

Henry Davis: Palo Alto user interface expert. The inventor of icons.

Tim Field: Palo Alto hardware designer of the Ethernet transceiver.

Main events:

Xerox is embarking on The Office of the Future, diversifying from their copier business. The effort is to be *based* on Xerox PARC's groundbreaking research, but it is not, contrary to popular ignorance, actually being *done* by PARC. Rather, it's a separate division, SDD, assigned to make a product. Dan and Janet are hired into the El Segundo group, and Grant is hired to be a manager for the operating system, in Palo Alto.

The OIS (Office Information Systems) effort is slow to get off the ground. There is much corporate intrigue, and the computer eventually called "Star" is called the "Display Word Processor" at first. Grant is in way over his head managing the operating system; the Ph.D. engineers mostly ignore him, and his calls to stick to the schedule and follow the Xerox development process fall on deaf ears. In a few months he transfers to the "Planning" department, and tries to act as an interface to the main Xerox bureaucracy. Grant has a crush on Janet, but she's married.

Janet works at TRW and her husband Ken works at Hughes Aircraft. They have an active social life with Ken's friends at Hughes, and most of them are bemused, at best, by Janet's work at Xerox. Ken makes fun of it constantly, which leads to a growing tension between them.

Dan becomes the manager of Records Processing. Janet has an interview at Hughes, gets an offer, and turns it down to become the Release Manager on Star. This leads to an explosive fight with Ken. Grant resolves to transfer down to El Segundo to work on the Tor electronic printer project, since he thinks Xerox has a better chance of marketing and selling laser printers (he was right, by the way).

Eventually, Janet gets a divorce from Ken, and Grant moves down to El Segundo to work on Tor. He thinks that, now that she's divorced, he has his chance! However, she just doesn't see him that way. They go out once, but eventually he gets the idea that it's not going to happen.

Even though he's in El Segundo, his colleagues still see him as their interface to Palo Alto. Since they're using Pilot, the OS he used to be in charge of, he still has to go there and stay involved. Eventually, his search for a new chip leads him to Fuji Xerox, the Japanese subsidiary, and they offer him a temporary assignment as liaison.

Star is introduced at the National Computer Conference in Chicago, to major headlines. Janet and Dan are there, and Janet notices Steve Jobs and his Apple retinue attending every hourly demo. She gives one of them her business card, they invite her up for an interview and offer her a job on the Lisa, and she accepts it. There are (mostly) no hard feelings on the part of the El Segundo people; they realize, as she does, that Xerox has no chance of success in the computer business.

Grant accepts the job in Japan. Dan feels, initially, that

Janet's leaving for Apple is a betrayal of all they'd worked for, but in the end they part friends.

Book 2: The Big Bucks - Love and the Birth of the Internet

The Big Bucks takes us through the 80s, before the Internet burst on the scene but was slowly taking shape. The main characters end up working at 3Com in "networking" which did not mean "Internet" yet. There were other ways the internet (with a small 'i') *could* have gone, and many "experts" were sure it would. Our characters get to experience this without knowing how things would turn out.

At the same time, we see the personal lives of the main characters, who do not fall into any of the stereotypes of modern media; there are no hippies who stay up all night on online bulletin boards, and no one resembles any of *The Big Bang* characters. They buy houses, remodel them, date and get married, go dancing, go fishing, and lead normal lives.

Dramatis Personae:

Dan Markunas, Janet Saunders: continued from Book 1

Grant Avery: from Book 1, but since he's now in Japan, he makes only a cameo appearance in this book.

Matt Finegold (new): a Ph.D. student at the University of Minnesota at the start of the book. He has a boring dissertation topic but longs to get into networking. Matt is from New York.

Miriam Finegold (Matt's wife): a clinical psychologist, also from New York. She is desperate to get out of Minnesota, being a New York chauvinist at heart.

Cassie: a young woman who works for Janet at 3Com.

Walt Campbell: a building contractor, whom Janet employs on her own house and later recommends to Matt.

Other important characters:

Kristen: HR lady at 3Com, alias "Miss Smarmy."

Larry Whitlock: one of Janet's direct reports at 3Com, alias "Leisure Suit Larry," Larry is a killjoy who is constantly reminding Janet and Cassie to stop having fun and do their regular jobs.

Logan Arnold: Matt's manager in his graduate program. Logan is not a professor but rather a full time employee of the University.

Mohan: one of Janet's direct reports at 3Com

Pete: a plumber, good friend of Walt's

Terry Franklin: 3Com engineer and manager, Dan's boss for a while

Main events:

As the book opens in 1981, Janet prepares to move up to the Bay Area to work on the Apple Lisa project, and Dan relinquishes his job as manager of the Records Processing group. Dan decides he really wants to work at a startup and get rich, and since almost all startups are in the Bay Area, he takes a job reporting to Martin Whitby in Palo Alto. This will give him a chance to interview while he's up there.

Matt is in the Ph.D. program at the University of Minnesota, working on a project for the Cray supercomputer, which he is bored with. Miriam is struggling in her own doctoral program, working for free at a psychological clinic to get in her required hours. Matt's manager Logan asks him to look into getting Minnesota onto CSNet, an early offshoot of ARPANET (the precursor of the Internet). He quickly decides that networking is more interesting than the Cray.

Dan, stuck in El Segundo, falls into a rhythm of going to Palo Alto for the day once a week, and interviewing at startups after he leaves in the afternoon. It quickly becomes depressing, as they are either uninterested in him, he in them, or else they want him immediately but he owns a house down South. He publishes a paper on his Star project.

Janet finds the Lisa project depressing after the initial

excitement wears off. They are not interested in the business market, despite Lisa's $10,000 price, or in a standard local area network, either. Nonetheless, she quickly becomes a manager of the Lisa applications. She buys a house in the West San Jose area, close to Apple's campus.

She gets interested in fixing up her house, and ultimately finds a contractor, Walt Campbell, who does her bathroom. Walt is more like an engineer than most contractors; he loves to tell the client exactly what he did, and Janet proves a receptive audience. She always pays him on time, since she senses that being slow to pay is a prime complaint that contractors have about their clients. They have a great working relationship and she continues to use him on other contracting jobs.

Dan finally gets a call from a startup in the Bay Area. They have read his paper on Records Processing and are planning to do a visual, analytical database, a perfect fit for him. They are three high-powered, egotistical guys who have found venture backing from some VCs dying to have a "software play." They have a hodgepodge of engineers who didn't interview each other and don't even get along well. The startup, Analytica, is an unhappy place that's nonetheless creating a good product, called "Reflex", although Analytica will have no chance of actually marketing it. Dan leaves shortly after it ships, for 3Com.

Matt discovers a community of PC and Apple II users at the University, and together they install the Datapoint ARCNet after hours one night. This leads to him having a summer internship at Datapoint in San Antonio, Texas. Datapoint's LAN was actually pretty darned good.

ARCNet is an immediate hit, and gets a retroactive blessing from the University and the unions, as they also create an official committee to choose a "real" LAN strategy. Matt sits on it, finds it mind-numbingly boring, and one day, gives his business card to the 3Com salesman. He gets flown out to California to interview at 3Com, and is offered a job.

Dan has bought a house very close to Janet's, and they re-establish contact. He recruits her to 3Com, where she is put in charge of the internal Ethernet. Dan works on email, and Matt works on their Directory service. Janet has three people under her; Cassie, Mohan, and Larry. Larry is a boring corporate drone whom Janet secretly can't stand. Cassie is a young woman who's eager to learn, and Janet takes her under her wing.

On one of Janet's home improvement projects, Walt's plumber friend Pete comes over, and the three of them have a great chat about fishing, which Walt and Pete like to do together, and which Janet used to do with her dad as a child. After she leaves, Pete suggests to Walt that Janet is nice looking. Walt dismisses him, saying "I don't date my clients."

Matt hears of Janet's contractor Walt, and hires him for his own home project, in Palo Alto. Walt is wary of jobs in Palo Alto, since he's found it to be a place of entitled people who are impossible to work with, but he goes to visit anyway, and gets the job. Miriam is suspicious of Walt since he's not "our kind," i.e. he hasn't done jobs in the Palo Alto area. She has house envy for her wealthy colleagues and changes the job to add a kitchen island, because all her rich friends have one.

Since they live in an Eichler, which has no crawl space and thus all wiring & plumbing is in the concrete, this is a major change. Walt gamely goes along with a re-estimate. As such jobs do, it spirals into more and more additional expense, which infuriates Miriam. She blames Walt and questions his honesty.

Janet feels horrible that she recommended Walt and the job has turned out so badly. Her friends begin to suspect that she has some feelings for him, but she denies it. Larry over-hears Matt, Dan, and Cassie plotting to get the two together, and starts malicious rumors about her. She finds out and tells him to mind his own business. When she tells her father Len about this, he sympathizes, but adds that he likes Walt. She begins to change her opinion on the idea. Walt does not.

Matt takes the initiative and pays off Walt for his work, with a handshake deal. Miriam is furious, but soon finds a local contractor to finish the job Walt started.

Pete is getting married and Walt is to be his best friend, so the conspirators hatch a plan to get Walt and Janet together at a dance class, the pretext being that Walt will need to dance at the reception. Janet doesn't show up, since Cassie gave her the wrong information. The plot is on hold, as Janet tells Cassie that she doesn't need or want a fixup.

Meanwhile, Leisure Suit Larry, as Cassie calls him, suddenly quits, apologizing to the whole company for his inappropriate email. No one has any idea what he's talking about. Unraveling this mystery takes Dan and Terry the rest of the book, and if you want to know what happened, you'll just have to read the book!

Pete has gotten married, and his wife fixes on Walt as a single friend of Pete's who needs a wife (whether he wants one or not). Cassie calls Pete, and she manages to find Cassie's phone number and calls her. They plot to have Pete and Walt invite Janet and Cassie on a fishing trip at the beginning of salmon season.

The trip happens, and they catch their limit of salmon fairly quickly and head back to shore. The magic has still not happened, but Pete finally takes drastic action and the couple are united! (You'll have to read the book to find out that bit, too.)

Almost a year later, they all meet at the wedding of Janet and Walt. We find out what the email thing was about, and Pete, while pretty drunk, hears them all recounting it, grasps the silly things they get up to, and utters the title line: "And you all get the big bucks!"